DANGEROUS PURSUITS

DANGEROUS PURSUITS

Jo Bannister

SEVERN
HOUSE

First world edition published 2020
in Great Britain and the USA by
SEVERN HOUSE PUBLISHERS LTD of
Eardley House, 4 Uxbridge Street, London W8 7SY.
Trade paperback edition first published
in Great Britain and the USA 2021 by
Severn House, an imprint of Canongate Books Ltd,
14 High Street, Edinburgh EH1 1TE.

British Library Cataloguing in Publication Data
A CIP catalogue record for this title is available from the British Library.

ISBN-13: 978-0-7278-9087-0 (cased)
ISBN-13: 978-1-78029-718-7 (trade paper)
ISBN-13: 978-1-4483-0439-4 (e-book)

This is a work of fiction. Names, characters, places and incidents are
either the product of the author's imagination or are used fictitiously.
Except where actual historical events and characters are being described
for the storyline of this novel, all situations in this publication are
fictitious and any resemblance to actual persons, living or dead, business
establishments, events or locales is purely coincidental.

Typeset by Palimpsest Book Production Ltd.,
Falkirk, Stirlingshire, Scotland.

ONE

Rachel Somers, running. Not for pleasure; not for prizes. With the blood pounding in her ears and fear pumping through her veins. With her shirt torn and one shoe lost; with her face and her hands scratched by the undergrowth she's forced her way through and the brambles she cannot allow to slow her. Running as if the hounds of hell are snapping at her heels; as if she doesn't mean to stop, as if she doesn't know *how* to stop, as if only the bursting of her young heart will stop her. Her eyes wide with terror, and disbelief, and something akin to indignation, because this sort of thing *does not happen* to girls like Rachel. Except that it has.

On the edge of the cornfield, green-gold under the blaze of the August sun, the man straightened up stiffly and shook his head. 'I think he's lost.'

Don't say that. Keep looking.

'I *am* looking. I've *been* looking for the last fifteen minutes. I can't find him. And actually, it's not my job to find him – it's yours. He's your baby, it was you who put him down and forgot where – plus, you're the one with the nose. I don't know why you bring him if you're going to drop him in the long grass and run off the moment something catches your eye.'

A reproachful look from the toffee-coloured eyes. It was a hare. A *hare* . . .

'That hare was just minding its own business. It didn't need chasing. I'm fairly sure it didn't *want* chasing.'

Sullenly: Chasing is in my blood.

The man shrugged, not entirely sympathetically. 'Well, I don't know what else we can do, short of borrowing a scythe and cutting Mr Burton's barley for him. Come on, let's go home.'

I can't leave without him!

'Yes, you can. You've got a spare, identical in every way except slightly less chewed. Patience, I don't think you've any choice. Spiky Ball is lost. It's time to bring on the substitute.'

The unusual thing about this conversation, had there been anyone to overhear it, was not that the subject of it was a jelly-pink ball with some of its squidgy protuberances chewed back to stumps. Old and treasured toys get lost on walks every day of the week, and tearful small children have to be hauled away before nightfall, only slightly mollified by the promise of a replacement. It wasn't that this particular toy had acquired enough personality to be identified not only by name but by gender.

No, what was remarkable about *this* conversation was that one of the parties to it was not a small child but a dog: a slim white lurcher, with one tan ear and one speckled one, and a long scimitar tail currently flying at half-mast in distress.

Gabriel Ash knew dogs couldn't talk. It was one of the things he'd known from earliest childhood. The sky is blue, things fall down not up when you drop them, and animals can't talk. Though he was not a gambling man, he would have staked quite a lot of money on the fact, until he acquired Patience.

So far as he was able to figure it, there were two possibilities. One was that the mental breakdown he'd suffered, six years ago now, had not resolved as completely as he'd believed, leaving him with a tendency to confabulate – in this case, to attribute to a perfectly normal dog the ability to voice thoughts and ideas that originated inside his own head. The other was that Patience could in fact talk, even if Ash was the only one who heard her. Of the two, he found the first slightly less alarming. Madness was something he'd had practice at dealing with.

He sighed. He was not an unkind man. 'Five more minutes. We'll keep looking for five more minutes. After that it'll be too dark to see him even if we step on him, and we're going home. Yes?'

I suppose, the dog agreed reluctantly.

But they didn't give it five more minutes. While Ash was

bent over, peering dutifully among the stalks as best he could without trampling the crop, Patience suddenly stiffened into the point she'd inherited from the better-bred side of her family.

Gabriel . . .

He looked where she was looking, saw the hawthorns shaking fifty metres up the path, saw a figure detach itself from the deep shadows gathering under the hedge. 'Please – oh, please help me!'

Ash thought at first it was a child. But it was a young woman, so breathless with exhaustion she could barely get the words out. 'Of course,' he said quickly, hurrying towards her. 'What's happened? What can I do?'

Ash had sons, not daughters, so it was not much more than an educated guess that she was sixteen or seventeen years old. But he didn't need to be an expert to see the stigmata of violence: the flimsy shirt torn at the breast, the cotton skirt at the hem; bloody tracks across her skin from the brambles; one bare foot where she'd lost a red and white trainer. And more than that, the porcelain pallor and vast, stretched eyes, the gasping breath racking her thin chest, the tremors shaking the hands she reached towards him, and the brain-lock that stopped her getting out any kind of coherent explanation. 'Someone . . . He tried to . . . In there.' She darted a terrified glance over her shoulder, as if the culprit might erupt through the hedge at any moment.

Ash, glancing too, moved protectively towards her. As he did so she sank to her torn knees in the grass of the corn-field's headland. Ash knelt beside her. 'You're safe now.' But it was important to be sure what she was trying to say. 'Did someone attack you?'

'Yes! He . . .' She waved a wild arm back at the hedge. 'I got away.'

'Just now?'

His questions were upsetting her. 'Yes! Please – I want to go home . . .'

'I'll take you home,' Ash promised. 'Where do you live?'

Again the unsteady gesture towards the tangle of trees beyond the hedge. 'On the other side of the spinney.'

Highfield Spinney was half a mile across and dusk was

falling. 'I'll come with you. Or we'll take my car. That's my house' – he pointed – 'over there.'

She was torn. She didn't know this large, shambling man; didn't know if or how far she could trust him. But she did know what lay behind her. 'I don't want to go back in there.'

'Of course not,' agreed Ash. 'We'll go to my house. My children's nanny will be there. We'll call your parents so they know you're safe, then I'll drive you home. All right?' She took his arm gratefully. 'And we'll let the police know what's happened. My name's Gabriel Ash,' he added as an after-thought, 'and this is Patience.'

The girl clung to his arm, too shocked to respond in the usual way until he prompted her. 'And you are . . .?'

'Rachel Somers,' she said then. Her teeth were chattering. A fresh horror crossed her face. 'I've lost my phone!'

Ash would have thought this was the least of her problems, but then he wasn't a teenage girl. He used his to make the few calls that wouldn't wait until he reached home or his shop. He didn't understand how much of a teenage girl's life was bound up in that small parcel of electronics. 'We'll use mine.'

The first flicker of an emotion that wasn't fear canted her thin dark brows. Regrettably enough, it was irritation. 'You know my mother's number?'

'Er . . . no.'

'Me neither. It's in my phone.'

So he took her to Highfield Road, and while Frankie Kelly, her charges dispatched to bed, was finding a jacket to cover Rachel's torn clothes, Ash was calling the local police. He would have called 999, except that he had Detective Chief Inspector Gorman's number on speed-dial.

Gorman cut right to the chase. 'Are we talking rape here, Gabriel?'

'I don't think so. She hasn't given me chapter and verse, and I didn't like to quiz her, but I think she got away before anything much happened. But she's very shocked, and she's torn her clothes and scratched herself pretty badly.'

'And this just happened.'

'She appeared in the field behind my house ten minutes ago. I don't know how long before that she was attacked.'

'I'll have the area car do a circuit of the spinney. They might spot his car, or him if he's on foot. It's too dark now, but tomorrow we'll search the wood. What was she doing there, anyway?'

Ash hadn't thought to ask. 'Can I take her home? Or do you want to see her first?'

'Take her home,' said Gorman. 'I'll meet you there.'

The Somerses' house was up a long lane off the county road, with Highfield Spinney starting where the back garden ended. A light showed at the rear of the house, but no one came when Ash rang the bell. Rachel took his hand. 'Come round the side. I left the back door unlocked.'

'When you went into the spinney?'

'There's a wicket gate,' she said. 'I was looking for my cat. He wasn't in the garden, so I took his feed bowl into the wood. To coax him in, you know? I was only a couple of metres from the gate – I never meant to go any further. But then . . . then . . .'

Ash nodded his understanding. 'It's all right, you don't need to tell me. The police would probably prefer you to speak to them first, anyway.'

'Police?'

'DCI Gorman's a friend of mine. I called him before we left, he'll be here shortly. Is your mother at home?'

'Her car isn't here,' said Rachel. She shivered inside Frankie's jacket. It was a warm evening, but now the adrenalin was subsiding she was feeling chilled. 'She said she'd be working late.'

'Your father?'

'Not in the picture.'

Under a bulkhead light, a small black and white cat was waiting on the back steps, rigid with disapproval. Rachel scooped it up, held it against her. 'So here you are,' she mumbled into its fur. It put its ears back and hissed at Ash, on principle.

He opened the door and ushered Rachel inside. 'Hello?' But there was no reply. 'Do you want to phone your mother or shall I?'

'I will. I've got her number in my diary.'

Ash went upstairs with her, turning lights on as he went. It occurred to him that, with the back door open and a potential rapist just beyond the garden gate, the house would have to be searched before it could be considered secure.

But before he could start there was the sound of cars in front of the house, and a moment later the sound of voices. One he recognised as Dave Gorman's. The other was a woman's.

The door flew open as Ash went to open it. The woman wrenched her key from the lock and shouldered past him, terse with alarm. 'Who the hell are you? Where is my daughter?'

'I'm here, Mum.' There was no more room in the hall: Rachel waited on the stairs. 'I'm all right.'

Her mother threw her handbag into a corner, her keys onto the hall table, and strode towards her, staring into her face, taking in the scabs and scratches. 'Are you? What happened? What on earth are you wearing? You didn't hurt your hands? Where's Gethin? Rachel – tell me what happened!'

The cat was called Mephistopheles, and he made up for his lack of stature with the sex drive of a Spanish jackass. Female cats as far away as Wittering blushed and giggled when his name came up in conversation. Being shut in at night was not part of his plan for fathering every kitten within a five-mile radius, but the human who called herself his mistress knew his weakness. His other weakness. When it came right down to it, Mephistopheles could not ignore a meal he could see and smell in order to pursue other forms of gratification which might prove elusive.

With dusk approaching, the light above the back door dispelled the deep shadow under the hydrangeas. The cat wasn't there. Rachel had no presentiment of danger, no reservations about going into the wood, at this time of day or any other. She'd spent the last four years in this house, had treated Highfield Spinney as her playground. Experience told her that her cat was probably within spitting distance as she shook the bowl encouragingly, and that given a moment to consider his options he would appear, purring and weaving round her ankles like a very small Morris dancer.

Tonight was different. Tonight, experience was no guide.

The first she knew was a hand grasping her arm. More startled than alarmed, she let out a yell and dropped the cat's bowl, and tried to turn to see who it was. But his other arm snaked around her neck, keeping her back to him. His breath was heavy in her ear but he didn't speak. He forced her against a tree-trunk and, releasing his grip on her arm, began to tug at her clothes.

Shocked as she was, Rachel recognised the moment as possibly the only chance she would get, and she took it. She drove both elbows back into his belly and scraped the side of her trainer down the front of his shin. The shoe came off, but – winded, hurt, and wrong-footed by her counter-attack – his grip weakened and Rachel flung herself free.

He was between her and the house so she ran the other way, deep into the wood. She doubted he knew it better than she did. She chose the rougher, narrower tracks, ignoring the low branches that whipped her face, and though at first she could hear the heavy-footed blundering behind her, soon enough he lost her among the shadows.

She had never heard his voice. She had never seen his face. She had never seen more than a vague shape crowding over her shoulder. The bulk of him pressing her against the tree had felt massive and muscular, but her own vulnerability may have distorted her judgement. She didn't think she'd know him again if DCI Gorman produced a suspect.

'And you're sure you're not hurt?' demanded Pru Somers. 'I can see the scratches. What about your hands? If he hurt you, you have to tell us.'

'I'm fine, Mum,' Rachel sighed wearily. 'Thanks to Mr Ash.' She cast him a tremulous smile.

Ash was puzzled. This was the second time Mrs Somers had enquired after her daughter's hands. In the same circumstances, Ash imagined most parents would have other concerns.

Gorman had noticed too. Being a policeman, he didn't settle for being puzzled: he asked. 'Her hands?'

'My daughter is a pianist,' said Mrs Somers, looking at him

as if he should have known. 'Any damage to a pianist's hands is unthinkable.'

They had moved into the sitting room, where there was enough seating for Mrs Somers and her daughter, the two men, and Detective Constable Emma Friend who was taking notes. They were ranged round a low coffee table, currently occupied by a drift of magazines, a plate of biscuits and a mug with an inch of cold coffee in it.

Now Pru Somers rose abruptly from the sofa and went to the front window, peering out. 'And where's Gethin? He should be here.'

'Who's Gethin?' asked Gorman.

'My partner,' said Pru. 'Gethin Phillips. He should be here.'

'What time does he usually get home?'

'It can be any time. He's an architect – a partner, he makes his own hours. But he said this morning he'd be finished by mid-afternoon. He suggested we go out somewhere, but I knew I wouldn't be home till late.' She turned to Rachel. 'Was he here when you got in?'

Rachel shook her head, the straight dark hair still tangled from the wood. She'd changed her clothes, and DC Friend had bagged what she'd been wearing for evidential purposes. 'I haven't seen him.'

'And what time did you get home?' asked the DCI.

'About seven. I do a masterclass in Norbold on Monday evenings. I caught the six forty-five bus.'

'The only car on the drive when we arrived was Gabriel's,' said Gorman.

Pru Somers barked a terse little laugh. She was a small, intense woman, expensively dressed, wearing a cap of short dark hair and vivid lipstick. 'That means nothing. Did you check the garage?' she asked her daughter. Then, by way of explanation: 'Gethin's car is his baby, he puts it in the garage every night.'

Rachel shook her head. 'I didn't know he was meant to be here so I didn't go looking for him. I suppose he could have been in the study, or upstairs.'

Gorman nodded at his DC, who put down her notebook and

slipped out by the back door. Two minutes later she was back. 'There's a red sportscar in the garage.'

'That's Gethin's,' nodded Pru. 'If the Morgan's here, he should be here.'

'Could he have' – Gorman was a city boy at heart – 'walked down for a paper?'

'The nearest shop is three miles away,' said Pru coldly.

To Rachel, Ash said quietly, 'Did you scream?'

'What?'

He had everyone's attention. 'You were attacked not far from your garden gate. If you screamed – which would be the natural thing to do – Mr Phillips may have heard you. He might be in the spinney right now, looking for you.'

Rachel bit her lip and nodded. 'Yes. I screamed.'

Gorman stood up. 'Then we'd better find him. Probably better, for both of them, if he isn't the one to catch up with this joker. Emma, grab a couple of torches from the car and we'll go and look for him. With any luck he'll hear us calling. If not, we'll need some more bodies – we can't put off searching the woods till morning if there's a chance that someone's been hurt.'

Ash would have liked to go home now. He'd had enough excitement for one evening. But he couldn't in decency leave two people to search half a mile of woodland in the dark. 'I'll get my torch too.'

'Is Patience with you?'

Ash shook his head. 'I left her at home.'

'Typical,' growled Gorman. 'All the places you take that bloody dog, and the one time she might actually come in useful, she's had an early night!'

Pru stayed with Rachel, and locked the back door. Ash, Gorman and Friend split up at the wicket gate: Ash could see the flicker of torches through the trees, and hear Friend's high, clear voice travelling further than Gorman's gruff rumble. He called too. 'Mr Phillips? Are you there?' But he heard no reply.

After ten minutes they were to regroup at the wicket gate. Ash was already on his way back, swinging out to cover a different track, when he heard Friend calling again. Not, this time, the missing man's name. 'Sir? Over here.'

Gorman and Ash converged on her voice. Gorman reached her first. 'Oh, bugger.'

He knelt down among the ferns and the leaf-litter, and shone his torch close, and felt inside the man's collar for a pulse. He couldn't find one, and when he saw the injuries to his head he wasn't surprised. He straightened up stiffly.

Ash said, 'Is he dead?'

'I'm not a doctor,' grunted Gorman. 'But yes, he's dead.'

'Who is he?'

Gorman glared. 'Who do you *think*?'

'I think,' Ash said carefully, 'he could be either Gethin Phillips or the man who attacked Rachel. I think, if Phillips caught up with him and they fought, that could be either of them.'

After a moment Gorman nodded. 'True.' He played the torch the length of the still body. 'It's Phillips.'

'How do you know?'

'Most rapists don't go trawling for victims in their slippers.'

TWO

The sun was up before DCI Gorman had finished at the spinney. His mind and body ached for his bed, if only for a couple of hours, but on a hunch he took the scenic route home via Highfield Road. As he'd guessed, there was a light on in Ash's study at the front of the big stone house that had been his mother's. Gorman tapped on the window, quietly enough not to disturb the rest of the household, and Ash beckoned him to the front door.

He made coffee and toast. A glance at Gorman's haggard face, and he put extra coffee in the coffee and extra butter on the toast. 'You should be in bed.'

'So should you,' countered Gorman. 'At least I'm paid to stay up nights, worrying.'

'I'm more of a gifted amateur,' conceded Ash.

Gorman chuckled. They weren't old friends – three years earlier, all Gorman knew about Gabriel Ash was that he wandered round Norbold holding mumbled conversations with his lurcher: the people at Meadowvale Police Station called him Rambles With Dogs. But they had become good friends. They were much of an age, they shared the same values, and even in their most marked differences – Gorman was very much a physical presence, Ash more of an intellectual one – they dove-tailed rather than clashing. Even before he learned that Rambles was once a government security analyst, DCI Gorman – but he was a detective inspector then – had discovered that attending to Ash's instincts paid dividends.

'All right, Sherlock,' he said, 'so what do we think happened out there?'

Ash squinted at him. Gorman's square, crumpled, frankly ugly face could be deeply uncommunicative when the need arose, but there was a certain dogged intelligence in his gaze. He'd spent the last nine hours considering the options, and wanted to know if Ash had come to the same conclusion.

Pensively, Ash blew steam off his coffee. 'The girl wasn't able to add anything helpful?'

'No. Shock, of course. I'll talk to her again today, see if she's remembered anything else. I'll need a statement from you too. But essentially, what she said is all we have to go on.'

'Scenes of crime officer . . .?'

'. . . Will have another look round now it's daylight. And we'll get an autopsy report, but it won't tell us much that we don't already know. That Gethin Phillips went into the spinney in his slippers and someone beat his head in.'

'Any strange vehicles parked on the edge of the wood?'

'No. The patrols didn't spot anyone on foot, either. But absence of evidence . . .'

'. . . Is not evidence of absence,' Ash finished with a smile. 'You and Hazel must have had the same training sergeant.' He thought for a minute longer. 'Rachel went into the spinney looking for her cat. Someone grabbed her and she screamed. Phillips heard her from the house and hurried outside, without changing into his shoes, to see what had happened.

'Rachel hadn't realised he was at home so she didn't know help was coming. When she broke free she was more concerned with getting away from her attacker than with reaching the house. She fled, and he ran after her. Then the sound of pursuit died away. She assumed she'd put enough distance between them that he'd given up.'

'But?' prompted Gorman.

'Perhaps what happened is that Phillips caught up with him. They fought, the attacker got the upper hand, put Phillips out of commission, then he disappeared into the trees. He may have got clean away while we were all bent over Phillips' body and before the reinforcements turned up.'

Gorman was nodding slowly. 'That's about how I figured it. We've got dogs in the spinney, but he won't still be there. He must assume that we've found the body by now.'

Surreptitiously, Ash added more milk to his mug. The brew was as strong as creosote, and Ash hadn't had his taste-buds destroyed by twenty years' worth of police station coffee machines the way Gorman had. When he worked in the anonymous office behind Whitehall, they'd inclined towards Earl Grey tea.

'Will the dogs be able to track him?' he asked.

Gorman shrugged. 'They should be able to follow his line out to the road, and we'll find traces of a vehicle having been parked there. It's too dry for tyre-tracks, but we can hope for flattened grass, broken twigs; if there is a God, the bastard might have dropped a cigarette butt, a cash-machine receipt or something else we can use. It doesn't happen often, but it does happen.'

Ash knew how seldom; how long policemen had to wait between gifts like that. He said, 'How is Mrs Somers coping?'

Gorman frowned. It brought his hairline, naturally rather low, into close proximity with his eyebrows. 'Pretty well, to say she came home to find her daughter had nearly been raped and her partner had been murdered. It's more like she's been let down by a temp agency: damned annoying, obviously it's going to put her to a lot of trouble, but by God she's not going to rearrange her entire diary because of it.'

'Temp agency?' echoed Ash, bewildered.

'Yeah, sorry – she's the manager of that big hotel at Westbroke, The King's Head. And she's treating all this like a professional challenge – tight-lipped determination rather than tears.'

'Perhaps that's just who she is,' suggested Ash. 'Or who she's learned to be. I imagine tearful women find it hard to get jobs managing big hotels.'

'Maybe,' allowed Gorman. 'Everyone handles grief their own way. She may feel she has to be strong for her daughter. It's just, it's easier when everyone behaves how you'd expect.'

'Easier for whom?'

The DCI stood up, stretching stiffly. 'I'd better move. You'll have the boys up and about any time.'

Ash nodded. 'The funny thing is, in summer they're up before seven. During term time, I have to drag them out of bed in order to get them to school by nine.'

Unmarried and without children of his own, Gorman gave a tired grin. 'Gabriel, you went to enough trouble getting them back – don't grumble about them now.'

'Grumbling's allowed,' said Ash. 'It's selling them to white slavers that's frowned on.'

At the front door Gorman said, 'You know the really remarkable thing about all this? That Hazel was miles away when the shit hit the fan. I can hardly remember the last time that happened. Where is she – Byrfield?'

Ash nodded again.

'I'll be glad when this damned wedding's over,' yawned Gorman. 'I don't know why Hazel has to organise it. I know for a fact that the bridegroom has a mother and two sisters. You'd think they'd be glad to be getting a new countess. Ensuring the succession, and all that.'

'I don't think the dowager countess altogether approves of the bride,' murmured Ash. He'd met the Earl of Byrfield's mother once. She hadn't approved of him either. 'But Pete's sisters just want him to be happy.'

'I'll just be glad when things can get back to normal around here. You know, stuff happening and Hazel refusing to believe what everyone else wants to believe, and usually being sort of right, or at least wrong in the right sort of way.'

Ash smiled. 'Careful, Dave. You almost said you missed her.'

'Yeah?' Gorman headed down the path. 'Well – don't tell her that.'

There's a kind of bush telegraph that serves the persistently inquisitive. No one ever admitted to calling Hazel Best, ninety miles away in Cambridgeshire, surrounded by samples of oyster satin and canapés, to tell her what had happened in Highfield Spinney. Hazel herself was uncharacteristically vague about how she came to be halfway back to Norbold when the first report of the incident was on the radio.

However it was, Gabriel Ash was walking Patience into town to open his shop – an hour late, but no one expects punctuality from a second-hand bookseller – when the familiar sapphire-blue hot-hatch fell into step beside him, the passenger-side window rolled down. 'Get in.'

'I've got Patience with me,' said Ash, as if his friend might not have noticed the white lurcher trotting at his side; as if Hazel wouldn't have been astonished to see him walking alone.

'I'll vacuum the seats later. Get in.'

Ash was about to say that he wasn't thinking of dog hairs on Hazel's upholstery but the recriminations if he cheated his dog of her morning walk. But he thought better of it, cast Patience an apologetic look, and did as he was bid. Patience sat on his lap.

'I can't leave you alone for five minutes, can I?' said Hazel.

Ash blinked at her. 'It was five days, and I didn't ask you to come back. Dave Gorman is quite capable of investigating even a serious crime without your assistance. Whereas Pete Byrfield, whose qualities as both a farmer and a man I know and value, will probably not manage to get himself to Burford Parish Church in time for his own wedding if you aren't there to tie his cummerbund for him.'

Hazel shrugged nonchalantly, the fair hair bunched roughly at her neck tossing on the collar of her cotton shirt. 'There's time enough yet. I'll go back for the dress rehearsal – they can manage without me till then.'

'And Dave can't?'

Hazel frowned at him. 'I didn't come back to hold Dave Gorman's hand,' she said tartly. 'Dave Gorman is the senior detective at Meadowvale Police Station, and I am – as Division never tire of pointing out – a lowly uniformed constable. I see old ladies across roads. I lecture children about staying safe online. If Dave Gorman needs help with a murder inquiry, he'll turn to Scotland Yard, not to me.'

'Then why . . .?'

'To make sure you're all right, of course! Good grief, Gabriel, you found a body! That's enough to knock the wind out of anyone's sails.' She did not add, Even people with no question marks over their sanity; which didn't mean that she didn't think it, or that Ash didn't hear it. He was good at hearing things that hadn't actually been said.

'It wasn't me who found him, it was Emma Friend. And you're right, he wasn't a pretty sight. I'm still glad we found him when we did. If we hadn't, that girl and her mother could have stumbled across him.'

'I suppose there's no question that it was murder?'

'It's pretty hard to commit suicide by beating your own

skull in,' observed Ash. 'Plus, we know there was a dangerous man nearby. It's hard to read it any other way.'

'The girl had a narrow escape.'

'I hope, when the shock recedes a little, it'll be some comfort to her mother to know that Gethin Phillips may have saved Rachel's life.'

Hazel parked outside the bookshop. There was always plenty of room. Rambles With Books had built up a faithful clientele in its first year, but you don't often find people queuing three deep outside second-hand bookshops. There were no would-be customers tapping their watches to mark the fact that the shop should have been open before now.

Hazel put the kettle on while Ash checked the mail and Patience took up her post under the long table where some of the more interesting offerings were displayed. Ash had been putting together a collection on English waterways, with an early edition of *Three Men in a Boat* in pride of place.

He looked up to find Hazel eyeing him critically from the doorway of the tiny kitchen. 'What?'

'You have got something decent to wear for the wedding?'

Ash looked down at himself. He'd never been much of a fashion icon. The best that could be said of his clothes was that they had been of a certain quality when they were bought, which explained them lasting long enough to be somewhat out of date now. Left to his own devices he inclined to tweed jackets and cords in a narrow range of muddy browns and sludgy greens. He would occasionally venture out in a brighter sweater if either Hazel had bought it for him, or his sons had, for his birthday. Somehow, even a bright sweater started to lose its zing when Ash wore it.

'You want me to hire a morning suit?'

Hazel laughed out loud at the mere thought. 'I don't think so, Gabriel, no. You've got a lounge suit, haven't you? Does it still fit?'

'It's more that it fits again,' he mumbled. He'd lost so much weight during his PTSD years that it had more or less hung from his shoulders straight down to his shoes. The recent upturn in his fortunes had restored some substance to his gaunt frame, leading him to hope that he might get another ten years out of his good suit.

'We'll buy you a new shirt. Not white – it's not a funeral you're going to. Maybe pale pink. And a tie to match.'

Ash looked doubtful. He hadn't had good experiences with pink.

'And, Gabriel.' She caught his eye with her own, green-gold like her name. 'Patience is not invited.'

'I really don't know why you want me there anyway,' he said in a low voice.

'Oh, I don't,' retorted Hazel briskly. 'Pete does. He says that, since the vicar insists on using his proper name in the ceremony, it'll be a comfort to him to have someone nearby with an even funnier one.' The 28th Earl of Byrfield rejoiced in the Christian name of Peregrine.

'Speaking of names,' said Ash, 'how's the dowager countess coping with the fact that her son is marrying someone called Tracy?'

'Not well.' Hazel made no attempt to hide her trademark grin. 'She tried to convince herself it must be short for something more appropriate. Elizabeth, perhaps, or Margaret. But Tracy Olroyd is the perfect wife for Pete, if only because she's so totally unfazed by his dreadful mother. She said that if the DC wanted to tell people it was short for Tatiana she could introduce her sister Cindy as Cassandra.'

Ash chuckled. Six months ago he'd thought it would be Hazel marrying Pete Byrfield. He'd thought he was going to lose her. 'This could have been your wedding. You've no regrets?'

'None,' she said, so immediately that it was plainly true. 'I love Pete dearly, but I'm not *in* love with him and I never was. I don't believe he was in love with me. I think he'd have been a good husband to me, but we'd both have been aware that we were settling for second best. Whereas he and Tracy were made for one another. You only have to see them dipping sheep together to know that.'

'You never told me how they met.'

'They were at agricultural college together, years ago. They lost touch, then someone organised a class reunion and they met up again. She's been running a big sheep farm up in Yorkshire.'

Ash considered for a moment. Then: 'This someone who organised the reunion . . .?'

Hazel regarded him levelly over her mug. 'So what if I did?'

'I'll be glad when this damned wedding's over,' growled Sergeant Murchison, glaring down at Hazel. She was tall; he was taller.

'You're getting married, Sarge?' she said innocently. 'Congratulations. Who's the lucky woman?'

'Not me,' he retorted gruffly. 'I'm already married, as you know fine well. I'm about as married as a man can be without committing bigamy.' Hazel had met the significant Mrs Murchison and knew what he meant. 'I *mean*, when can I get a week's work out of you without you buggering off to Cambridgeshire?'

This was so monstrously unfair – she knew it, and she knew that Donald Murchison knew it – that Hazel took no particular exception to it. 'Sarge, I'm on leave. I booked this leave three months ago. Cambridgeshire or the Costa del Sol, I'm entitled not to be here. I'm only here now because I stuck my head round your door to see if you needed any help, and you were inconsiderate enough to say that you did.'

The station sergeant hid a smile somewhere in his jowls. 'Don't you know there's a murder on?'

'Why do you think I stuck my head round your door?'

Murchison had a long list of things he needed to cover today, and a short list of bodies to cover them. An unattached PC, who was unlikely to be seconded by officers senior to himself for the simple reason that they didn't know she was here, was like manna falling from a particularly overcast heaven. Even if he only had her for a few hours, he could make use of her. 'Do you fancy doing a bit of family liaising?'

'Sure.' There were almost no parts of her job that Hazel Best wouldn't tackle with some enthusiasm. 'Who needs liaising with?'

'CID have finished with the Somers family for now. But someone ought to swing by them from time to time, see if there's anything they need. They're pretty shocked.'

It would be uncharitable to suggest that she'd anticipated the request before putting her head round Sergeant Murchison's door, so let's just say that Hazel was unsurprised. 'I bet they are. Shall I change?' She was still in civvies. She might be struggling to get a transfer to CID, but looking like a detective and picking up the oddments of work the detectives hadn't time for let her edge her feet under the table a bit at a time. It let people get used to the idea that CID was her second home, even if no one had actually given her a key.

'Not unless you want to. Just go there, hold their hands for a bit, answer any questions they may have about what happens next. You know the routine. Tell them we have all available resources dedicated to finding this man. Tell them Detective Chief Inspector Gorman is like a lion in pursuit of a murder suspect.'

'A lion, Sarge? Don't they lie around in the sun most of the day, except when they're making little lions?'

'A lion,' insisted Donald Murchison. 'Who died and made you David Attenborough? A lion is what they want to hear, a lion is what you tell them.'

On the way out to her car, Hazel glanced through the canteen window to see the lion yawning over a mug of coffee and the sports results.

THREE

Shock affects people differently. Some families it binds like glue; others it splits like an axe. Hazel knew better than to draw any conclusions, or even form any opinions, from the chilly atmosphere that met her at the Somerses' house. She was accustomed to being blamed for the failure of the real police to solve even quite complex crimes in the hour (less commercials and credits) that was generally sufficient for their television counterparts. She reminded herself that, while this was the sea she swam in, most victims of crime were experiencing it for the first time, and didn't know what they could reasonably expect. Family liaison was a gentle way of telling them.

Pru Somers answered the door with her phone in her hand. 'Just a moment.' She gestured Hazel towards the sitting room, finished the call with a few curt words and followed her in from the hall. 'You have some news for me?'

'Not really,' admitted Hazel. 'Only that everything that can be done is being done. Our detective chief inspector' – no, she thought, the lion simile really wouldn't wash – 'won't rest until he finds this man. I wish I could tell you we have a suspect. We haven't, yet. But we are gathering information and looking for evidence, and someone who was in the spinney for long enough to attack your daughter and fight with Mr Phillips will have left traces of himself. Even microscopic traces can be enough to set us on the right track. Don't think that, because I can't tell you much today, nothing much is happening. All the techniques at our disposal are being employed right now. Collating the information and analysing it will take a little longer, but modern forensics puts killers in prison every day. Even the ones who thought they'd got clean away.'

'Of course,' said Mrs Somers briefly. She was a small, wiry woman who'd made a good career by convincing people she was a big strong one. 'So if there's no news, why are you here?'

Hazel told herself the woman wasn't being rude, just direct. 'To see if there's anything you need. Or if you have any questions. If I don't know the answers myself, I'll get them for you.'

Pru Somers shook her head, too quickly to have given the offer any consideration. 'I don't think so. Not at this time.'

'What about Rachel? How's she bearing up?'

For a moment Pru looked faintly puzzled, as if she'd forgotten that her daughter was involved. 'She's all right, I think. She's practising right now. At least' – she cocked an ear towards the door – 'she should be.'

'Perhaps I should have a word with her. See if there's anything she wants to ask.'

'Not while she's practising.'

According to the notes she'd been handed, Mrs Somers was something high up in the hotel business. Perhaps that explained the abrasive manner, the self-confidence and the tendency to impatience. Or perhaps Hazel was mistaken, and she actually was just rude.

But probably, she thought charitably, this was how she dealt with shock and grief: head on, combatively, punching her way through. It was how she met obstacles to her career, and it was how she dealt with issues in her private life. It might make her professionally successful but it didn't make her easy to like; but then, being likable wasn't her job. Her job was to get through the next days and weeks intact, without letting the grief tear her apart; and to support her daughter while she too struggled towards acceptance. No one could make their situation less traumatic – certainly not the police, not even if they'd had the culprit under lock and key already. Only their own strength of character would see them through; and if that meant Pru Somers giving short shrift to the offer of a shoulder to cry on, Hazel wasn't going to take offence. The woman had lost someone immensely important to her. Her daughter's safety had been bought at the cost of her partner's life. There were no pamphlets to tell you how to feel about that, how to deal with the maelstrom of conflicting emotions. Just ending each day sane would be a major achievement.

'If you're sure there's nothing I can do.' Hazel made a move towards the door. 'But call if you need any help, any kind of advice . . .'

Rachel Somers was hovering at the foot of the stairs, listening to their exchange. She was pale and hollow-eyed, her hair a dark waterfall either side of her face, the scratches still livid on her cheeks and the backs of her hands. She didn't look as if she'd slept last night; she didn't look as if she'd sleep tonight either.

Hazel gave her a grave smile. 'You must be Rachel. I'm Hazel, from Meadowvale Police Station. If there's anything I can help you with, either of you, please let me know.'

'We will,' said Pru Somers firmly, holding the door for Hazel to leave.

You can't force either help or sympathy on people: all you can do is offer, and offer again, even after it's been thrown back in your face. Hazel took her leave and walked back to her car.

But as she opened the door she heard gravel crunch behind her. It was Rachel, hurrying to catch up. 'Actually, there is something you could do for me.'

'Name it.'

'That man. The one who helped me. The one with the dog.'

Hazel smiled. 'Gabriel. Gabriel Ash.'

'You know him?' The girl seemed surprised.

'Oh yes. We're old friends.'

'Oh. Then . . . will you thank him for me? With everything going on, I don't think I told him how glad I was of his help. I don't know what I'd have done if he hadn't found me.'

'Of course I'll tell him,' said Hazel. 'He'll be pleased to have been able to help. Helping people is his speciality.'

The girl looked puzzled. Hazel considered explaining, decided against. 'I'm on my way over to his house now. Do you want to come? He'll be glad to see you, to see that you're all right.' In all the circumstances, *all right* was probably optimistic, but Hazel couldn't think of a better term. 'I'll bring you straight back if you just want to say hello and thank you.'

The offer clearly came as a surprise. But Rachel decided quickly, nodding her head. 'I'll just tell my mother.' Hazel thought she heard raised voices, then the girl was back.

But in the act of climbing into the car she hesitated again, looking down at herself – an oversized grey T-shirt over grey leggings – in shy dismay. 'I'm not really dressed for visiting.'

Hazel smiled. 'We're visiting a man who's been known, while stone-cold sober, to pair a striped tie with a checked shirt. You look just fine.'

It probably took longer to drive round Highfield Spinney than to walk through it. Hazel didn't hurry. 'I was saying to your mum, I hope you'll both feel free to call me if there's anything we can do to help. Something terrible has happened to you: you don't have to cope with it on your own.'

'Mum doesn't like asking for help,' murmured Rachel.

'I don't think anybody likes asking for help. But there are times when the best of us, the strongest of us, needs it. Maybe, if she finds it hard to ask, you could ask for her.' Hazel negotiated the junction with the county road. 'I've been out of town – you'll have to forgive me if I don't have all the information. But I gather Mr Phillips was your stepfather?'

The girl frowned at her, then looked away. 'No. He and Mum weren't married. Actually, she's still married to my father, though we haven't seen anything of him for years.'

'Divorce proceedings can drag on,' said Hazel, with more feeling than she intended.

'They never got any further than a legal separation. I don't even know where my father is now. I suppose, if it mattered enough to her, Mum would have done something about it.'

'People can be a bit wary of a second marriage if the first one didn't work out.'

Rachel shrugged. 'Maybe. Or maybe neither she nor Gethin really wanted to commit. After four years, I don't think they were as keen on one another as they used to be. I think it was mostly habit that kept them together.'

'Habit can be another word for being comfortable together.' But Hazel filed the information away for future reference.

Ash was in the front garden, weeding. Gardening was one of the many topics on which his knowledge was more holes than net: Hazel was fairly sure she recognised, among the detritus in his trug, many of the seedlings she'd helped him plant out two months earlier. 'I've brought you a visitor.'

He looked up with a polite smile that broadened to genuine warmth when he saw Rachel emerge from the car. 'Miss Somers! What a pleasant surprise. We were thinking about you only this morning, wondering how you were doing.'

Rachel looked uncertain. 'We?'

'Er – Frankie and I.' Actually Ash had been talking to Patience, but now people were forgetting that he used to be mad he saw no reason to remind them. Holding conversations with your nanny was socially acceptable; holding them with your dog was not. 'She'll be sorry she missed you. She took the boys into town to buy them new shoes.' Until his sons came home, he'd forgotten how many shoes growing boys got through.

'I'll put the kettle on, shall I?' said Hazel, patting Patience absently as she headed up the path.

Rachel hung back. 'I think Mr Ash is busy . . .'

'Nonsense,' said Hazel briskly. 'Gabriel is to Capability Brown as Herod is to Dr Barnardo. Distract him from his gardening and his plants will be eternally grateful.'

Ash couldn't really argue. He knew where his talents lay. 'Come in and tell me how you and your mother are managing. And if there's anything I can do to help.'

Hazel was putting mugs on a tray. 'There are some biscuits in the barrel,' he added.

'Found them,' mumbled Hazel through a mouthful of crumbs.

They took their coffee out to the flagstone terrace behind the house. Patience flopped, panting, in the shade of a gunnera.

'I've wondered if I should call,' said Ash. 'But I thought your mother probably had enough to deal with, without perfect strangers dropping round. How is she?'

Rachel shrugged. 'It's a bit hard to tell. Mum never gives much away. She's doing what needs doing and dealing with what needs dealing with. Emotionally? – I don't know. She seems more angry than upset. But then, she's always found anger a useful default position.'

'Anger stops you feeling pain,' Ash said quietly. 'It can get you through situations when almost nothing else could. But it can't last forever, and it would eat you up if it did. When the anger starts to subside, that's when the awareness of what she's lost will threaten to overwhelm her. That's when she'll need all the support you can give her.'

'Well, maybe,' said Rachel doubtfully.

Hazel said nothing. But she knew Ash was talking from experience. The sense of loss had tainted his life every day for seven years. For four of those years he'd grieved for the family he believed had been murdered. For the last three he'd grieved for the wife who had let him think that. Cathy Ash was still out there somewhere, with an Interpol warrant pursuing her; but Hazel had no doubt that if she turned up at Highfield Road one day, out of luck and out of money, Ash would take care of her. Despite everything she had put him through, Hazel believed he was still in love with her. Or perhaps he was still wedded to an idea, to a time when, to the best of his knowledge, they were in love with each other.

'What about you?' asked Ash.

'Me? I'm fine,' said Rachel negligently.

Ash shook his head. 'You can't possibly be fine. You went through a terrible experience. The fact that something even worse happened to Mr Phillips doesn't diminish what happened to you.'

'Gethin wasn't my father. We weren't that close.'

'I understand that. But he was, at the very least, someone you shared your home and your life with. And . . .' He thought better of the next sentence and left it unsaid.

Rachel Somers knew what he was thinking. 'And he died defending me from someone who tried to rape me. And my mother's stoking her anger as much as she can, because she doesn't want anyone to know that she'd give anything if only he hadn't been home last night.'

Ash leaned forward, his face compassionate. 'I'm sure that's not what she's thinking, Rachel. You have to forgive her if she can't express her feelings very well just yet. She must be terribly conflicted, knowing that one member of her family died defending the other, but you mustn't ever think that she blames you for what happened. When her emotions have had time to settle down, she'll be proud of what Mr Phillips did, and very grateful to him for keeping you safe.'

Tears welled abruptly in Rachel's eyes; she looked away. Kindly, Hazel changed the subject. 'Shoe-shopping, hm? That'll set you back a bit.'

Ash nodded ruefully. 'That's why I thought I'd take the day off, catch up on the gardening and stuff.'

Dashing away the tears on her sleeve left Rachel looking puzzled. Hazel explained. 'Most days it costs Gabriel more to open his shop than he makes by selling books.'

'Nobody ever opened a second-hand bookshop in order to get rich,' agreed Ash.

'So why . . .?'

'Because working is better for people than sitting at home watching game shows on television. Because I have two young sons, and I don't want them to grow up thinking that work is an optional extra. Because I enjoy meeting the kind of people who come into a second-hand bookshop, and I feel I'm providing a service for the reading public. I'm in the fortunate position that I can indulge myself in an occupation that's only really profitable in the spiritual sense.'

'And it keeps him out from under Frankie Kelly's feet,' added Hazel pragmatically. 'Have you met Frankie?'

'Oh yes,' said Rachel quickly. 'She was very kind when . . .' She didn't finish; but then, she didn't have to. 'Mrs Ash must find her a great help.'

The awkward pause lasted barely a moment before Hazel said, perhaps more shortly than she meant to, 'There isn't a Mrs Ash.'

Ash couldn't let that pass. 'Well, there is. But we're . . .' He struggled briefly. 'Separated.' That was certainly the word.

It was clearly dangerous ground: Rachel hurried off it. She said, 'I like your house. Is it very old?'

'About a hundred years, I think,' said Ash. 'It was my mother's. I used to live in London. I came back here after she died.'

'We came to Norbold four years ago, soon after Mum and

Gethin got together,' Rachel volunteered. 'Except Mum says it's not Norbold, it's Whitley Vale.'

Which pinged on Hazel's snob radar. The road past the Somerses' house would certainly reach the picture-postcard village of Whitley Vale eventually. But she'd have gambled all the money in her purse that when the family wanted milk, they bought it in Norbold.

Ash suspected she was about to say as much. He interjected quickly, 'I gather you're a pianist, Rachel.'

The girl just nodded.

Hazel watched her curiously. People who are learning to play are usually quite bashful about their accomplishment; people who think they *can* play are usually rather proud of it. Rachel Somers seemed to acknowledge it as simply a statement of fact, that ascribed no particular virtue to herself. As if Ash had said 'You're quite tall' or 'You have brown eyes.'

'Are you any good?' she asked.

'Pretty good,' said Rachel, still without any particular inflection. 'Possibly not as good as Mum thinks. Certainly not as good as Mum thinks I should be.'

Ash chuckled wryly, Hazel – unburdened by parenthood – more openly. 'A mum's reach should exceed her grasp,' she said, 'or what's a heaven for?'

FOUR

A bout then, the return of Ash's family was heralded by the sound of the Volvo in the drive and voices raised in desultory argument. Ash listened a moment, then nodded. 'Oh, this is a good one. Who'd win in a straight fight between a T-Rex and a Challenger tank? This one can go on for hours.'

'As could the fight,' said Hazel, 'but for the fact that the combatants missed one another by sixty-five million years. Rachel, I think this is our cue to leave.'

Rachel stood up as well. She looked absurdly young and fragile in her girlish outfit, her hair like a brown silk curtain to hide behind. Diffidently she said, 'I really just wanted to thank you properly. Your help was all that made it bearable.'

'I'm sorry it didn't end better.' Ash glanced at Hazel. 'I don't suppose there's anything new with the investigation?'

It wasn't the right question. The last thing that victims of serious crimes want to hear is that, barring good luck early on, investigations take time and results are often slow in coming. Hazel scowled at him. 'Proceeding as per our best efforts. They're still searching the woods. Whatever they find will go straight to forensics.'

'What kind of thing?' asked Rachel.

'All kinds of things. Forensic science is now so good you can almost say that any activity by any person in any place is going to leave detectable traces. The man we're looking for walked through the spinney to the back of your house; he probably waited there for some time, then he grabbed you. After that he fought with Mr Phillips, and then he made his way out of the wood, probably moving rather faster this time. It's inconceivable that he did all that without leaving something behind – footprints, fibres from his clothes, maybe spots of blood. You got snagged by the brambles, probably he did too. Criminal cases have been solved before now by linking a few fibres of polyester to the carpeting in a particular kind of car. It doesn't take much. We will get this man, Rachel. We might not get him today, but we will get him.'

When they reached Hazel's car, Rachel hesitated, half-turning to look up Highfield Road towards the spinney. 'Maybe I should walk home. It isn't very far.'

Hazel stared at her. 'Your mother will skin me alive if I let you walk home through that wood!'

Rachel managed a wan smile. 'He won't be there now. He'll be a hundred miles away, and never show his face round here again. That's what I'd do if I'd done something really bad.'

She was probably right. Hazel still wasn't going to let her walk. 'Not yet. It's too soon. For you, I mean. You will want to go into the spinney again some time, but not yet. It'll be pretty traumatic – maybe more than you expect. If you like, I'll come with you the first time. But not yet.'

'I suppose not,' said Rachel, getting into the car.

Hazel cast her a sideways glance as she drove. 'I don't know if you realise it, but you're dealing with this pretty well. There are six-foot paratroopers who'd have fallen apart under the strain of what you've been through. Are all musicians this tough?'

Rachel barked a little laugh. 'Maybe we are. We have to be. The nature of what we do is, there's a lot of work for precious little reward at the start. Even when you feel you're finally making progress, you're always comparing yourself to people who're better than you – to musicians who will always be better than you. It takes a degree of mental toughness to keep going. To settle for being the best you can be, rather than the best.'

'Does your mother play?'

'Piano? Not so much these days. She gets a better tune out of playing me.'

Hazel grinned, though she wasn't entirely confident it was a joke. 'Pony Club Mother syndrome.'

'What?'

'You see it a lot at horse shows. Women who never rode, or only at a modest level, pushing their offspring to live out their own dreams. They buy the best ponies, they drive the best horseboxes, they shout instructions like the sergeant major at a passing-out parade – and nine times out of ten, by the time the kids are old enough to say no, they burn their boots and never get on a horse again. At least nobody gets killed playing piano. Horse-riding is a risk sport. If you're going to get hurt doing it, you want it to be your dream, not someone else's.'

They'd reached the end of the Somerses' long drive. 'You can drop me off here,' said Rachel.

Hazel frowned. 'You don't want me to see you to your door?'

The girl laughed. 'I don't need an escort up my own driveway! It's a kind thought, but really, it's not necessary. I'm not going to alter how I live because of what's happened.'

'I'm not suggesting you should,' said Hazel seriously. 'But I do think you need to be careful. Until we catch this man, we don't know if it was a random attack or if he singled you out. If he did, it's possible he could come back. After the dust has settled and he starts feeling safe again.'

But Rachel shook her head decisively. 'He's wanted for murder. He'll be at the other end of the country by now, or abroad. He'd be crazy to come back to Norbold. Or even' – she gave a shy grin – 'Whitley Vale.'

'I expect you're right. Still, be careful. This man was dangerous when he was a potential rapist. Now he's a killer, he has nothing left to lose. If you think someone's watching you, call us right away. It doesn't matter if you're mistaken. We'll be glad if you're mistaken.'

'I *will* be careful,' promised Rachel. 'And I will call, if anything worries me. I still think we've heard the last of him.'

Hazel let her go, and didn't follow her up the drive. But she turned the car's engine off and listened through the lowered window until she heard the sound of the front door closing. She thought the girl was probably right. But in fact she was wrong.

The next incident came two days later. Two fourteen-year-old girls walking their dogs along the canal towpath on Thursday morning heard the sound of heavy breathing behind them and turned to see a man shambling after them, claw-like hands reaching towards them. They screamed and fled, and next time they looked back he was gone.

'Description?' asked Detective Chief Inspector Gorman.

Detective Sergeant Presley checked his notes. 'Not much of one. They thought he was big, but they couldn't say how big because he was bent over. Dark clothes – nothing specific; dark hair. He didn't speak, just gasped at them.'

'Gasped?'

'Gasped,' confirmed Presley.

'We're looking for a killer and child molester with emphysema?'

The sergeant gave a stoical shrug. 'I bring you the witness statements, I don't necessarily explain them.' He nodded at the paperwork on Gorman's desk. 'The PM on Phillips?'

The DCI nodded. 'It doesn't tell us much we didn't already know. Marks on the face – superficial, insignificant – probably from overhanging branches. No injuries, offensive or defensive, to his hands or arms, so there wasn't anything you could call a fight. Two blows to his head, from left and right, one from behind, one from the side: fractured skull, bleeding to the brain, death supervened.'

'What kind of weapon are we looking for?'

Gorman gave him a cynical leer. 'You'll like this. We're searching a wood for a length of wood with the bark still on.'

'Terrific,' said Presley glumly. 'What are we doing for the rest of the day?'

'A fingertip search of the towpath, of course. See if this time he managed to drop his business card.' Gorman reared back in his chair, scowling. 'This description. It doesn't sound like a real person, does it? It sounds like the bogeyman. These girls – I suppose you believed them?'

'If you mean, do I think they're telling the truth as they remember it, then yes,' said Presley carefully. 'Both mothers were there too, everyone was obviously upset but I didn't get any sense that I was being lied to. Respectable families, so far as I could tell. But if you mean, should we take their statements as factually accurate, then probably no. They're a pair of fourteen-year-old girls who've had a nasty shock: how much of the detail is what they remember and how much is hysteria, I couldn't say. But something happened to them on the towpath, and if their statements are a bit overblown, I'd still put some faith in them.'

Gorman nodded, considering. 'There's nothing to say this is definitely the same guy.'

Presley raised an eyebrow. 'We don't get a lot of kiddie-botherers, thank God. You think it's a coincidence that we get two in one week?'

'Coincidences *do* happen.' Even to himself, Gorman sounded unconvincing. 'Get down there – take SOCO – see if there's anything to find. See if there were any witnesses who weren't terrified fourteen-year-old girls.'

'What do I say if the local rag turns up?'

'What you always say when a reporter from the *Norbold News* asks you for a quote,' the DCI said wearily. 'Refer him to me.'

'What will you tell him? That there's nothing positively linking this to the murder of Gethin Phillips? They'll love that.'

'I probably *will* tell him that, because right now it's true. If there's any speculating to be done, the *News* can do it. They've never had any problems before.' Gorman gave a disparaging sniff.

'If there *is* a connection,' said Presley, a note of warning in his voice, 'it's a game-changer.'

DCI Gorman glared at him from under one lowered eyebrow. 'You think I need telling? You think I'm not already sweating bullets over the thought that somebody who should be in John O'Groats by now has decided, against all reason, to stay in Norbold and see what else we have to offer in the way of young girls? If these two incidents *are* connected, we're looking for a man with no control over his urges, not even when his own safety requires it; who's willing to kill anyone who gets in his way. Offhand, I can't think of a more dangerous combination. If these two incidents are connected, all Norbold needs to be as scared as I am. And if the *Norbold News* asks to quote me on that, I shall let them.'

Tom Presley nodded. There was nothing more he could usefully say. 'I'll get down there, see what I can find.'

He found nothing. No corroborative evidence, no other witnesses. Presley did everything there was to be done, then waited with grim expectancy to see what would happen next. Alerted by a stop-press in Thursday's *Norbold News*, the town waited with him.

For another two days.

On Saturday night, around eleven o'clock, fifteen-year-old Skye Pascoe was found sobbing in the bathroom of her father's flat, trying to wash dirt and blood off her clothes and herself. He'd been ready to give her an ear-lashing – he'd been listening out for the door for an hour and a half – until he saw the state she was in. When he'd coaxed enough of an explanation from her to realise what had happened, he called the police.

It was policy at Meadowvale Police Station that, whenever possible, interviews regarding rape allegations should be conducted by female officers. Complainants found it easier to talk to another woman, so more information was obtained more quickly; while the demeanour of rape suspects could be markedly different in the presence of a female officer rather than another male, making it possible to infer something about their attitude to women in general. The senior female CID officer at Meadowvale was DC Emma Friend; there wasn't a junior one. She asked Hazel to ride shotgun.

Meadowvale also had a dedicated rape suite, not so much an interview room as a sitting room with coffee-making facilities and a small examination room off it. While Skye was dressing, the clothes she'd worn for her night out having been bagged and tagged for forensics, Dr Miriam Green gave the officers a summary of her initial findings.

'I can't, as a medical examiner, tell you it was rape. You know that. I can tell you there has been recent sexual activity, that she was handled roughly both internally and externally, and I see no reason to doubt her statement that she was a virgin until tonight. I'll get the swabs off for analysis: they may or may not tell us more.'

'But if you've got a semen sample . . .?' asked Hazel.

'You'll still have to find a suspect to match it to.'

'Usual thing, then,' said Friend, forcing a smile. 'All the

wonderful modern technology is worth diddly-squat until we've done a bit of old-fashioned detective work.'

Dressed now, hugging herself, the bruises on her arms darkening as they watched, the girl – small even for fifteen – stood in the doorway to the examination room. 'Can I go home now?' She was close to tears.

'Very soon,' nodded Emma Friend. 'We'll ask your dad to come in now – is that all right? Then we'll take a quick statement – to get the details before they start getting jumbled in your memory. Then we'll take you home.'

Skye nodded miserably. Her flame-coloured hair, combed through now, cast a shadow across her ashy face. Her eyes were stretched with shock, hunted, fugitive.

A PC showed Edwin Pascoe upstairs. He took the chair he was offered and sat hunched over the mug of coffee Hazel passed him, frozen in grief, saying nothing. After a minute Skye slipped her hand into his, as if she were the appropriate adult, and they exchanged a broken smile.

'In your own words,' said DC Friend, 'tell us what happened.'

She'd been late. She'd promised her father she'd be home by half nine, and it was later than that before she left her friend's house. To make up time, she'd cut across the park. It was August, even an hour after sunset it wasn't pitch black; she could see well enough to find her way towards the gate on the far side of the lake that would bring her within a hundred metres of home.

She never reached the gate. He grabbed her as she hurried past the stand of willows at the end of the lake: an arm around her throat, a hand over her mouth. He dragged her into the deep shadow under the trees, knocked her down and threw himself on top of her, tearing at her clothes.

By then she'd known what to expect. After it was over, after he'd left her sitting sobbing on the grass and disappeared among the trees, she pulled her torn clothes disconsolately around her, found her shoulder bag, got up and walked home.

'Can you give us any kind of a description?' asked Emma Friend. 'Anything at all.'

'He was big,' said Skye. 'And he seemed to be bent over.

You know – as if there was something wrong with his back? And when he ran, he sort of shambled.'

'How old would you say he was?' But the girl didn't know.

'When you say big,' said Hazel, 'do you mean tall, or fat, or both?' But Skye couldn't say. She'd just got an impression of substance.

'What was he wearing?' asked Friend.

Skye shook her head again. There had been neither the time nor the light for her to see. Something dark, maybe. And she thought he had dark hair.

'Clean-shaven or bearded?'

The girl thought for a moment. Clean-shaven; she'd have noticed a beard. Felt it.

Friend tried a few more questions but got nothing more by way of answers. 'I'll get someone to take the pair of you home now. We'll talk again soon. If you think of anything else you can tell me, I'll be right there.'

After the girl and her father had gone, the police officers finished the coffee. 'What do you think?' asked Hazel.

Friend regarded her askance. 'I think she was raped.'

'Well, yes. What I mean is, that sounded awfully like the man on the towpath. If this was him, and that was him, surely it's odds-on it was him in Highfield Spinney as well. In which case he's attacked three times in a week, and killed once.'

The fact that she was now a reasonably experienced detective constable did not prevent Emma Friend from shuddering. 'It's beginning to look that way, isn't it?' A slight pensive frown crossed her brow. 'Hazel – do you think you ought to have a word with Gabriel Ash?'

Hazel was taken aback. 'Gabriel? What about?'

There was no very tactful way of putting it, so Friend just did the best she could. 'About watching his back. After this week's events, Norbold is going to be a hostile place for big, dark men who stoop and shamble, and can't point to a happy marriage as their get-out-of-jail-free card.'

Hazel stared at her in astonishment. 'You're not suggesting . . . *Gabriel*? Oh come on, Emma, you've known him as long as I have. There isn't a man in England less likely to be responsible for these attacks.'

'I'm not suggesting that he is. I'm suggesting that, to a frightened town ready to jump at shadows, he might *look* suspicious. He matches the descriptions we've been given. Even if they weren't very good descriptions, there are more people who wouldn't fit them than who would. He was nearby when Rachel Somers was assaulted and Gethin Phillips killed. He walks his dog on the towpath and in the park. And there are a lot of people in Norbold who already think of him as a bit strange and unpredictable.'

'You know as well as I do, there was a good reason he went off the rails!' declared Hazel indignantly.

'Of course I do. And you and I both know it's not likely to happen again. But most people don't know that. To most people he's a little odd, someone who isn't quite the same as them, someone who even now they might be more comfortable avoiding. The last guy on the busy bus to have a seat to himself.'

'Hazel, you know what people are like. Most of the time they don't mean any harm, but they don't think. And it's always easier to blame an outsider for any kind of trouble. I'm just saying, now would be a really good time for him to avoid drawing attention to himself. And if he feels the need to hold long and convoluted discussions with someone, to do it with a consenting adult in private, *not* in a public place with his dog!'

Gabriel Ash was indeed a big, dark-haired man who had to be reminded to stand up straight. Stooping had become a habit: it was his way of not looming over people in an intimidatory manner. During what he now cheerfully described as his doolally days, he'd discovered that if there's one thing that makes people more uneasy than a village idiot, it's a big village idiot.

And it was true that he was a doting wife short of the perfect family, and that he had done some strange and unpredictable things in his time. On the other hand, he made a genuine effort these days not to be overheard conversing with his dog.

But he couldn't honestly refute the charge of being an outsider. He'd been an outsider all his life. Before Cathy betrayed him; before he knew Cathy. He'd been a serious child, a studious teenager, and as a young man all he looked for in a car was reliable transportation. He couldn't remember ever being incapably drunk, and he didn't know the words to any rugby songs. He rather suspected he was the most boring person most people had ever met.

In spite of which, he looked at Hazel much as Hazel had looked at Emma Friend when she passed on the DC's warning. 'I think she must have been joking,' he decided.

'I don't think she was.'

'Meadowvale considers me a suspect? Dave Gorman thinks I might have attacked four girls and murdered a man?'

'That's *not* what she was saying,' Hazel said testily, torn between her fondness for Ash and her professional loyalties. 'Of course it isn't. She was concerned – concerned for you – that people who knew nothing about this except what they'd seen in the paper and heard on street corners might put two and two together and get the square root of bugger all. She was just suggesting that you be a bit careful. Don't let yourself get drawn into arguments. Don't go round annoying people.'

Gabriel Ash was also the least argumentative person most people had ever met. 'Leave my axe-murdering hat at home, you mean.'

She hadn't wanted to upset him, but she knew that she had. In truth, it wasn't something anyone wanted to hear about himself, that those around him thought he had the potential to be a violent criminal. It didn't have to matter. It wouldn't have occurred to Ash any more than it had occurred to Hazel, and the fact that it *had* occurred to Emma Friend was significant and had to be shared. What he would do with the information, what he could do with it, was for Ash to decide. Hazel took some comfort in the knowledge that he was an intelligent man: when he stopped being offended and thought about it, he would understand why she'd told him.

'Just, if you need to know the time, don't ask the first teenage girl you meet – wait for her granny to come along.'

FIVE

Next, a mixed group of youngsters cooling off in that stretch of the canal which the local council had furnished with a beach were approached by a dark-haired man with wild eyes and ragged clothes. Alarmed, they retreated across the canal, where passers-by helped them up onto the towpath. Mumbling obscenities, the man disappeared back into the bushes.

That night, someone heaved half a brick through the window of Rambles With Books.

DCI Gorman didn't hear about it from Gabriel Ash. He heard about it from Hazel. Now he was sitting on Ash's big table, watching Ash clear up the debris with a dustpan and brush. Patience had been banished to the kitchen where she wouldn't get sherds of glass in her paws.

'I don't suppose you've any idea who it was.'

Ash looked up, irritation in his gaze. 'No, Detective Chief Inspector, I haven't. I rather thought it was the job of CID to establish that.'

'Of course it is,' agreed Gorman. 'We'll put this murder inquiry on hold, shall we, and focus all our resources on finding out who broke your window?'

Ash forbore to comment.

'Well, if we don't know who it was,' said Gorman, 'I imagine we've a pretty good idea why.'

'To steal my valuable stock?' hazarded Ash. 'To raid my till before the armed guards from the Bank of England come to empty it?'

Gorman breathed heavily at him. 'Have you had words with anybody about what's going on? Has anybody threatened you, or given you a funny look, or . . .?' He gave a little thought to what he'd just said, and sighed. 'OK, I probably can't arrest people for giving you funny looks: there'd be too many of them and some of them would be my officers.

So, anything out of the ordinary? Anyone seeming to have a problem with you?'

'Miss Hornblower wasn't very happy that I sold an early edition Dickens before she got a chance to look at it.'

'Was she carrying half a brick at the time?'

'A handbag and a floral umbrella, as I recall.'

'Well, we won't dismiss her just yet, but perhaps we should keep looking.'

Ash finished clearing up and let Patience out of the kitchen. 'It was probably just kids.'

'It may well have been just kids. And if your head had got in the way of that half-brick, you'd have a fractured skull now, whether it was kids who threw it, or a parent, or someone else with an overdeveloped sense of civic duty. You need to take this seriously, Gabriel. It isn't just vandalism, it's an attack on you. It's a warning. It may be the only one you get.'

Ash regarded him frankly. 'So what do you want me to do, Dave? The glazier will be here to replace the window by lunchtime. I've told you what happened, I've told the insurers. What exactly do you think I should do to prevent it happening again?'

'You could shut the shop for a few days.'

'This didn't happen when the shop was open. Anyway, closed shops attract more vandals than ones that are open for business.'

'I'm not really thinking what's best for the shop. I'm thinking what's best for you.'

'I know you are,' said Ash with a tired little smile. 'But I don't see what it would achieve. If it's just random vandalism, it'll be some other shop next time. If it *is* directed at me specifically, surely we can take some comfort from the fact that the boldest stroke he was capable of was to heave a brick at a shop window in the middle of the night? It's a long way from breaking my glass to breaking my legs.'

'And if he isn't the only one this idea has occurred to? Gabriel, you know what a mob is, don't you? It's a group of people whose IQ is in inverse proportion to its size. What if next time it isn't half a brick in the middle of the night but a dozen big guys with baseball bats at ten in the morning?'

Ash didn't have an answer. Probably there wasn't one. 'This is a small town. People know where I live. If someone has a problem with me, I'd rather they come here than go to my house – to my children's home. If I shut the shop, that's where people will come looking for me.'

'You could go away for a couple of weeks,' suggested Gorman. 'Take the boys on holiday.'

At least Ash gave it some thought. 'Are you confident of charging someone in the next fortnight?'

'Of course not,' snorted Gorman. 'Hopeful – always hopeful – but I can't put my hand on my heart and say I expect to.'

'Then the likelihood is we'd be returning to a situation no better than it is today. In fact, it could be worse. If there are no more incidents while we're away, the sort of people who did this' – he gestured at the window – 'will think it's all the proof they need that I was responsible. Dave, I've worked too hard at being accepted in Norbold. I'm not giving it up without a fight.'

Gorman sniffed. Like many former rugby players, he was significantly endowed in the nasal department. 'You know who you sound like, don't you?'

Ash thought about that too, then nodded ruefully.

'And do you remember what you and I both told her when the boot was on Hazel's foot?'

Ash gave his gentle smile. 'We told her that her safety was more important than her dignity. She said that the only place the issue could be dealt with was right here. And she was right. She stayed and fought, and won.'

'She could have stayed and fought and lost,' the DCI pointed out. 'Even if it was the right decision for her then, that doesn't mean it's the right decision for you now.'

'Perhaps I should book a holiday,' said Ash pensively.

Gorman eyed him warily. He hadn't expected it to be this easy.

'For Frankie and the boys,' added Ash, for the avoidance of doubt.

Frankie Kelly understood immediately why he wanted her to take his sons to the West Country, but she didn't like leaving him alone.

'Patience will be here.'

The nanny looked at the lurcher; the lurcher looked calmly back. 'And if you're cornered by a mob of vigilantes, I'm sure she'll be a great help to you. Almost as much, indeed, as a feathered whoopee-whistle.'

Ash didn't dare look at Patience for fear of what she might say. 'I honestly don't think there's much to worry about. But Mr Gorman was concerned, so I said I'd get the boys off-side for a couple of weeks. They'll like the West Country. Sign them up for surfing lessons.'

'They'd like it more if you came too.'

'I know. But I'm not doing.'

Frankie pursed her lips. She was a tiny Filipino woman with two children older than the Ash boys back at home. She was a mainstay of life at Highfield Road. 'Would you consider asking Miss Best to stay while we're away?'

Ash could guess what it cost her to say that. She was by no means a prude, but she had firm ideas of what was proper behaviour, and generally speaking she would not have approved of a single woman moving in with a married man. But she was aware of the particular circumstances of her employer's family background, and knew that, however it might appear to casual acquaintances, Gabriel Ash and Hazel Best were really good friends and nothing more. She knew this because both parties had told her so, more than once.

'As my own personal police protection?' he said. 'I suppose I could ask her.'

But that was not, and Frankie Kelly knew it was not, the same as saying he *would* ask her.

The following day Frankie drove Gilbert and Guy south. Before they were out of Highfield Road, Gilbert was complaining that he was old enough to sit up front instead of in the back like a little kid.

Ash watched them go with a mixture of relief and regret. If there was going to be trouble, he wanted his sons to be somewhere else; but in the two years they'd been back he'd grown unused to having the house to himself. When he waved one last time and went indoors, it felt absurdly big and absurdly empty, and he was astonished to find tears in the corners of his eyes.

He'd offered Frankie his mother's car – he still, even after so long, never thought of it as *his* car – to save putting mileage on her own. Unaccountably, she preferred her modern automatic to the eighteen-year-old Volvo, but undertook to keep the fuel receipts.

He caught Patience watching him, expressionless. 'What?' he asked defensively. 'I'm not allowed to miss my children?'

It'll be nice, just us again, said the lurcher. Like old times.

'I remember those times,' said Ash darkly. 'I don't remember enjoying them all that much.'

You hadn't just been rescued from the dog pound, and the prospect of a one-way ticket to the great kennel in the sky.

Ash allowed her that one. 'On the other hand, everyone I knew thought I was mad.'

Everyone you know *still* thinks you're mad. They're just more polite about saying so now they know you've got money.

Ash laughed out loud. 'You are such a cynic!'

And you're a man engaged in a dialogue with his dog, who thinks he *used* to be mad.

They walked into town via the park. The new window at Rambles With Books had come through the night unscathed, although Ash had declined the glazier's suggestion of security shutters. The value of the stock didn't justify the expense, and Ash didn't think that steel gratings would enhance the calm, contemplative ambience that he aimed at.

He opened officially at ten, though he usually reached the shop at around nine thirty and would admit anyone he found on the doorstep, slavering for a volume of nineteenth-century poetry. It didn't happen often enough to be a problem.

What happened more often, if she was off duty, was that Hazel would turn up around twenty to ten, put the kettle on and see what he'd got in the way of biscuits. He glanced at the clock over the counter and began a countdown, and before he'd reached single digits the bell jangled as the unlocked door opened and then closed. Ash, bent over the long table arranging books, smiled secretly to himself. Apart from anything else, he liked the bell on its annular spring, which danced musically when the door disturbed it. He'd found it in an antiques shop, and the sound immediately took him back thirty years to when many local shops had one, so the shop-keeper could get on with her housework between customers. Ash's mother had disapproved of supermarkets as a flashy, newfangled idea that would never catch on.

'You're nearly out of custard creams,' said Hazel.

'People keep eating them,' said Ash.

'I heard about your window.'

'Yes?' He took the mug she offered, the one inscribed with the words: 'Etonians Do It Up Against The Wall'. He hadn't been to Eton, but he had been to a grammar school and Hazel teased him because of it. 'Did you hear anything else, anything useful – like who broke it?'

'Some pillar of the community with an IQ smaller than his shoe size,' she hazarded, 'who probably doesn't support his own children but takes as a personal affront any threat to anyone else's. I'm sorry, Gabriel, this is what happens when enough people are frightened. If they could have found a hunchbacked foreigner with a squint to blame, they'd have chased him with pitchforks. They couldn't, so they focused on you.'

'It's that description,' said Ash ruefully. 'It isn't very flat-tering, but it is tolerably accurate.'

Hazel dismissed that with a shake of her fair head. Her hair was down below her shoulders again, the ripe-corn curls constantly attempting to escape their elastic band. 'It isn't a description at all. It's an idea, a stereotype. It's the storybook child-snatcher: dressed in black, bent over, long grasping fingers. In all probability, the man who killed Gethin Phillips and raped Skye Pascoe doesn't look anything like that. Neither Skye or Rachel saw enough of their attacker to give a proper description.'

'The girls on the towpath did. And there were other witnesses to the incident at the beach – people on the other side of the canal. They can't all be imagining things.'

She shrugged. 'You know as well as I do, eyewitness testi-mony is about as reliable as the British weather. Half the time we don't see what's actually there, we see what we expect to see. After the attack on Rachel, everyone was primed to see the sort of man the public consciousness associates with that kind of crime.'

There was a pause then. From the way Hazel was dipping into the biscuit barrel on autopilot, Ash realised she was cogitating so didn't distract her. After a couple of minutes she looked up again, brows drawn together in a pensive frown. 'I don't suppose . . .' And there she stopped.

Ash knew what was required of him now. 'What are you thinking?'

'I'm not sure,' she admitted. 'It's probably stupid anyway. Only . . .'

Ash waited patiently. Experience told him that she'd get to the point eventually.

'Look,' she said, 'you, me and the rest of Norbold know you meet all sorts on the canal towpath. Not just joggers and dog-walkers but glue-sniffers and meth-heads and even the occasional honest-to-goodness tramp. Any other week, the mothers of those two girls and the parents of the swimmers would have been down at Meadowvale insisting that we increase patrols along the canal and clean the place up. We would all have assumed that the kids had had an encounter with an undesirable rather than a dangerous element.

'But this week, two girls were attacked and a man was killed. The murder was front-page news in the local rag; the attack on Skye Pascoe made the local radio. People had an image of this man in their heads before ever they saw him. And I suppose what I'm wondering is whether the heavy-breather on the towpath was the man we're looking for at all. Or was he just some worn-out, beat-up homeless guy trying to panhandle a bit of loose change?'

They regarded one another in speculative silence. It wasn't the answer to anything, it was only a question; but she was wrong to say it was a stupid one.

At length Ash said, 'How can we find out?'

'I'm not sure we can. None of those witnesses lied to us: they all reported what they thought they saw. If we ask them again, they'll tell us the same thing. But maybe there's another interpretation.'

Ash was in favour of anything that cast doubt on the description that even he thought he fitted better than anyone he knew. But there were other facts that there was no room for doubt about, including a man's body in the morgue at Norbold Royal Infirmary. 'Suppose you're right, and there has been a degree of hysteria. Suppose we set the canal incidents aside for the moment. The man who attacked Rachel Somers and Skye Pascoe, and killed Gethin Phillips, is still a deeply dangerous man.'

'Yes. But he may not be the out-of-control obsessive that he would be if he'd attacked four times, twice in broad daylight.'

Ash was nodding slowly. 'You should talk to Dave. He may need to reconsider the kind of man he's looking for. And he may be able to do something about that bloody description.' Gabriel Ash almost never swore. It was an indication of how uncomfortable the finger of suspicion made him feel.

Hazel said quietly, 'No one who knows the first thing about you thinks you had anything to do with this.'

'I know,' he said tersely. 'Unfortunately, there are more people in Norbold who *don't* know me than who do. And you have to admit, I look more like a storybook villain than the man on the Coventry omnibus.'

Hazel regarded him fondly. 'Well, maybe, on a bad day. I have told you about not stooping, haven't I?'

'You have.'

'I will talk to Dave. He may not think there's any mileage in it. Or he may think that, while I could be right, if we're going to make a mistake it has to be on the side of caution. If there's any chance those kids did see the killer, he can't discount what they say they saw.'

Ash might have been hoping for something more concrete and immediate to exonerate him, but he knew she was right. In time her insight might alter the direction of the inquiry; in the short term it changed nothing. Disappointed but resigned he said, 'Too soon to break out the champagne, then.'

Hazel smiled. 'Maybe a little. Don't be discouraged, Gabriel.

Dave will find this man. It's a murder inquiry: he's throwing everything he has at it. For Pru Somers' sake, for Rachel's, and for yours. When the breakthrough comes, everything will change overnight. It could be tonight. Tomorrow night you could go to bed knowing that the man who killed Gethin Phillips is in custody.'

'And if it takes longer than that?'

'Try to be sensible. Be aware of what's going on around you, and don't do anything to make people uneasy. The *Norbold News* stuck pretty much to the facts, but folk have also heard stories and rumours in pubs and the queues at supermarket checkouts, and they're just about ready to panic. It wouldn't take much to provoke an outbreak of mass hysteria. The town's like a forest at the end of a dry season: one carelessly dropped match and the whole place could catch fire.'

Ash knew she was looking out for him. He recognised with the same old wonder that it was because she cared about him, and that made it easy to forgive her for giving him hope only to snatch it away. 'If you've any suggestions . . .?'

'Go away for a few days. Take Patience, and the boys, and Frankie, and go to the seaside.'

He appeared to give it some thought. 'It's a good idea.'

Hazel had expected not so much an argument as a point-blank refusal. She peered suspiciously at him. 'It is?'

'Which is why I sent Frankie and the boys off to Cornwall this morning. In case things get out of hand.'

'When are you going to join them?'

Ash gave her the ghost of a smile that made her want to slap him. 'Apart from the sea views, the beaches, the surfing and the cream teas, what has Cornwall got that Norbold hasn't?'

She breathed heavily. 'This is not a good time for heroics, Gabriel. If you get yourself beaten up for looking like a nervous teenager's description of a meth-head, it'll divert resources from the murder inquiry. Dave Gorman won't thank you for wasting man-hours he needs to find the killer.

'Look, the fact that he remained in the area after committing murder, that he couldn't resist attacking at least one other girl, means he too can't bring himself to do the sensible thing and leave town. So he's already made one mistake, and he will make others. We will find him, and then everyone will know it wasn't you. By the time you get back from Cornwall, it'll all be over.'

Ash was less confident. Though DCI Gorman worked hard to tie up his cases, his clear-up rate was no higher than the fairly dismal national average of eight per cent. This was more important than most of his workload because it concerned not only attacks on children but a man's death. Being important meant CID were working flat-out; it didn't necessarily mean they would succeed. On the other hand, Hazel was right: if the perpetrator was too driven to be cautious, sooner or later he'd attack when there were more people close enough to help, or bigger people, or people who were ready for him, and his reign of terror would be over. Of course, that probably meant there would be more victims.

It also meant that, until then, there would be people patrolling the shadows of Norbold armed with baseball bats, and they would probably rack up more victims too.

'If I leave town, it'll look as if I have a reason to run away.'

'If you stay, it may turn out that you had.'

Ash sighed. 'I know you have my best interests at heart, Hazel. Perhaps you're right, and I'll end up wishing I'd taken your advice. But I've got a lot invested in this town. A home, a family, a business. People who used to cross the street when they saw me coming don't any more. I don't want to jeopardise that. I don't want to feel like a pariah again.'

Hazel felt a twinge of compassion. It was easy to forget that, when she first met Gabriel Ash, he was an object of ridicule throughout Norbold. Apparently it hadn't been that easy for *him* to forget. 'Well, maybe it'll all blow over,' she murmured.

But it didn't.

SIX

A sh shut the shop at six, brought his accounts up to date, and walked Patience home via the park.

They were waiting for him at the corner of Highfield Road: five men, aged between twenty-five and forty. None of them were carrying a baseball bat, but two of them wore baseball caps, the peaks shading their faces. One wore a hoodie with the hood up, though the heat of the summer day had yet to dissipate. Ash glanced at them, moving into the road to pass. He didn't recognise any of them.

One of them rumbled, 'Just so you know, mate – we're going to be watching you.'

Ash could have kept walking. The men made no move to detain him. It might have been the sensible thing to do: he wasn't sure. But he thought the inference was plain enough that failing to deny it could seem like an admission of guilt. He heard the low vibration at his side that was Patience growling, which gave him a certain amount of confidence. She wasn't a big dog, but she was fast and well-armed, and not many people are angry enough to stand their ground in the face of a snarling dog.

He said, 'There seems to be some misunderstanding here. I'm willing to discuss it, if that's what you want.'

Generally speaking, the last thing a mob wants is a rational discussion. The man who had spoken before responded first. 'We're not here for a debate. We just want you to know . . .'

'That you're going to be watching me. You said. You're going to find it rather boring. Taking my dog for a walk is about the most exciting thing I do all day.' This was slightly disingenuous. It was the most exciting thing he did on a lot of days; but perhaps the men neither knew nor cared about his intermittent forays into criminal investigation.

'What, in the woods?' said another of the men, jerking his head towards the far end of the road. 'Down by the canal?'

'Sometimes,' agreed Ash. 'They're good places for walking dogs. You see a lot of dog-walkers there.'

'And kids,' said the first man.

Ash sighed. 'Was it you who broke my window?'

There was a longish pause. 'No.' It might have been the truth.

'All right. Well, I'm not going to pretend I don't know what this is about. You think it was me who attacked one girl in Highfield Spinney and another in the park, and frightened some other young people down by the canal. Don't you?'

'That's right.'

'So you must also think I killed Gethin Phillips. Yes?'

But it wasn't the murder of a grown man that concerned them. It was almost as if they'd forgotten for a moment that a man had died.

'Er . . . yes.'

'But if that was what had happened, that's what his step-daughter would have told the police. And she didn't. She said she was attacked, that she struggled with her assailant and made her escape – and several minutes later, and half a mile away, she stumbled out of the spinney and saw me and my dog in the adjacent field. And I wasn't out of breath from fighting and then running to get ahead of her, and although she was covered in scratches and bruises, I wasn't.'

He held out his hands for inspection, palms down, the knuckles clearly undamaged. 'It's nine days ago now, so any bruises would have faded. But the police saw me within minutes of the attack, and then again at intervals over the next several days. Do you really think they wouldn't have noticed if I'd been in a fight?'

He might not have convinced them but he had shaken their confidence. 'Er . . .'

'Listen,' Ash said kindly, 'the whole town's on edge over this. Of course it is. People are worried about their children. Me too: I've sent mine down to Cornwall for a fortnight. You made a mistake. I hope I've been able to set your minds at rest.'

They gave it one last shot. 'Talk's cheap . . .'

A sharp, clear voice cut through the atmosphere of confused belligerence. 'What's going on here? Get away from him!'

Ash thought for a moment it was Hazel, but it wasn't. When the shoulders in front of him parted he saw the slight form of Rachel Somers stalking down Highfield Road from the direction of the fields. 'Gabriel, are you all right? Do you want me to call the police?' She had her phone, recovered during the search of the wood, ready in her hand.

'No, everything's fine,' he assured her. And, turning to the men: 'Isn't it? The police are busy enough trying to find whoever killed Mr Phillips – we don't need to trouble them over a misunderstanding. Do we?'

Their certainty already undermined by Ash's manner, they were further wrong-footed by the arrival of a girl who, judging from their puzzled expressions, they failed to recognise. The man who was the closest thing they had to a leader tried looming at her, in the hope that she'd prove easier to intimidate than Ash. 'You get about your business, miss. This is nothing to do with you.'

Indignation blazed like fireworks in Rachel's eyes. 'If it isn't my business, you stupid man, I don't know whose business you think it is!'

Ash felt the need for introductions – careful ones, that preserved as much of the family's privacy as possible. 'Gentlemen, this is Mr Phillips' stepdaughter.'

'Actually, I'm not,' Rachel said sharply. 'Gethin was my mother's partner. But yes, it was me that he died protecting. I'm Rachel Somers. Gabriel came to my aid as well; and then he went into the spinney to look for Gethin, when the man who killed him might still have been there. And if you think I don't know the difference between a vicious thug and a brave man who put himself in danger to help me, you need your tiny heads examining!'

The spokesman wouldn't have let his own daughter speak to him like that, but he didn't know how to react to being insulted by one of the young people in whose name he'd come here. Furthermore, his troops were getting uneasy and starting to drift back towards the cars they'd left round the corner. Deprived of support, he decided a dignified withdrawal was his best option and the incident ended as it had begun. 'Just so as you know – we'll be watching you . . .'

'Are you all right?' Rachel said again, anxiously, after the men had gone.

'I'm fine. They were just . . .' Ash shrugged. 'They're scared, and they don't know what to do about it.'

'So they thought they'd come here and threaten you?' Her voice soared with the excess of adrenalin.

'They weren't very threatening,' said Ash mildly. 'Not really.'

Yeah, right, drawled Patience.

'I thought they were,' confessed Rachel.

Ash smiled. 'No one would have guessed.'

She returned the smile, tremulously. 'They always say attack is the best form of defence.'

'They do say that, don't they?' He looked up and down the road. There was no one in sight now, and no cars he didn't recognise. 'Rachel, what are you doing here? How did you get here?'

'I wanted to apologise. I heard about your shop being vandalised. I feel guilty about that. It only happened because you helped me.'

'I'm not sure that's true. I had a certain reputation in this town long before we met. When something like this happens, when people are alarmed, they tend to look askance at anyone who isn't quite like them. They'd have suspected me even if I hadn't been walking my dog near the spinney that night.'

She was looking at him with what Ash was astonished to recognise as compassion. It came as a shock that a girl who'd had to fight off a rapist thought he was the one who needed sympathy.

He cleared his throat. 'Who brought you? Your mother? Where is she?'

'I walked,' said Rachel.

Ash stared as understanding dawned. 'Through the spinney?'

She shrugged. 'I was going to have to do it sometime. I did it today. I'll go back the same way. It'll be broad daylight for ages yet.'

'Indeed you will not,' he retorted, exactly as if one of the boys had proposed hang-gliding off the garage roof. 'I'll drive you home. Rachel, don't be foolish about this. Unless we believe in multiple unconnected attacks, the man who attacked you didn't leave town afterwards. One other girl has been badly hurt. You can't afford to assume that the man responsible won't return to the spinney at some point. I'm driving you home, and if you feel any gratitude to me at all, you won't go back into the woods until he's been caught.'

Ash drove her up to the front door.

'Please come in,' said Rachel. 'I'm sure my mother will want to say hello.'

'All right.' Something occurred to him. 'Did she know you were going to walk through the woods?'

The girl shook her head. 'She was asleep when I went out. She hasn't been very well since – you know. She wanted to get back to work, but she really isn't up to it.'

'Don't disturb her if she's sleeping.'

'I'll go and see.'

Pru Somers wasn't sleeping. She was in the kitchen, leaning white-faced over the sink. She looked round at the sound of their voices. 'Where have you been?' she demanded querulously. 'I've been worried.'

'I needed some fresh air,' said Rachel. 'I told you I was going out.'

'Did you?' Pru drew a hand across her damp forehead. 'Perhaps you did. I'm not entirely with it today.'

'Would you like me to call a doctor, Mrs Somers?' asked Ash from the doorway.

She looked at him as if she'd only just noticed him there. 'Ah, Mr Ash. Again.' She looked at her hand, at her forefinger, as if inspecting it for damage. 'No, it seems to be working. So if I want to see a doctor, I'll be able to phone one myself.'

'Mum!' hissed Rachel, embarrassed.

'I'm sorry,' Ash said, 'I didn't mean to intrude. I just wanted to see Rachel safely home. I'll get off now.'

'No, I'm sorry,' said Pru, relenting. 'I'm snapping at everyone. I don't know why I think being rude to people will make me feel better. Especially people who've done nothing except try to help.'

'You're still in shock. You both are. Right now, all you can do is get through each day, somehow, and hope the next one will be slightly better.'

Pru tilted her head to one side in a gesture that reminded him of Hazel. 'And are you a doctor, Mr Ash?'

'No, I sell second-hand books, Mrs Somers. But I do know something about loss, and grief.'

She sat down tiredly on a kitchen chair. 'Something like this' – she flicked her fingers as a substitute for finding better words – 'makes one horribly self-centred. Of course I'm not the first person to have lost someone I loved. But that's how it feels. In here.' She laid her palm flat on her breastbone. The neck of her thin summer blouse was open to the third button. 'As if no one has ever before had their life ripped apart like this.'

'You probably should see a doctor,' ventured Ash. 'You don't have to struggle through on your own. If you mention it to your police liaison officer, I'm sure she'll arrange it. Who was it, do you remember?'

'A blonde girl. Hazel something.'

Ash smiled. 'Hazel Best. She'll certainly want to know that you're feeling like this. She'll get you some help.'

Pru was watching him again in that calculating, almost predatory way. 'Did you ask for help? When it was your turn?'

'No,' he admitted, 'I didn't. I punched my boss and spent six weeks in a psychiatric hospital instead.'

Pru Somers laughed out loud. It wasn't the reaction Ash had expected, and it was a brittle laugh with more strain than amusement in it, but it brought a little colour back into her cheeks and he thought that talking was doing her some good. 'That wouldn't work for me. I'm pretty well my own boss.' She glanced at the kitchen clock. 'The sun's well over the yardarm now – can I offer you a drink?'

'I'd better not,' he said, 'I'm driving. Could I have a soft drink instead?'

'We'll all have a soft drink,' Pru decided. 'Rachel, will you make them? Bring them into the drawing room.' She led Ash through the house.

He wondered for a moment if he was supposed to say something, if she was actually inviting him to comment. If she wanted to talk about her situation and needed someone to talk about it with. But if he was mistaken, it would be so gross an impertinence that he didn't dare risk it. He took the chair she waved him to and admired the painting over the fireplace instead.

But then she reached for an onyx box on the coffee table and took out a cigarette, and he wasn't quick enough to mask his disapproval before she saw it. She put the cigarette back. 'Ah. You've guessed.'

After a moment Ash nodded. 'How long have you known?'

'I suspected a couple of weeks ago. Now I'm sure.'

'Have you told Rachel?'

'Not yet.'

Rachel came in with a pitcher and three crystal tumblers on a tray. 'Have you told Rachel what?'

Ash went back to admiring the picture.

Fragments of expressions flitted across Pru's face – irritation, anxiety, self-pity – before it slumped into weariness, as if her reason for telling the truth was that she was just too tired and dispirited to make up a lie. 'I'm pregnant, dear.'

Rachel didn't drop the tray. Perhaps the crystal tumblers were too valuable. She put it down carefully on the coffee table and slowly straightened, slender as a wind-whipped reed. 'No.'

Pru barked a bitter little laugh. 'You think I'm too old? I'm forty-two! It really isn't that unusual.'

'But . . . Gethin . . .'

'Is dead? Yes, Rachel, I had noticed. But he wasn't sick, he wasn't an invalid: he got his head beaten in, because you had to go running round the spinney after that damn cat! Six weeks ago he was fine.'

'Six weeks . . .' The girl's voice was hollow with a cocktail of emotions Ash couldn't quite identify. A degree of shock, of course. Finding out she was going to acquire a sibling, or at least a half-sibling, after seventeen years as an only child, would always have rocked her. The precise circumstances of Gethin Phillips' death would pile guilt on top of the shock, and would have done even without her mother's jibe. Perhaps, too, they would have money worries, with half the household's income ceasing immediately and the other half likely to drop in the not-too-distant future;

and perhaps Rachel was wondering how her life, how her ambitions, would be affected.

All that was entirely understandable. What he didn't understand was the flash of anger he was almost certain he saw in the depths of her dark brown eyes. She said, 'I suppose it's his?' and Pru Somers slapped her face.

Ash had been about to make his excuses and leave. Now he wanted to leave even more but didn't think he should. He raised broad, placatory hands. 'Come on, people, let's not get stupid, shall we?'

It may not have been the best phrased intervention – Ash was more used to separating fractious pre-adolescent boys – but it had the desired effect of interrupting the imminent battle at the opening-salvoes stage, before it could progress to all-out war. Ash seized the initiative while it was within reach.

'Please,' he said, '*please* don't start taking out your pain on one another. You are each of you all the other has left. You need to comfort and support one another, even if it takes strength you don't think you have, because the strength will come with the effort, and it's how both of you will find healing.

'You've gone through huge and terrible events, and it's no wonder you feel so angry that you find yourselves striking out at people who don't deserve it. I'll tell you something you don't want to hear: it'll be a long time before it starts getting better. Before you start feeling you might get through a day without wanting to slit either your own throat or someone else's. But it will happen. It will get better. Just a little, at first; more later. You will come through this. And when you have, the last thing you'll want to think is that you've hurt one another.'

Rachel had her hand, her long-fingered pianist's hand, to the red mark on her white cheek. Her eyes were full of tears.

Pru wasn't crying. She was watching Ash, listening attentively. Then she gave a fractional nod. 'Yes. You do know what you're talking about, don't you? So how long did it take?'

'Before I started behaving like a rational human being again? Four years. And then I had help.'

'How long before the process was complete?'

He gave her a haunted little smile. 'I'm quite hopeful for the year after next.'

Pru filled the tumblers from the jug of lemonade, and passed one to Ash and the second, after only a brief hesitation, to her daughter. She took the third to the armchair on the other side of the coffee table and sipped reflectively for a moment. 'I don't feel anything,' she said quietly. 'Almost nothing at all. Is that very abnormal? Or wicked?'

'You're asking the wrong man about normal. But I can tell you what I was told, by a highly qualified and expensive therapist, which is that in extreme situations the word loses all meaning. People react differently. Shock acts on us in different, even diametrically different, ways. One is crushed, another becomes belligerent, a third seems almost unaffected because his coping strategy is to internalise. Which is normal? – all of them. It's just different personalities trying to find a mechanism for coping with events no one's prior experience could prepare them for.

'As for wicked,' he went on, 'how could it be? Your family are the victims here. What happened was not your fault. It didn't happen because of anything you or Rachel did or didn't do. You didn't make it happen, or allow it to happen, or fail to stop it happening. You weren't careless, or reckless, or foolish. There *was* wickedness at work, but it wasn't yours. You feel numb because your mind is trying to protect itself from the enormity of this tragedy. In time, the numbness will fade. Then you'll feel the pain and loss so acutely that you'll understand why, right now, your mind daren't let you feel at all.'

Pru searched his face with sharp, intelligent eyes. She would not in normal circumstances – that word again! – have found what she saw prepossessing. He was around her own age, both taller and bigger-boned than Gethin Phillips, though a habitual self-deprecating stoop tended to disguise the fact. He had dark eyes set deep in a troubled, broad-browed face, and dark, slightly disorganised hair, and his clothes were not merely conservative but positively old-fashioned. He looked like a maths teacher in a struggling comprehensive school. If they'd met in the street, she wouldn't have given him a second glance.

But he'd been where she was now. He knew what it was like, and he knew the way out; and there was a candour in what he said that invited trust. Pru Somers wasn't a great one for trusting people, but she needed someone to trust in now. Someone to hear the unbearable confession.

'I can't see him any more,' she whispered. 'I can't see his face. He hasn't been dead for ten days, and without pulling up a photograph, I can't picture his face. I lived with him for four years. He fathered this child.' Without looking down she touched her belly. 'I loved him. And already I can't remember what he looked like.'

Compassion was a tight knot under Ash's ribs. 'I think that's pretty normal too. It's as if we don't *need* to remember the faces of people we see all the time, and it takes a little while for the brain to adjust its filing system. But it won't last. At some point you'll be thinking about him, and you'll see him clearly again. I promise.'

Pru walked him out to his car. Already she'd packed that uncharacteristic vulnerability away behind her brisk, business-like face. 'Thank you for bringing Rachel home. I'm sorry about all the drama. It really isn't like us at all.'

Ash gave a sombre smile. 'If there's anything I can do, you will let me know?'

'There won't be,' said Pru.

SEVEN

'Any progress with the investigation?' asked Ash.

Hazel gave him a long look. 'How would I know? I'm on leave.'

'So you haven't seen Dave Gorman in the last few days. You haven't asked him if searching the spinney turned up anything useful?'

She scowled at him. 'I may have stuck my head through his door in case there was anything I could help with. I told him what we'd been talking about, incidentally. I think the same thing had occurred to him – that the incidents on the towpath might turn out to be a red herring. He said, would I be comfortable about shutting down that aspect of the inquiry, and I said no, and he said he wouldn't either.' She sighed. 'Which is pretty much what we thought.'

Ash was brushing Patience. 'So *is* he making any progress?'

'Not that you'd notice,' admitted Hazel.

'The fingertip searches turned up nothing?'

'The fingertip searches turned up lots. Both Highfield Spinney and the towpath are places where the public has unrestricted access, and people leave rubbish. The spinney was particularly fruitful. There wasn't one cigarette butt where the killer had a quick smoke while he was watching for Rachel: there were hundreds. There were seven odd shoes, all but one for the left foot. Who the hell hops home after a walk in the woods?' she demanded parenthetically. 'You don't want to know how many used condoms were lifted and bagged, and Wayne Budgen found a Norwegian coin with a hole in it.

'Any one of these things may have been left by the man who attacked Rachel Somers and murdered Gethin Phillips, but how are we going to know? We may have his DNA in the evidence locker right now, but we'll only find out if we track him down the old-fashioned way, by being smart, dogged and just plain lucky, and when we arrest him he's wearing one shoe and reading the *Bergen Examiner*.'

Ash was regarding her in amusement. 'You're starting to sound like Dave Gorman.'

She didn't think he meant it as a compliment, but she took it as one. 'It's part of my new plan. To get into CID by disguising myself as one of them. Like a duck-hunter using one of those quacking devices, you know? I'm hoping everyone will get so used to the idea they'll finally make it official.'

Ash forbore to comment. 'So what's the hypothesis? Phillips heard his stepdaughter scream, and hurried out into the spinney in his slippers, and tackled the man who was chasing her. He gave her time to get away, but the assailant was stronger than Phillips – or at least more ruthless.'

'And fractured his skull with two blows to the head, probably with a length of branch he'd lifted from the ground. That's one murder weapon we're never going to find.' Hazel had made it her business to read the autopsy report. 'Dr Green reckoned at least one of the blows was delivered from behind – that Phillips had turned away and was no longer defending himself. The assailant could have made his escape at that point. Instead, he hit him again.'

Ash nodded. 'This is a deeply dangerous man.'

'I think we already knew that, Gabriel,' said Hazel flatly. 'A man who rapes young girls and brains someone who intervenes? We're not in ASBO country any more. This is big league.'

Ash put away Patience's brushes. Her cold damp nose touched the back of his hand in acknowledgement, and he stroked her head. 'Rachel was here today. She walked through the spinney.'

Hazel stared. 'Why?'

'Mostly to prove to herself that she could, I think.'

'You didn't let her go home the same way?'

'Of course not. I drove her. Her mother was there.'

Something about the way he said it suggested that he'd meant to say more but thought better of it. Hazel considered. 'What do you make of Pru Somers?'

'I thought she was a bit of a cold fish when we first met. I think I did her an injustice. She's going through hell: she just doesn't want anyone to see. Perhaps she's trying to stay strong for Rachel's sake.'

Hazel, who hadn't warmed to Rachel's mother, was made to feel a little ashamed by Ash's generosity. 'Any way you look at it, her life's been turned upside down. She had a partner and a daughter until some bastard waiting in a dark wood decided she could only keep one of them. A fortnight ago they were a family; now there's just the two of them. Well, two and a bit.'

Ash's head came up sharply and his eyes widened. 'So you guessed, too.'

'Guessed what?'

'That Pru's pregnant.'

'No!' exclaimed Hazel. 'Seriously?'

'Well, yes.' He hadn't intended to share Pru Somers' confidence, had genuinely thought Hazel already knew. 'So what did you mean by two and a bit?'

'I was thinking of the cat. A baby on the way is much more interesting.'

'Why? It can't have any bearing on what happened.'

Hazel gave it some thought. But actually, she couldn't see how either. 'How does Rachel feel about it?'

'I'm sure she's pleased,' said Ash diplomatically.

'Did she say so?'

'Well – no. But surely it's a given?'

Hazel sighed. 'Gabriel, you are such an innocent. You think every baby is wanted? That, even when its parents are thrilled, its siblings will be too? Especially its much older siblings, who've spent years tweaking the family dynamic to suit themselves?'

Ash was frowning. 'You think Rachel will be jealous of Pru's baby?'

'Er – yes! Her whole relationship with her mother will be affected, and it wasn't her idea and she wasn't consulted. It would have been a game-changer, even if Gethin Phillips was there to help raise it. As it is, Pru will need Rachel to fill the gap. She's bound to wonder what it'll cost her – financially, in terms of time, and having to share her mother's attention with a demanding infant. She's been an only child for seventeen years. She has no relationship with her father. It was her and Pru, and then her and Pru and Gethin. Now Gethin's gone, and Pru's going to need Rachel to step up, and a few months down the line there's going to be this tiny stranger elbowing her out of what has always been her place in the household.

'It's a lot for anyone to deal with. For a seventeen-year-old girl on a guilt trip over the death of the baby's father, who thought she knew what her future held, except that now the needs of her mother and her new brother or sister will mean a fundamental reassessment, it must be devastating.'

Ash hadn't understood that. He'd noted Rachel's stunned expression and just thought she was surprised by the news. He hadn't realised, as Hazel had realised immediately, how it would affect her life for the foreseeable future. 'When she gets used to the idea . . .' he ventured.

'Oh, I expect she'll do what's required of her. Most people, dumped into a difficult situation, find a way of coping. And I imagine she'll get fond of the sprog when it arrives. But she'd be less than human if she didn't harbour some resentment about how it had thrown her hopes and dreams into the cement-mixer without so much as a by-your-leave!'

'I wonder . . .'

Hazel could always tell when her friend was thinking. He had a way of tuning out of the present and re-tuning to some station beyond the range of normal equipment, his eyes sliding out of focus while he listened to it. 'Gabriel?' she prompted him after a minute.

'Oh – yes. Sorry. I was wondering – and I don't know if it's a good idea or not, tell me what you think – if I should ask Laura Fry to meet with her.'

Hazel's fair brows arched. 'Laura doesn't come cheap.'

'That's of no consequence,' said Ash dismissively, 'I'll pick up the bill if that's the only obstacle. Do you think Rachel would find it helpful?'

Laura Fry was a highly trained, highly qualified trauma therapist with an office overlooking the park in the middle of Norbold. Ash had been discharged to her care after spending six weeks as a psychiatric inpatient, and had spent many hours working through his grief with her. He had found her guidance helpful – it was she who'd advised him to adopt an abandoned dog, so she got Patience's seal of approval as well – and he hadn't had to pay her that time because his former employers in the government offices behind Whitehall had covered it.

'I think it probably *would* be helpful,' said Hazel after a little thought. 'But I'm not sure how happy Pru Somers would be about sending her daughter to a trick-cyclist. She strikes me as the kind of woman who thinks you deal with trauma by stiffening the sinews, tightening the upper lip and generally manning up. She might be offended if you suggest it.'

Ash, who shied away from anything resembling a scene, was positively alarmed at the prospect of offending Pru Somers. 'I could sound them out. Skirt round the whole baby issue – talk about what happened to Rachel and her stepfather. Except I mustn't call him that. Strictly speaking he wasn't, and Rachel doesn't like people thinking he was.'

'I wonder why,' said Hazel. 'It's a harmless enough little social fiction. They were a family unit, even if he and Pru weren't married.'

'I'll have a word with them,' Ash decided. 'Once I've had a word with Laura.'

'Gabriel! I haven't seen you for ages. Gone mad again, have you?'

Laura Fry was a narrow, severe-looking woman with diamond-sharp eyes and greying hair folded into a rigorous French pleat. Her association with Gabriel Ash went back almost six years now, to when he returned from London to his late mother's house in Norbold, to a time when the therapist was his only lifeline, almost his only connection with the world. Then, and for some years afterwards, she would never have addressed him in that light, avuncular fashion. The fact that she did so now was testament to the progress he'd made.

Her pleasure in seeing him was in no way feigned. He was one of her successes. Most of her clients benefited to a greater or lesser extent from her expertise. But it was unusual, even in Laura's wide experience, to see someone who first came to her as human wreckage return as what Ash was now: a man with a stable home life, a rich personal life and the respect of much of his community. She took her fair share of the kudos for that, but it helped that – whatever the world thought – he had never been mad in the first place. Subjected to more emotional stress than any human being was designed to cope with, he had bent. He had never broken.

Ash smiled wryly and took the chair she offered. Not a couch: Laura had never encouraged her clients to get that comfortable. 'I don't think so. Though you're probably a better judge than I am.'

Laura gave an economical shrug. 'The longer I do this job, the less convinced I am that any of us is entirely sane, me included. I incline towards auto-analysis.'

He frowned, puzzled. Laura was one of the few people he knew who was probably cleverer than he was, and he struggled to keep up with her thought processes. 'Auto-analysis?'

'If people think they're sane, and if they can behave as if they're sane, that's probably good enough for all general purposes. You look pretty sane to me, Gabriel.'

'Well – thank you.' It had sounded like a compliment, mostly. 'To be honest, it's not me I wanted to talk about.'

Her hatchet profile sharpened a little more. 'You're the only one I *can* talk to you about. You know that.'

'Of course. I don't want you to breach any kind of privilege, I just need some advice. Can we talk hypothetically?'

'We can try,' said Laura cautiously.

Ash tried to steer away from the details, but Laura Fry didn't live in a barrel with the bung in: she knew what he was talking about and therefore also who he was talking about. She stopped him before he'd gone very far at all.

'You want to know if trauma therapy would help. I'm a trauma therapist, Gabriel, of course I'm going to say yes!'

He dipped his head in acknowledgement. 'I suppose what I'm asking is, if I can get them to come – the mother and the daughter, or either of them – will you see them? And bill me?'

Laura sat back in her swivel chair, her keen eyes speculative. 'The second-hand book trade doing well, is it?'

'Oh yes,' said Ash, 'sometimes I actually make a profit. I

have a very good pension, Laura, as you know perfectly well. I'm not looking for what I believe are referred to as Mates' Rates.' Whenever he used an expression from the common vernacular, he invested it with capital letters, or even italics, as if he was quoting from a foreign language and might not be understood.

'We can talk about that later. Certainly, in principle, I'd be happy to see them, together or apart, and I think they'd find it useful. If they'd rather leave it until they actually know how they feel, it would still be useful then.'

'I'll find a way of broaching it with them.' Already in Ash's mind was the looming cloud from which he expected thunder and bolts of lightning to come. 'While I'm here . . .'

'Is it normal to talk to your dog?' guessed Laura. 'Yes, Gabriel. Perfectly normal. I've told you that before.'

For a split second he was tempted to wipe the patronising smile off her face by asking, 'And how normal is it for her to talk back?' But that really would have been madness, and he skirted the abyss carefully.

'That isn't what I was going to say. I was going to ask about men who attack children. Who are they, what kind of people are we looking for? What exactly is their motivation?'

Laura Fry sucked in a thoughtful breath. 'There's one very easy answer, and one very hard one. There are some clearly abnormal individuals that anyone would have their doubts about, but an awful lot of them look, behave and in most respects are pretty much like everyone else. It would be a lot easier if they weren't. There are no diagnostic features that will enable even a practised professional to spot one across a crowded room. You will only know what they're thinking by what they say and what they do.' She gave a brittle smile. 'I'm sorry, I don't suppose this is what you want to hear. It would be nice if everyone's granny was right and abnormal sexual urges really did make your ears drop off. Then we could concentrate on looking for a guy with a pulled-down bobble hat.'

'Why is it so much more prevalent than when I was a child? You never heard of such a thing, then.'

'The fact that you didn't hear about it doesn't mean it wasn't going on,' Laura pointed out. 'They were different days. A lot of people's response to difficult subjects was to pretend there wasn't a problem. If we don't talk about it, it'll go away. It isn't true now and it wasn't true then, and my colleagues put their children through college dealing with the fall-out in human misery.

'We don't share the same taboos now. Which is usually a good thing, although there is a point at which recognising that shit happens and you can and will get over it is more help than even a really good therapist. Feeling free to talk about these things makes it more likely that people will complain when they happen to them; but it also makes the rest of us feel that it's a more common problem than it used to be.'

'What's the hard answer?' asked Ash.

'How we live now is different to how we lived when I was growing up, and even when you were. The stable nuclear family of two parents, two-point-four children and up to four grandparents is largely a thing of the past. The cards get shuffled more often. The grandparents sail off around the world, or join a commune in the Himalayan foothills. The parents get bored with one another and split up; and dad finds a new pseudo-wife, and mum finds a new pseudo-husband, and the kids spend alternate weekends with each. And it's manageable, if everyone exercises common sense and goodwill.

'The problem is that the roles get blurred and everyone can get a bit confused. It's fine for your dad to bath you: is it all right for your stepdad? Only if he's got children of his own? And if it's all right when you're small, when does it stop being all right? What about when stepkids start looking at one another not as rivals, and not as brother and sister either? They're not related genetically – at what point should we get worried? *Should* we get worried? If we don't, how will that affect the family dynamic?'

She rolled a pen between her fingers, put it to her lips. Though she'd given up smoking twenty years earlier, bits of her still missed the physical ritual. 'It's not just humans: many species have built-in inhibitors to prevent in-breeding. Sometimes the males leave the group when they reach sexual maturity, sometimes the females do. Male lions will father as many cubs as they can on a pride of lionesses, but usually they'll either move on or be supplanted before their own daughters are old enough to breed. One presumes they don't do this because of any moral imperative, but because their DNA has figured out that this is the best way to leave healthy offspring. Incest becomes self-limiting because there are fewer healthy offspring to continue the line.'

Quite unconsciously, she took a puff on the end of her pen. 'Another thing that male lions will do on taking over a new pride is kill any young cubs they can get at. This brings the mothers back into season, ready to mate afresh, and it also means the resources of the pride aren't being used to raise another lion's offspring. It looks brutal to us, but genetically speaking it's a sound policy. It is not in one male's best interests to treat another male's offspring as if they were his own.

'We like to think that human beings have higher motives than simple self-propagation, but perhaps our genes are less civilised than our brains. Emotions can get confused by the variety of extended families and open families and more-or-less families and families-till-a-week-next-Wednesday that we expect them to deal with. The anchors that held firm for millennia have dragged. It's a credit to the human race that most people manage to handle the situation without too much grief. But if the appropriate instincts don't cut in, a door can be left open for various unwanted behaviours to sneak through.'

'You mean, these men really are the product of a broken home?' said Ash with a tiny smile.

'Some of them. Some of them will have come through a broken marriage. And some will have had all the advantages available, and still managed to go astray in terms of how their minds process interpersonal relationships. I'm sorry, Gabriel, I did warn you. Most of the men who brutalise children are indistinguishable from most of the men who don't. Therein lies the problem.'

Ash thought for a moment. 'So, basically, if we're looking for the bogeyman we could be missing the point.'

Laura raised a thin, articulate eyebrow. 'I didn't know it was your job to be looking for anyone.'

'Oh, I'm not,' he assured her hastily. 'It's really none of my business. I'm just a second-hand bookseller trying to make a living. At least, trying not to make a loss.'

'And?' she said astutely.

'And,' said Ash slowly, 'I'm a second-hand bookseller who just happens to fit the description some of these youngsters are giving of a man who frightened them.'

Laura gave a rather unkind laugh. In some ways she was not an easy woman to like, but she had saved more souls than many who are. 'I'm not sure I can help you with that, Gabriel. I could write you a certificate saying that, in my professional opinion, you're as sane now as ever you were, but it might not have the desired effect.'

Ash could see that. 'Perhaps I'd better just hope they find this man soon.'

'Amen to that,' said Laura Fry.

The first postcard arrived from Cornwall. It showed Newlyn beach, with a white surf running. Gilbert had written:

Frankie says to tell you we arrived safely. She got us wetsuits today. Mine is grey and black. Guy's is green. He looks like a sprout.

EIGHT

On a whim – or at least, on a suspicion coalescing in the depths of his detective's soul – Dave Gorman took the scenic way to work on Friday morning, via the canal. He parked his car near the bridge and, hands in pockets, feeling the sunshine on his back, strolled along the towpath. Not because he was expecting to find any clues that had been missed by Presley and the scenes of crime officer, more to get a feel for the place. For the sorts of things that happened there on a normal day.

A couple of narrowboats came down the canal as he watched, chuntering along at walking pace. Others were tied up along the bank, where a small community of water gypsies had become so established that they now got milk and postal deliveries. They were not, for the most part, either hippies or dropouts: their average age was about sixty, and those who were not counting the days to retirement had already reached it. Some of them lived on their boats at weekends, some for the summer, some no longer had any other home.

A woman with iron-grey hair stuck her head out of a hatch as he passed. 'Are you looking for someone?'

Gorman introduced himself, and got his warrant card halfway out of his wallet, and both of them pretended that the woman had looked at it. 'Were you around last weekend? There was an incident on the towpath about here last Thursday morning, and another up by the beach on Monday afternoon.'

'No, but I heard all about it,' said the woman, nodding keenly. 'Those poor children! It's a good job I *wasn't* here – I'd have taken my windlass to the dirty bugger! I'm still a long-weekender: Thursday night to Sunday night. Roll on January!'

'January?'

'When I get my pension.'

DCI Gorman couldn't help wishing he could throw in the towel come January as well. 'Who would have been on the boats last Thursday morning?'

The woman pointed. 'Harry and Jane Phoenix,' she said, 'Jenny Sweetbriar and Sam Warwick Castle.' It was only then that Gorman realised the curious surnames actually belonged to the boats. 'But nobody saw anything. Your people have already talked to them, and nobody even noticed the girls. And anyway, you can't see the beach from here.'

'Yes, I know,' said Gorman. 'Maybe I'll talk to Mr – er – Castle anyway.' The *Warwick Castle* occupied the next berth along, and there were sounds of industry coming from the stern.

'Just a minute.' The woman disappeared briefly down the hatchway, returned with a plate of buns. 'I've been baking. Tell Sam to bring the plate back anytime.'

Rather like the fourth Wise Man, expunged from history for lack of ambition in the gifts department, Gorman followed the sounds of spanner on engine, spanner on thumb and breathless nautical swearing. In the *Warwick Castle*'s cockpit, the sole had been lifted and a man was up to his biceps in a diesel engine cannibalised from a tractor. The fumes were making him cough.

His name was Sam Meredith, and for seventeen years he'd been conducting a war of attrition with the narrowboat's engine that would only end when one of them died. It was looking increasingly likely that would be Meredith.

'It's this bloody asthma,' he wheezed. 'Twenty years ago my doctor said I had to get out in the fresh air more. He suggested I take up boating. Silly bugger! Look where it's got me. Lungs like a bag-lady's underwear.'

Gorman explained his purpose again, and Meredith abandoned the recalcitrant engine, accepted the plate of warm buns and replaced the cockpit sole so that his visitor could step aboard. 'Tea with them, boy?'

It was a while since anyone had called Dave Gorman *boy*, though he had been called a great deal worse and Sam Meredith must be pushing seventy. He was tall but cadaverously thin, bent by hours arguing with his engine, and he wore oil-stained denims

with a black rag that may once have been a handkerchief stuffed
into a pocket. The oil was grained so deeply into his hands and
even his hair that it would probably never come out.

He put two mugs on a tin tray and carried it forward, and
he and Gorman sat companionably on the cabin roof, drinking
tea and eating buns in the sunshine.

'Thursday week, hey?' he said thoughtfully. 'Bit of a rum
do, that. Poor little maids.'

'Were you around during the morning? Did you see what
happened?'

'I was here, yes. Doing a bit of maintenance.' He glanced
darkly back towards the cockpit. 'But I didn't see nothing. I
told that young constable I didn't.'

'I know,' said Gorman. 'I'm scraping the bottom of the
barrel, checking we haven't missed anything. Well, if you didn't
see the incident, did you see anyone odd hanging around?'

Sam Meredith thought, then shook his head. 'Last Thursday
morning? He'd have had to be bloody odd for me to notice
him last Thursday morning. Bloody engine tried to kill me,
didn't it? Insisted there was an airlock in the fuel line. It was
just a ruse to get me blowing into it. A gob full of diesel
is *just* what the doctor had in mind for my asthma!'

For a minute Gorman said nothing more, just drank his tea
and ate his bun and pictured the scene. The stick-thin old
boatie in his oil-stained denims, diesel running down his face,
staggering about with his eyes squeezed tight shut and his
arms waving in front of him, the diesel fumes threatening to
turn his lungs inside out.

'So . . . you jumped down onto the towpath?'

'I did,' agreed Meredith. 'I stuck my head in the bloody
canal, didn't I? Couldn't think what else to do. Here' – he
frowned suspiciously at Gorman – 'how did you know?'

'Just a lucky guess, Mr Meredith,' said Gorman, a touch
smugly. 'Just a lucky guess.'

The next subject tabled for discussion at Rambles With Books
was how to suggest to Pru Somers that she and Rachel might
benefit from seeing a therapist without having her explode
with indignation.

'You're the family's liaison officer,' Ash said. 'Would the suggestion be better coming from you or from me?'

Hazel thought about it but still wasn't sure. 'You don't think maybe it's too soon?'

Ash didn't claim to be any kind of an expert; but he did know that, in his case, it had been almost too late. His emotions had become so tightly knotted that even the experts had broken their fingernails on them. 'I'm afraid things will only get worse unless they get some help. Pru isn't going to get less pregnant as the weeks go by. Rachel isn't going to get more comfortable with the fact that the baby's father died protecting her.'

'She told me things were pretty well over between Pru and Gethin,' Hazel remembered. 'It rather looks she was wrong about that.'

'Wishful thinking,' murmured Ash.

For a moment Hazel put herself in Rachel Somers' shoes. If her father had remarried after her mother's death, how would she have related to a new stepmother? It was something she'd never asked herself. Fred Best had never contemplated a second marriage: his wife might have been a Payne when he married her, but she ended up the best of the Bests. But what if he'd felt differently? He'd been younger than Ash when he was widowed: what if he hadn't wanted to face the next thirty or forty or even fifty years on his own? Hazel had been thirteen when her mother died. Wouldn't it have felt like a betrayal to have another woman sleeping in her mother's bed? Whether she was a nice woman, whether Hazel liked her, would have been immaterial; indeed, liking her might have resulted in a burden of guilt.

'Maybe,' she said slowly. 'That poor kid's emotions must be in tatters. I wonder how they got on, Gethin and Rachel? Has anybody said?'

'Not to me – but then, why would they? And I don't suppose Dave Gorman thought to ask. It wouldn't have much bearing on his inquiry.'

'It may have a bearing on how we help them, though. If Rachel was fond of Gethin, she'll be grieving for him; and if she wasn't, she's probably feeling she should be. And I doubt her mother's making things any easier. I need to pay them another visit, don't I – see how they're hanging together. If you like, I'll sound them out about Laura Fry at the same time. Hell's bells, but I'll have to be tactful!' Hazel could do tactful, because she genuinely liked people and cared about their feelings. The only time she was likely to get it wrong was when she became too invested in getting answers.

Ash nodded gratefully. 'Coming from you, it might seem just part of the trauma management service. Coming from me it might seem impertinent and intrusive.'

These were not two adjectives she commonly associated with her friend – curious, perhaps, and he had a way of pursuing his curiosity until the virtue of perseverance trespassed upon the vice of obstinacy, always with that same polite, diffident, gentle manner that hid an adamantine core – but Hazel took his point. Proposed by her, wearing her stupid little uniform hat, metaphorically if not actually, the offer might be declined but it would not cause offence. 'All right. But you're going to owe me.'

Ash's smile warmed her heart. 'Even more?'

She phoned ahead, hoping to see Pru Somers at a time when Rachel would be otherwise occupied. Bereaved and pregnant, Pru was once more working twelve-hour days so the best she could offer was eight in the evening.

'Will Rachel be about?'

'Not this evening – she's going to a concert in town. She'll be back around ten. Come later, if you want to see her.'

'No – no, that's fine,' Hazel said quickly. 'It was really you I wanted to touch base with.'

'Has there been some progress with the inquiry?'

'I'll have all the latest information for you this evening,' promised Hazel. It was true, but it was also disingenuous. All the latest information amounted to sweet FA, and she knew it.

Still, it gave her an excuse to beard DCI Gorman in his den. Every time she visited, it looked more like the aftermath of an explosion in an office supplies shop. 'I'm seeing Pru Somers tonight. Anything I can tell her?'

Gorman blew out his cheeks. 'I don't suppose "Police

inquiries have come to nothing and CID have moved on to something easier" would do?'

'I don't think so, no,' said Hazel with a sympathetic grin. 'I take it we don't think an arrest is imminent?'

'Hey, I can arrest any number of people on suspicion of being weird sods. It's been suggested to me that Gabriel should be top of the list. I'm tempted to ask him to drop in for a cuppa and a chat about the Great War poets, just so I can tell people I've had him in for questioning. But the guy who jumped Rachel Somers, killed Gethin Phillips and raped Skye Pascoe? I'm beginning to think he's related to the Yeti and the Loch Ness Monster – lots of people have seen him, but then he vanishes back into the mist.'

Hazel thought he looked tired. Of course, he'd be losing sleep to this. It was a detective's worst nightmare: a child-molester who was prepared to kill rather than be caught. The lack of progress in no way reflected the effort being invested in the case. 'Is there *anything* I can tell Pru Somers that'll make her feel slightly better?'

'No-o,' he said slowly. 'But there's something I can tell you that might make *you* feel slightly better. You may be right about the incidents at the canal. One of them, at least. I went down there this morning. I still didn't find anyone who'd witnessed the incident on the towpath last Thursday. I *did* find someone matching the description the girls gave, who was suffering from a diesel-induced asthma attack just about the time those girls were passing. Reeling around on the towpath, waving his hands about in front of him because he'd been temporarily blinded.'

Hazel stared at him. 'You think that's what they saw?'

Gorman shrugged. 'Hard to be certain. But the timing fits, the description fits, and it would explain why no one else saw anything odd. Sam Meredith snorting diesel fumes is just part of life's rich tapestry down there.'

That was when the front desk phoned to say that Mr Pascoe wanted a word with one of the lady detectives who'd inter-viewed his daughter. Gorman frowned. Emma Friend was out of the office, and he didn't have any other lady detectives, or even any other female ones. He looked askance at Hazel.

'He must mean you. Go and get him, will you? Bring him up here.'

As soon as she saw Edwin Pascoe's face, Hazel knew something had happened. He wasn't at Meadowvale to enquire about progress into his daughter's case, or to bring some new information that might be helpful. Something had happened that had hurt him even more than he'd already been hurt; it showed in the angular planes of his face, rigid as steel, and in the fathomless depths of his eyes. He barely looked at Hazel; and when she took him upstairs to see DCI Gorman, he barely looked at him either.

None of this was lost on Gorman. Half rising as Hazel tapped on his door and ushered the visitor inside, he gestured towards the comfortable chair. Hazel took the uncomfortable one, kept for visitors who weren't being encouraged to stay. 'What can we do for you, Mr Pascoe?'

Pascoe took a deep breath, the way a man who wasn't a sidesman at his parish church might have taken a stiff drink, and made no attempt to answer the question. 'I've come on my own because I think it might be slightly easier. But you will want to talk to my daughter. I understand that, and so does she.'

Hazel and Dave Gorman exchanged a puzzled glance and waited for him to go on. Presently he did.

'I'm sorry to have to tell you that we've been wasting your time. Skye was not raped. Skye was entertaining a young man in one of the old boathouses beside the canal. Apparently they were enjoying themselves so much they didn't notice how late it had got. When Skye realised I'd be waiting for her and would see the state of her clothes, she decided to go for the sympathy vote and say she'd been attacked. She got her friend to slap her around a bit, for authenticity.

'Mr Gorman,' he said, leaning forward, his voice thick with pleading, 'believe me when I say my daughter is not a bad girl. She can be thoughtless, she can be impulsive, but she would never deliberately do anything to harm another person. She never anticipated how seriously her story – her lie – would be taken. She thought it would get her off the hook with me,

and that's as far as she thought. She never imagined that a
description made up to protect the young man in question
would be circulated around Norbold, and frightened and angry
men would round on someone who vaguely answered that
description.'

Gorman's gaze sharpened. 'I didn't know they had.'

'Gabriel,' murmured Hazel. 'It's all right, he defused the
situation. For now.'

Gorman leaned back in his chair. He'd need time to figure
out if this was good news or bad news, but the immediate priority
was to be sure it was accurate news. 'Skye told you this? It
isn't something you figured out for yourself?'

Pascoe shook his head. 'She told me everything, an hour
ago. Some inconsistencies were creeping into her account.
When I asked about them, finally she broke down and
admitted it was all made up. Floods of tears, abject apologies
– terrified she's going to prison for perjury. I'm sure it's the
truth this time. I'm only sorry I didn't realise earlier that we
were being lied to, you and me both.'

Hazel said quietly, 'Forgive me, Mr Pascoe, but there was
physical evidence. She'd been roughly handled.'

Skye's father gave a painful smile. 'Yes, I know. It was her
first time. I think it might have been the lad's first time as
well – neither of them seems to have had much idea what they
were doing, only that they were prepared to keep trying until
they got it right. It wasn't rape – she was an entirely willing
participant. If they hadn't lost track of the time, she'd have
sneaked home and cleaned herself up before I saw her, and
no one would have known anything about it. Instead of which
she's managed to confuse a murder investigation, and I am
more sorry for that than I know how to express.'

DCI Gorman stood up and offered his hand. 'You did absolutely the right thing by telling us as soon as you found out.
I can imagine how difficult that must have been, both for you
and for Skye. I will need to speak to her at some point. But I
think you can reassure her that a prison sentence is unlikely.
I think a thorough' – he was about to say *bollocking*, amended
it at the last moment – 'telling off will serve the purpose.'

Relief had gone some way to filling the hollows in Edwin Pascoe's eyes. He took Gorman's hand with gratitude. 'You try to raise them right,' he growled. 'You try to give them values, and some kind of a moral code. And then their hormones start rampaging, and they demonstrate all the morality of cats on heat!'

Hazel saw him out. 'Don't be too hard on Skye, Mr Pascoe. I think it may have been her first time at lying to you, too. If she'd had more practice, she'd have done a better job.'

Pascoe flicked her a thin smile and hurried on down the steps, glad to have accomplished a difficult task.

'Well, that's a turn-up for the books,' whistled Gorman when Hazel returned. It took a fair bit to surprise him these days, but that had done it. 'Did you see it coming?'

Hazel shook her head. 'Not for a minute. It seemed to fit the pattern.'

'No,' said Gorman pensively, 'it established the pattern. Before Skye Pascoe got frisky with her boyfriend, all we had was the episode in Highfield Spinney. It was Skye's story that made us think there was a serial attacker. Well, I'm reasonably happy that the girls on the towpath saw Sam Meredith having an asthma attack. So maybe the kids swimming in the canal also saw what, by then, they were programmed to see: a pervert rather than a druggie, a vagrant, some old dodderer who'd temporarily escaped the clutches of his carers, or even someone having a laugh at their expense.'

'A hoax?' Hazel was more shocked than a police officer of three years' experience had any right to be.

'There's always someone ready to make a bad situation worse by playing on people's fears,' said Gorman grimly. 'With half the town jumping at shadows, it wouldn't have taken much to make a bunch of teenagers shriek and leap in the canal.'

Hazel thought she was following his train of thought. 'So everything after the Highfield Spinney incident may have been either a lie or a misunderstanding. Well – isn't that a good thing?'

'Yes,' rumbled DCI Gorman, 'and no. We're looking for the wrong guy. We shouldn't be looking for a serial offender, someone who can't stop attacking young girls. We should be looking for a man who attacked one girl and killed the man who came to her aid. Maybe his motivation is not that he can't keep his hands off teenage girls. Maybe it's Rachel Somers, and only Rachel Somers, that he's interested in.'

NINE

When Hazel kept her appointment with Pru Somers, Gorman came with her. Pru heard them out with a degree of restraint that would have surprised her employees. Patience had never been her strong suit.

'So what's worrying us now,' concluded DCI Gorman, 'is that Rachel may not have been a random target after all. Can you think of anyone who might have singled her out specifically?'

Pru frowned with a moment's thought, then shook her head. 'No. Of course, no. If I knew that someone was threatening my daughter, don't you think I'd have mentioned it before now?'

Hazel intervened before Gorman could answer. 'It's just, this new information puts a different slant on what happened. We hoped that if you thought of it as something personal rather than the first of a string of attacks, a name might occur to you. Not necessarily someone you'd recognised as a threat to Rachel, but possibly someone whose interest in her didn't seem entirely appropriate. Someone who seemed to have a crush on her – who always made sure of serving her in shops, or carrying her books home from school, or something like that. Something as trivial as that.'

Pru did them the courtesy of thinking again, at greater length. But the result was the same. 'I really don't think so. I'll talk to Rachel – or you can talk to Rachel – but if she noticed anything like that she never mentioned it to me.'

'No discarded boyfriends who could still be carrying a flame for her?'

Pru regarded her coolly. 'My daughter is a concert pianist in the making, Constable Best. She doesn't have time for boyfriends.'

'What about her father?' asked Gorman.

Pru rounded on him with eyes like knives. 'You think

Rachel's father attempted to rape her in Highfield Spinney? What planet are you living on, Inspector?'

Dave Gorman didn't mind her abbreviating his title, though it was new enough that he was still rather fond of hearing it. He didn't mind the suggestion that he was out of touch with reality – he'd been accused of worse. But he was beginning to find her unrelenting hostility somewhat wearing. 'That's not what I'm suggesting, Mrs Somers. I'm wondering if there's any possibility that rape was not in fact the purpose of the attack – that, conceivably, it was never intended as an attack on Rachel at all.'

'You think she made it up?'

'I didn't say that, either,' said Gorman woodenly. 'Will you try to work with me here? Sometimes estranged fathers go to extreme lengths to see their children. Is there any chance that Rachel's father staked out the back of the house simply for the chance to talk to her? That he startled her, and since she never saw who'd grabbed her, she jumped to the obvious conclusion and let out the yell that brought Mr Phillips running. Is there any chance that's what happened?'

Pru Somers was staring at him with incredulity. Finally she shook her head. 'Inspector Gorman, Rachel's father showed minimal interest in her for the first nine years of her life. He left us when I realised what a talent she had and how many sacrifices we were both going to have to make to nurture it. I have no idea where he is now, or even whether he's alive or dead. He doesn't send her birthday presents, he doesn't send her Christmas cards. Whatever makes you think a man like that might be suddenly overwhelmed by such paternal love that he'd kill someone in order to see her?'

'I'm just asking the questions, Mrs Somers,' said Gorman wearily. 'Give me some personal details – full name, date of birth, the last address you had for him, his last known employers – and we'll see if the computer can track him down.'

Lips pursed disapprovingly, she did as he asked. Hazel took down the information.

'I take it, then, it was a fairly acrimonious separation,' said Gorman.

'Of course it was. I accused him of putting his comfort ahead of his duty to his daughter. I still believe that.'

'So you wouldn't expect him to resent your relationship with Mr Phillips too much? Enough to want a showdown with him, for instance.'

'Steven?' she exclaimed derisively. 'I doubt if he even remembers us by now. If he does, I imagine he's grateful to Gethin for taking us off his hands. And even if he isn't, posting snide comments on Twitter is much more his style than lying in wait in a wood!'

Hazel was following the exchange avidly. It hadn't occurred to her that Rachel might not have been the intended target so much as the means of bringing Phillips outside. The fact that it *had* occurred to Gorman impressed her deeply.

'If you're right and it wasn't someone who didn't mean Rachel any harm, we have to assume it was someone who did. And possibly still does,' said the DCI. 'If he came here to attack Rachel once, there's a significant risk that he'll be back.'

'Aren't you supposed to catch him *before* he comes back?'

'We're supposed to,' agreed Gorman heavily. 'Unfortunately, we can't always do all we're supposed to. Sometimes the best we can do is try. In the meantime, it's important that you and Rachel both take whatever measures you can to protect yourselves.'

In view of the tone of the interview, Hazel decided that now was not the right time to suggest to Pru Somers that either she or Rachel ought to see a therapist. She suspected that, however tactfully she broached the subject, Pru would throw her bodily down the front steps. The woman seemed to be never more than an incautious word away from fury. Perhaps it was understandable. Pru had lost her partner to a violent predator, and the fact that her daughter had escaped injury could only compensate her so far. Additionally, she couldn't know right now how she felt about a pregnancy that should have been joyful news but in the circumstances must be more of a worry than anything else. And on top of *that* she was suffering with morning sickness. Anyone who wasn't actually banging her head on the wall was probably coping pretty well.

Yet Hazel suspected that anger was Pru's default position, and her current mood owed less to the loss she'd suffered or the problems she faced than to her own temperament. Being mad at the world was a powerful tool in the hands of an ambitious woman.

'What do you want us to do?' demanded Pru. 'Fill the cellar with tinned goods and barricade ourselves in? Hire a bodyguard? What do you suggest?'

'I suggest you both exercise common sense and caution,' snapped Gorman. 'Stay out of that spinney. If the damned cat won't come in, leave it out. Don't leave Rachel in the house alone if you can help it, even in the daytime. If you go into town, take her with you or leave her with friends. You shouldn't be alone either, come to that. Keep your doors locked, and draw the curtains in the evening. Don't answer the door unless you know who it is. And if anything makes you uneasy, call Meadowvale and we'll send someone round.'

'Police protection?' Pru managed to make it sound at once a joke and an insult.

'We can do that too. We have a safe house in Norbold. It'll mean you and Rachel sharing a room, there's no piano and the cat will have to fend for itself, but you will be safe there. Do you want me to arrange it?'

They glared at each other like a couple of boxers at a weigh-in. Finally Pru said, 'I think we'll take our chances here, thank you.'

On the way back to Norbold the DCI growled, 'I suppose you think I could have handled that better.'

'Actually,' said Hazel, 'I was thinking that even personal tragedy is only a good excuse for so long, and after that people deserve a slap.'

Gorman barked an appreciative little laugh. 'Don't think I wasn't tempted.'

'*I* was tempted,' said Hazel, 'and I'm a nicer person than you are.'

There was a pause as Gorman drove. Then he said reflectively, 'Of course, she does have a point. Two women, one young, one pregnant, living in an isolated house where there's already been a murder? If they don't qualify for protection, who does?'

'Someone living in a country where people are prepared to pay higher taxes. We operate within legal constraints, practical constraints and financial constraints. You don't have the manpower to post a sentry outside their house.'

'We can do some drive-bys. And I expect you'll be paying them a visit from time to time . . .' He let it hang in the air like a question.

'I expect so, yes.'

The DCI knew perfectly well that not only was Hazel Best not a member of his staff but she was supposed to be on leave. He waited for her to remind him; when she didn't, conscience pricked. 'I know this isn't how you meant to spend your holiday. It's a case of the willing horse, isn't it? If you want to go back to Byrfield, I'll get someone else to take over family liaison.'

Hazel gave him a cheerful grin. 'Turn my back on a murder inquiry so I can arrange flowers and fold serviettes? There's plenty of time yet. As long as I'm there for the wedding, the bride and groom can make their own arrangements. Or not. If they both turn up at Burford Parish Church in flat hats and wellies, with a pet lamb under the bride's arm and a stray bullock tied to the altar rail, I doubt if God will hold it against them.'

'The vicar might.'

'Our vicar keeps chickens, and conducts services with his fishing rod and thigh waders waiting by the vestry door. When the mayflies are rising, he can deliver a sermon in eight and a half minutes flat, with dry flies tucked into the lace of his surplice.'

'They say the past is another country,' said Dave Gorman thoughtfully. 'Well, so is the country.'

Hazel realised he wasn't taking them straight back to Meadowvale when he turned right at the traffic lights. Highfield Road was quiet; even the net curtains remained untwitched.

Ash saw the big car through his study window and had the kettle on before the bell rang. He looked from Hazel's face to Gorman's and back again; then he reached for the coffee jar and wordlessly added another spoonful to the pot.

'We were over seeing Pru Somers,' said Hazel by way of explanation.

Ash went back for the custard creams.

'That woman is bloody impossible!' Gorman settled himself at the kitchen table with his arms around his mug as if someone might try to steal it.

Ash considered. 'We have to make allowances. So much has happened to her in the last fortnight, she probably doesn't know which end of the sky has fallen on her.'

'Then I'd hate to meet her when she's on top form.' Gorman took a savage bite out of his coffee. 'I tried to explain to her that Rachel may be in more danger than we thought, but all she was interested in was scoring points. I offered her the flat behind the Derby Road, but she was too damned snooty to take it!'

'Rachel's still in danger?' Ash's gaze was searching.

'There have been developments,' said Gorman pontifically. He explained how they had affected his assessment of the situation. 'So what looked like a series of random attacks has probably condensed down to one actual attack, one outright lie, a misunderstanding and a bit of hysteria. Incidentally,' he said, fixing Ash with a critical eye, 'you should have told me what happened here the other day. I shouldn't have had to hear about it from a third party.'

'It was nothing. Frightened people desperate to protect their families. I dealt with it.'

'And if they hadn't wanted to listen but had beaten the crap out of you instead?'

'That I would have told you about.'

'And I didn't get a chance to talk to Mrs Somers about counselling,' interjected Hazel. 'The mood wasn't exactly conducive. Maybe, if you get a chance, you could try?'

'Perhaps I should make a chance,' said Ash. 'If there was nothing random about the attack on Rachel . . .'

And at that point, mid-sentence, he got what Hazel thought of as his out-to-lunch expression. It was as if he became aware of some activity deep within his own synapses, some nexus of brain cells working the problem to greater effect than he himself was doing, and he disengaged from his present company and withdrew inside himself for a minute or two to follow their progress. His eyes, deep-set and naturally rather shadowed, slid out of focus, and his lips parted and pursed as if he was learning how to whistle, and for that minute or two nothing short of a nearby explosion would have recalled him.

Then he came back. 'We're assuming it was Rachel he was after. Is that a safe assumption?'

DCI Gorman stared at him. 'I don't think he was trying to abduct the cat!'

'Neither do I,' said Ash. 'But Rachel and the cat weren't the only ones there.'

Gorman shook his head. 'I asked Pru Somers if Phillips could have been the target. She really didn't think so.'

Hazel didn't like contradicting the head of Meadowvale's CID, but she thought she should. 'Pru didn't think her ex-husband would have come after him. That doesn't necessarily mean he had *no* enemies.'

Gorman regarded her doubtfully. 'He was an architect.'

'I'm not sure that's a guarantee of universal love and respect.'

'You think he could have been leading a double life? Architect by day, drug baron by night?'

Ash shrugged. 'Or maybe there's something in his professional past – something he built fell on someone, or a contract went bad, or . . . *I* don't know. But I'm sure even architects can make enemies if they try hard enough.

'What do we know for certain? We know he was in the spinney, and before he was in the spinney he was in the house. Suppose the attacker knew that too. If he wanted to get Gethin Phillips outside, getting Rachel to scream would have been a good way to do it.'

They regarded one another, the implications of this trickling down through the filters of their minds, losing cloudiness and gaining purity as they went. For another minute none of the three of them spoke. Then Gorman said grimly, 'So maybe we're not looking for a sex offender at all. We're looking for someone who went to that wood in order to have a barney with Phillips. Possibly, in order to kill him.'

'If I'm right. I may not be,' warned Ash. 'I certainly wouldn't want either Pru or Rachel to think that they were out of danger – not until we're sure.'

'Then we need to make sure,' said Hazel. 'How?'

'Now we're playing with my ball,' said Dave Gorman succinctly. 'We knock on doors and ask questions. We find out everything there is to know about Gethin Phillips. So far we've been thinking of him as an incidental victim, a quiet hero who died protecting his stepdaughter. If he wasn't that, what was he instead?'

TEN

Today, many of the doors that detectives knock on are digital ones. No one raised any objections when Hazel logged in on a computer in the CID room that Saturday morning and began trawling for information on Gethin Phillips. Dave Gorman knew he would need to interview Pru Somers again, but first he wanted to know everything there was to know. It was his guiding principle only to ask questions when he knew what the answers ought to be.

Two hours later, Hazel tapped on his door and opened it with her elbow, her hands full of print-outs and scraps of paper with notes jotted on them.

Gorman looked up. 'So who was he? A Mafia hit-man? The man who broke the bank at Monte Carlo? The inventor of the everlasting battery?'

'So far as I can tell, he was just an architect,' said Hazel apologetically. 'He designed houses, and commercial premises, and a small hospital in Barbados, and a concert hall in Inverness. He was a sound, traditional architect who was well regarded by colleagues and industry insiders, and almost totally unknown to the wider public. His bank records show his salary going in and normal household expenditure going out, and nothing more. He wasn't spending beyond his means, and he wasn't suspiciously wealthy.'

'Probably not struggling to pay off gambling debts or drug dealers, then.'

'No evidence of it. No unexplained payments in or out to suggest he was either being blackmailed or blackmailing someone else.'

Gorman nodded his approval. 'You're getting good at this.'

'Don't tell me, tell Division.'

The DCI regarded her speculatively. 'You're still interested in a transfer, then?'

'Oh yes,' said Hazel at once. 'But I'm not holding my breath any more. They've got me down as trouble looking for somewhere to happen, and they think it'll be easier to keep a leash on me if I'm in uniform. No one's going to come out and say it, because I haven't done anything they can justify punishing me for, but I don't think I'm going to get CID or any of the specialties. I think my only chance would be to try another Division, or another force, and hope my reputation didn't follow me.'

Gorman understood why she made the top brass at Division uneasy: he also knew how unfair it was. 'Would you think of doing that?'

Hazel sighed. 'I don't know, Dave.' They were alone, and they'd been through too much together to observe the conventions of rank. 'I sometimes think I ought to. But I've made a life in Norbold, I don't want to leave. And I've burned so many bridges in the past that I'm wary of setting fire to another one. Especially when I'm standing on it.'

'Don't give up just yet,' he suggested. 'There are people here who're in your corner. I'm one, and Superintendent Maybourne is another. I don't know how far our influence goes – mine not very far, I suspect, but hers may go further. Either way, we'll keep pushing for you to get what you deserve. Don't give up on us yet.'

Hazel had always been a realist: the last couple of years had tried to turn her into a cynic. She knew that, if Division had set their face against her, the unrelenting efforts of a DCI who'd been almost as much of a thorn in their flesh as she had would hardly change their minds. But she appreciated his support, whether or not it accomplished anything. She knew, and she knew he knew, that speaking up for her was not a good career move for him.

She smiled. 'Meanwhile, in the much less important matter of your murder inquiry . . .'

Gorman grinned briefly. 'So Phillips wasn't involved with drugs, and he wasn't involved in gambling, and if he'd caught someone burying a body he hadn't tried to turn what he knew into a steady income. That's three reasons people get killed ruled out. What else is there?'

'It could have been personal. If he was having a fling with someone else's wife, for instance.'

'Pru says she and Phillips were fine. She has the bump to prove it.'

'Rachel said things were pretty well over between them. Who do we believe?'

Gorman scowled. 'I make it a rule never to believe anybody until I'm all out of options.'

'Well, *somebody* wanted him dead!'

The DCI leaned back in his chair in order to gaze down his rugby-player's nose at her. 'Or it may have been a sex attack all along.'

'It may,' Hazel agreed, reluctantly. 'But we've been thinking that for nearly a fortnight and it hasn't got us anywhere. Maybe thinking outside the box will.'

'All right. On the clear understanding that we're only talking possibilities, let's suppose Phillips was the intended target. It was his body that ended up down the morgue, after all. We know his stepdaughter was molested in the spinney, that she screamed and that he hurried out to help her. We know there wasn't anything you could call a fight before someone knocked Phillips down. We don't know for certain that he intended to kill him.'

Hazel's fair eyebrows drew together in a pensive frown. 'He was hit twice round the head with a length of wood. That's not a couple of macho guys trading black eyes, only one of them doesn't get up again – that's assault with a deadly weapon. And the FME said he was hit from behind. Waiting till your opponent isn't looking suggests intent.'

'It does rather,' allowed Gorman. 'Still, even minor disagreements can get out of hand. People don't listen to reason, it gets personal, then it gets violent. People die in arguments over a parking space.'

'So . . .' Hazel was thinking on her feet. 'Phillips was involved in some sort of dispute with this other man, and the other man wanted to meet him and sort it out. But Phillips wasn't prepared to. Maybe he thought whatever it was would blow over; maybe he thought it would be better dealt with by us, or by solicitors.'

'He never came to us with it,' said Gorman.

'The other guy thought he was getting the brush-off. If

Phillips wouldn't meet him for beer and some straight talking in the Rose & Crown, he figured out a way to make him come outside and settle things.'

'He used Rachel as bait.'

Hazel nodded. 'Whoever grabbed her may not have intended to hurt her, but he was happy enough to frighten the life out of her. That was nasty, and it was ruthless. It wasn't the action of a decent man dissatisfied with the way his kitchen extension turned out.'

'So there *is* something in Gethin Phillips' background that we haven't yet got a handle on. Unless, of course, Rachel was the intended target all along. Did you have any luck finding her father?'

It was good to have something concrete to report, even if it was essentially a negative. 'Steven Somers is working in Glasgow. Runs a car dealership. Has three children with the woman he's been with since leaving Pru. I haven't spoken to him, I wasn't sure if you'd want me to, but it doesn't sound as if he has a reason to come looking for trouble down here. If he wanted to touch base with Rachel, he could start by remembering her birthday. And why would he want to beat up Phillips when he's obviously happier with his current lady friend than he was with Pru?'

'Doesn't sound very likely, does it?' conceded Gorman. 'Still, we'd better not rule him out just yet.' He looked up with a smile. 'Go home, Hazel. It's Saturday, it's lunchtime, and anyway, you're on leave. Go and address some wedding invitations or something.'

'There's nothing else I can do here?'

'Not today. Not unless you have access to a crystal ball. Go home.'

The post brought another card to Highfield Road. It showed a beach donkey wearing a straw hat. Guy had written:

I do NOT look like a sprout. Gilbert looks like a core jet. We're going to Surf School tomorrow. Wish you were here.

Ash left Patience at home. This was going to be embarrassing enough without feeling the lurcher's expectant gaze on the back of his neck. If it all went pear-shaped, at least he'd have the drive home to recover his composure before he told her.

He considered, briefly, walking through the spinney. But that would bring him to the back of the Somerses' house, and they weren't good enough friends for back-door visits. Or so he told himself as he took the longer, safer way round.

While he drove he tried out a few different approaches in his head. 'Congratulations, you've won this week's prize – a visit for two to the therapist of my choice.' 'My friend Laura needs a case study for her Fellow's dissertation – she'd be so grateful . . .' 'Let's go for afternoon tea. There's a nice little café by the park. Oh look, there's our friendly neighbourhood shrink waving from her window. Let's pop in and say hello.'

It was, of course, utter fantasy. Although his earlier profession had made him very good at spotting lies in other people, Ash had never mastered the knack of lying himself. These days he didn't even try. He could get into enough trouble sticking religiously to the truth.

Rachel answered the door. The wary look on her face melted immediately into one of welcome. 'Gabriel! What a nice surprise. Come in. Patience isn't with you? Sit down, I'll put the kettle on.' She had him established in one of the big armchairs in the sitting room before he got his first word out.

'Is your mother at home?'

'No, she went out. A doctor's appointment.' The smallest flicker of disapproval pinched her lips for a moment. 'She's going private, of course. Nothing's too good for *this* baby. She shouldn't be long. What did you want to see her about?'

Ash hadn't wanted to put his suggestion to Rachel alone. Ideally he would have spoken to Pru first, but at least to mother and daughter together. The direct question discomfited him. 'I just had . . . a bit of an idea . . . I don't know, it might not appeal to her, but I thought I'd ask.'

For an intelligent and reasonably articulate man, Ash recognised this as a pathetic performance. He could only think that talking to a teenage girl was making him behave like a teenage boy again: awkward, self-conscious, timid.

And he remembered something about those distant, unlamented days: that teenage girls punished weakness in teenage boys like wolves descending on a lame caribou. Rachel laughed out loud. 'Going to make an honest woman of her, are you?'

The staggering inappropriateness of the joke, or the timing, or both, struck Ash momentarily dumb. He didn't know how to respond: certainly not in kind, but how sharp a rebuke was called for? Was anger justified, was he entitled to a pained expression and a brief homily, or should he simply ignore it? This family were going through hell: if a seventeen-year-old girl had struck a wrong note in dealing with the trauma, who was he to criticise? Dealing with his own traumas, or failing to, he'd struck more than wrong notes: he'd struck his boss. He'd needed, and received, infinite resources of patience and understanding. Maybe now was the time to pass on some of what he'd been given.

Rachel must have sensed what was going through his mind. The brittle ribaldry cracked clean across and fell out of her expression, leaving a hurt child, lost and alone, desperate for reassurance. She stammered, 'I'm sorry – I didn't mean – I only meant . . . Don't listen to me, I don't know what I'm saying. Please don't hate me.'

Ash was out of his chair in a moment, both hands held out to her; and maybe that wasn't entirely appropriate either, a man in his forties offering to embrace someone else's teenage daughter; but when situations are extreme enough, sometimes the normal mores of social congress have to go by the board. The girl was in urgent need of a hug, and right now it was him or no one.

Rachel moved even faster than Ash had, pressing herself into the protection of his arms, seeking comfort in a way that reminded him of how Patience pressed against his legs in the vet's waiting room – unhappy and full of trepidation but still trusting in his strength and his goodwill. He held the girl until her anxious breathing steadied. He said quietly into the top of her head, 'Of course I don't hate you, Rachel. And I do understand how your feelings are in turmoil. I'm sorry I can't be more help.'

He took a deep breath. There might never be a better opening. 'But I do know someone who might. She helped me when I didn't know whether I was coming or going. I'm not sure I could have got through without her.'

Rachel stood back, her gaze searching his face. 'You're talking about a psychiatrist!' she realised at last, her tone startled and accusatory.

'She's a trauma specialist. Her clients aren't mentally ill, for the most part – they've been subjected to more stress than anyone should be expected to deal with alone. I always thought of her as a bit like a wagon train's Indian scout. She knew the paths and the pitfalls, and where it was safe to rest and where it was necessary to keep moving forward. She brought me out of a dark place. When your taps dry up, you call a plumber. When you can't think straight, that's another time you need to talk to an expert.'

'I don't want anyone picking my head apart, thank you!' retorted Rachel hotly.

'Neither did I. It was what I needed, just the same.' He didn't sit down again. There seemed no point. He moved towards the door. 'Tell your mother I called. And run this by her, see what she thinks. No one's going to force you to take help that you don't want. But in the same way that a bad tooth doesn't get better until you see a dentist, this may be the time when the least amount of help would produce the greatest amount of benefit. If you decide it would be a good idea, I can set it up. Let me know.'

Hazel called for him as Ash shut the shop at six, to offer him a ride home. Patience rolled her caramel-coloured eyes and disappeared briefly into an alleyway before springing into the back of Hazel's car. Hazel clipped on the seatbelt the dog so disliked wearing and got in behind the wheel.

'That's you off Patience's Christmas-card list,' said Ash mildly. 'She likes walking home through the park.'

Waiting for a gap in the traffic, Hazel gave him a long look. 'Gabriel, she's a dog. It's her job to fit in with the wishes of the Master of the Tin-Opener.'

Ash chuckled ruefully. 'I don't think she thinks I'm master of anything very much at all.'

'She's a *dog*,' repeated Hazel. 'Go on talking about her as if she's your maiden aunt and Laura Fry will start keeping spare appointments for you. Speaking of which . . .?'

Ash gave a disconsolate sigh. 'I tried. It didn't work out as well as I'd hoped.'

'You spoke to Pru?'

'She wasn't there. I talked to Rachel.'

Hazel winced. 'That may not have been the best approach.'

'I know that, now.' Ash explained how it had come about. After a brief reflection, he told her about Rachel's extraordinarily tasteless joke.

'That girl is harbouring an immense amount of resentment,' observed Hazel. 'I wonder why.'

Ash stared. 'Apart from being attacked by her garden gate, you mean?'

'I haven't forgotten.' Hazel frowned, the fair brows drawing together. 'But why would that make her angry with her mother? Why is she so angry about this pregnancy? Not just surprised but angry. It would make more sense if Pru was angry with Rachel.'

'I think they're angry with one another,' said Ash, 'and I don't think they understand it any more than you do.'

'And you do?'

He was silent for a moment, marshalling his thoughts. 'When I thought I'd lost Cathy and the boys – when I thought they were dead – I was devastated: turned inside out by grief, and guilt, and remorse. But underlying all that, and perhaps even more powerful, was the anger. The anger all but consumed me. When you and I first met, four years after they disappeared, I was still angry, all the time.'

'I never saw that,' murmured Hazel. 'I knew you were pretty fragile. You never seemed in danger of boiling over.'

'I think there are only two ways of dealing with that degree of rage: letting it out or keeping it in. If you let it out, you risk hurting and frightening people who don't deserve it, and sooner or later it will be necessary, for their safety and yours, that you're brought under control. Possibly after you've decked your boss in the street in Whitehall. If you keep it in, the effects may be less noticeable, you may be able to live an outwardly normal life by keeping the lid clamped down, but then the pressure will build and build until Krakatoa explodes and sends shock-waves seven times around the earth.'

'So what is the answer?'

'Decompression,' said Ash. 'Bringing the diver up a few metres at a time, giving the effects a chance to dissipate harmlessly. Well, more or less. I wasn't a model patient. But the process that began when I was sectioned, and continued when I was discharged into the care of Laura Fry, kept me from self-destructing.' He gave a gentle smile. 'Not to mention your contribution, and Patience's.'

'Do you' – she wasn't sure how to put it; wasn't entirely sure she wanted to know – 'still feel like that? Angry?'

Ash shook his head. 'Not even at Cathy, any more. What she did feels like ancient history, as if it happened to someone else. I'm not that person any more. I have my sons back, I have my life back, I have what passes for my sanity, and I'm content.'

'It's a lot to have forgiven,' ventured Hazel.

'I don't know that I have forgiven her. I've just moved on. What Cathy did is no longer relevant to me. Cathy is no longer relevant.'

'Laura Fry did that?'

'Not entirely, no,' Ash said honestly. 'Laura helped to create the conditions for me to move on when the time was right. She gave me the tools to build a new life when I was ready to.'

Hazel sucked in a deep breath. Close as they were, they didn't often discuss matters this profound, this personal. She found it oddly upsetting to be reminded how much he had suffered, to realise how hard he'd tried to keep the extent of that suffering from her. She found herself wondering if she would be any more perceptive today, knowing him better, or if she would still see only the cinder-covered flank of the volcano, grey and still and lifeless, and never guess at the white-hot magma boiling within.

She said, diffidently, 'Do you ever think that maybe it's time . . .?'

Ash didn't answer immediately, which might mean that at least he'd reached a point where he was able to consider it. 'To start divorce proceedings?' he said then. 'Perhaps I should.

In fact, I know I should. It's just . . . it seems such a big step. And I worry how the boys would feel about it.'

'I think,' Hazel said carefully, watching the road and not him, 'they'll support you whatever you decide. It's two years since they saw Cathy; they'll probably never see her again. Gilbert at least understands what happened between you, and he made his choice two years ago. I think – and it's none of my business, but what I think is – they're too young to consult and too old to keep in the dark. If that's what you decide, I think they'll accept a plain statement of fact that it's time to tidy up your affairs and this is how you're doing it. You may be surprised how matter-of-fact they are about it.'

He turned in his seat to study her face. 'You think it's the right thing to do?'

But Hazel refused to be put on the spot like that. 'I don't get to say what's right. This is one you have to figure out for yourself, Gabriel. Do what's right for you. The boys, and your friends, just want you to be happy.'

She turned into Highfield Road, pulled up in front of Ash's house. As they got out of the car, someone came down the path from the front door. It was Pru Somers, and she looked as if she'd been ringing the bell for some time before accepting that there was no one at home. As if she thought he might have been hiding from her.

Ash went to meet her. 'You were looking for me? I was at the shop. Is everything all right? Is Rachel . . .?'

He never saw the slap coming. Pru was neither a tall nor a sturdy woman, but she was clearly an angry one. Her face was flushed and her eyes crackled like gunfire, and momentarily the anger gave her a right hook way above her fighting weight. The sound of it filled the leafy street and Ash rocked with the impact, his eyes wide with shock.

'How dare you?' demanded Pru Somers, her voice soaring. 'How *dare* you tell my daughter she needs a shrink? Who in the blue blinding blazes do you think you are?'

'Please . . . Mrs Somers . . . I never meant . . . That wasn't my intention . . .' Ash stammered miserably, his cheek flaming. 'I wanted to help.'

'I'll tell you how you can help,' spat Pru, readying another scything blow.

As a serving police officer, Hazel had seen people visit much worse assaults on one another. She'd seen them visit much worse on Ash. So while she wasn't unduly alarmed, she was conscious that the best time to intervene in a fight is right at the start. She inserted her shoulder between them and made calming noises. 'Now then, Mrs Somers, I'm sure there's been a misunderstanding. Let's talk about this inside.' Though in point of fact she suspected there had been no misunderstanding at all, only a tendency to cack-handedness on Ash's part and over-reaction on Pru's.

It was a sensible suggestion, but Pru Somers wasn't going to sit down with Gabriel Ash and sip tea from his mother's best china. She'd already done most of what she came to do; if she wasn't allowed to hit him again, she'd settle for the visceral triumph of shouting at him in the street.

'You keep away from my daughter, do you understand? Keep away from both of us. We don't need your help, we don't want your help, and if you come to our home again I'll call the police. Do you understand?'

'Of course,' mumbled Ash. 'I am so sorry. I hoped that what had helped me might help Rachel. It was never my intention to go behind your back.'

'Oh, I know all about you, Gabriel Ash,' snarled Pru. 'For years everyone thought you were the local idiot, wandering round with that dog.' Her venom extended to an acid look at Patience, still sitting innocently in the back of Hazel's car. 'Then, for some reason, you weren't the local idiot any more, you were some kind of a closet genius. You know something? – I think Norbold may have got it right the first time. I don't know what you hope to gain by haunting my family, but it stops right now. I don't want to hear that you've spoken to Rachel again, not about anything. Look after your own children, and leave me to look after mine.'

With that she turned on one spiked heel and stalked back to her car.

There was a long silence. Then Hazel breathed out and said, 'I don't know about you, but I need caffeine.' Freeing Patience from her seatbelt, she led the way up the path to Ash's front door. After another long moment, Ash followed.

Highfield Road was not the sort of neighbourhood where the housewives hung net curtains mainly for the pleasure of twitching them. But an astute observer would have noticed shadows behind the bay windows on both sides of the street, and at least one well-polished brass letter-box propped open so that someone crouching behind it could hear everything that was said.

ELEVEN

'I realised I'd handled it badly,' confessed Ash, embarrassed, looking not at Hazel but into his mug. 'I hadn't realised just how badly. I'm still not sure why they were quite so offended.'

Hazel Best was very fond of Gabriel Ash. But still he regularly strained both her patience and her credulity. 'Most people,' she said, using the careful voice she reserved for small children and wool-gathering grannies, 'resent being told they might be mentally ill.'

'That's not what I said. I told Rachel that trauma therapy had helped me, that's all. I said if she wanted, I could set it up.'

'Rachel Somers is a seventeen-year-old girl in a particularly vulnerable state: of *course* her mother objected to you saying that to her. We knew this was going to take tactful handling. Whatever possessed you to talk to Rachel alone?'

Ash gave an awkward shrug. 'It just happened that way. I called, she was in, Pru was out. And there was that really weird thing she said about me and Pru. After that, I was surer than ever that she needed professional help.'

'It was pretty weird,' agreed Hazel. 'But Gabriel, think what that girl's been through. Her emotions must be tied up like spaghetti. Is it any wonder that she strikes a bum note from time to time?'

'Of course not. The wonder is that she's able to function at all. I *did* handle it badly,' he said again, shaking his head dolefully. 'Mrs Somers was right. I deserved a slap.'

Hazel chuckled affectionately at his hangdog expression. 'Yes, you did. Well, let's just be glad it wasn't worse. That Pru wasn't cleaning her shotgun when Rachel told her.'

Ash smiled dutifully, but he couldn't pass it off that easily. It wasn't the slap that rankled so much as concern that his ineptitude had discouraged the family from getting the help they needed. He was in many ways a mild, polite and un-assuming man, the sort of man who gave up his seat on public transport and always said please and thank you. But behind that, unsuspected except by those who knew him best, was a steely thread of obstinacy that would have done credit to a mule. He was already wondering how he could broach the subject again and get a more positive response.

Hazel was one of those who knew him well enough. She lowered a brow at him. 'Don't even think about it,' she said.

It is axiomatic that books will burn at Fahrenheit 451. Helped by a sprinkling of petrol, they'll burn very cheerily.

Ash was woken by the phone a little after three in the morning. It was DCI Gorman. 'Meet me down at the bookshop. Now, Gabriel.'

The fire service had been on site for twenty minutes, alerted by a new father giving his wife some much-needed sleep by driving their fractious baby round town. He actually saw three men running off, and the first flames gaining hold behind the new glass.

By the time Ash arrived the fire was out; only a little smoke was still rising from the sodden embers on the floor. At first sight the shop appeared gutted. But as the hammering of his heart steadied enough for a proper appraisal, he could see that much of the damage was superficial. A lot of the stock was charred beyond rescue, but many of the shelves and the long central table were only lightly toasted, the fire had never reached the little kitchen and office at the back, and the smoke-blackened walls would yield to a good scrubbing and a generous application of paint. Whoever had intended to destroy Rambles With Books had not succeeded.

The new front window had been cracked by the heat, and the fire-fighters had smashed it to gain access. Dave Gorman had spent a little time putting the pieces of glass back together, a little further up the street where they weren't in anyone's way. He ushered Ash up past the fire engine to see why.

'Not random, then,' said Ash after a moment. 'Not a couple of drunks having fun after chucking-out time.'

'No, Gabriel, this was personal.'

On the pavement, lime-green spray-paint on the glass jigsaw spelled out the word *Pervert*. Ash went on staring at it until Gorman steered him away.

'Why would someone think that?'

When DCI Gorman had done all he usefully could at the shop, he'd taken Ash back to Meadowvale. He knew that coffee wouldn't make everything all right, but of all the things that might make matters slightly better, coffee – even police station coffee – was the easiest to provide. He sat Ash in his office while he went to kick the machine on the landing into life, and came back with two nasty cardboard cups. After a moment he put his own down in order to fold Ash's hands around the other.

Ash blinked, and registered the rising steam, and looked through it at the DCI, his eyes hollow with disbelief. 'Why would someone think that?'

Gorman sniffed the faintly odd aroma that suggested the machine might be dispensing a regrettable blend of coffee and oxtail soup again. 'You tell me.'

'I can't imagine. I've never given anyone any reason to think any such thing.'

'You have a habit of being in the wrong place at the wrong time.'

'If the man who killed Gethin Phillips had chased Rachel Somers all the way through the spinney, I'd have been in the right place at very much the right time.' He became aware that Gorman was squinting at him. 'What?'

Under the fluorescent strips of office lighting, Gorman could see the mark of a hand on Ash's cheek. 'Where did you get the shiner?'

Ash felt the place gingerly. 'This?'

'That.'

So Ash told him about Pru Somers' visit, and what had provoked it.

Gorman listened with the stoic expression, slightly exasperated, slightly amused, that he kept for his dealings with Ash. 'Well, there's your answer.'

Ash stared at him. 'You think Mrs Somers torched my shop?'

Exasperation won. 'Of course not. This happened in the street, yes? Pru Somers shouted at you, told you to stay away from her daughter and then slapped your face, in a public place where anyone could have seen and lots of people probably did. Someone put two and two together and got five.'

'You think one of my *neighbours* . . .?' Ash sounded positively indignant at the idea. As if it might have a dampening effect on property prices.

'Hell's bells, Gabriel, for an intelligent man you do a damned good impression of a moron sometimes. Do I think one of the Highfield Road blue-rinse brigade sneaked into town with a sherry bottle full of petrol and a silver-plated cigarette lighter? – no. Do I think one of them couldn't wait to tell some friends, who were then overheard gossiping about it in the Happy Grape Wine Bar? – quite possibly.'

Ash passed a hand across his face. 'Why are people so ready to believe this about me? People I don't even know – and even, it seems, people I do.'

'Well, there was that description cobbled together by a bunch of over-excited teenagers. But more than that, it's because you don't slot into any of the pigeon-holes that people use instead of thinking. This town was probably more comfortable with you when it thought you were a fairy short of a Christmas tree. When it found out you had brains, and money, and a couple of kids they knew nothing about, and you kept being there or thereabouts when weird stuff was happening – well, they didn't know what to make of you any more. And people don't trust what they don't understand. It's like they only have room for so many templates in their heads. So if you're not going to play the village idiot any more, maybe you're the Demon King.

'And I have to say,' he added with asperity, 'you do go out of your way to invite misunderstandings. You had no business suggesting to Rachel Somers that she needed counselling. That's my job. We have leaflets. Mind your own business, Gabriel. What happened tonight was a direct result of you sticking your oar in where it was neither wanted nor needed. Clean up your shop, get another window put in, and go back to selling books. I'll look after the Somers family.'

The sun was peeping over the eastern horizon as he walked Ash back to his car. He didn't expect any more trouble tonight, but if he was wrong he'd rather it didn't take place in the Meadowvale car park. The editor of the *Norbold News* could be relied on for a pithy headline if that happened.

As Ash unlocked the car he hesitated and looked back at Gorman, his face perplexed. 'Is there really . . .?'

The detective knew what was coming. He'd been expecting it. 'No,' he said wearily. 'I made up the Happy Grape Wine Bar.'

Hazel's first instinct was to go and shout at Pru Somers. Her second instinct was to go and shout at Ash. Her third was to avoid taking sides. They were both doing the best they knew how in desperate circumstances, and it was hardly to be wondered at if either or both of them got it wrong, even very wrong, at times.

Her fourth instinct, best and most characteristic of all, was to take a bucket and a sponge round to Rambles With Books and start cleaning up.

The fire investigators had already left. It wasn't exactly a three-pipe problem. The deliberate nature of the fire and the reason for it were spray-painted on the broken window; if the author had absent-mindedly signed his work, everyone could have taken the rest of the day off. The rotund figure of Meadowvale's scenes of crime officer – no longer, in fact, an officer but civilian staff; but since the function was performed by an experienced ex-policeman who was invariably still addressed as Sergeant Wilson, the outsourcing process might never have happened – gave her a cheery wave as he too departed, the last man in England who should have gone out in public in a white plastic Babygro.

Ash wasn't there, which surprised Hazel a little. Gorman had told her that he'd seen Ash off the premises in the early hours of the morning, but she'd rather expected that he'd have found his way back by now.

Apparently she wasn't the only one to think that. She'd cleared one corner of the shop as a base to work from when a taxi pulled up in the street and Rachel Somers sprang out, almost throwing her money at the driver in her haste. Hazel watched her standing stricken on the pavement, staring open-mouthed at the devastation; then she spoke the girl's name and stepped out from between the smoke-blackened book-shelves. 'Mind what you touch, everything's filthy.'

Rachel switched her stare to Hazel, taking in the sooty T-shirt and the smuts smeared across her face. 'Is Gabriel here?'

'I think he must be at home. He was here soon after it happened, but I haven't seen him since.'

'Soon after *what* happened?'

'Someone torched the place,' Hazel said succinctly.

'*Why?*'

Hazel wiped her brow with the back of her wrist, spreading the smuts even further. 'Because the stupid people in this stupid little town have got the idea it was Gabriel who killed Mr Phillips and attacked you and some other young people.'

'Those men in Highfield Road. That's what they were saying. I told them they were wrong. I thought they believed me.'

Hazel shrugged. 'Maybe they did. Maybe the same idea occurred to someone else.'

'This is our fault, isn't it?' Rachel was close to tears. 'Mine and my mother's. He was only trying to help us. I was upset and Mum was angry, and she made a scene outside his house. Someone must have thought she was blaming him. That's why this happened.' She looked up at the wrecked shop-front, the charred books like ruined butterflies in the broken window. A fresh thought occurred to her, and her eyes raced back to Hazel. 'Was he hurt?'

Hazel shook her head. 'It was the middle of the night, he wasn't here. DCI Gorman woke him up, and then he saw him safely off the scene and back to his car. He's fine. He probably can't face the mess again just yet.' Even as she said it, though, it didn't sound much like Ash. He was not a man to avoid unpleasant duties.

'Just because he was all right when he left here,' said Rachel in a low voice, 'does that mean he got home safely? Does it mean no one was waiting for him?'

Hazel paused only long enough to throw the towel from the

back seat, the one she kept for Patience to sit on, over the driver's seat to protect her upholstery from the soot. She pushed the passenger door towards Rachel. 'Get in.'

The girl did. 'If he's come to any harm . . .'

'. . . Then the sooner we get there, the better,' Hazel finished tersely. She performed a U-turn in front of the shop and headed for the park and, beyond it, Highfield Road.

Rachel perched on the front of her seat like a jockey, urging the car to go faster. 'I feel responsible.'

Hazel forbore to comment. In her heart, where she was Gabriel Ash's friend before she was anything else, she too held Rachel responsible. Neither the attack on his property nor the threat to Ash's person would have happened if he hadn't tried to help her, and Hazel harboured the natural resentment of a friend.

But in her head she was a police officer and had to view events with a cooler, less partisan eye. Her head said that it was never appropriate to blame the victim of a crime. If other people had misunderstood his actions, Ash would never lay that at Rachel's door. She hadn't asked to be attacked in Highfield Spinney. The fact that the first man who came to her aid had paid with his life and the second had seen his business go up in smoke did not alter the basic rule that criminal acts are the responsibility of those who carry them out.

Hazel sucked in a steadying breath. 'I'm sure everything will be fine. If he was up before dawn, he's probably overslept. Anyway, we'll be there in a minute.'

Ash's car, the fawn Volvo estate that was built on the same lines as a tank and bought by his mother so long ago it was now old enough to vote, was parked in front of his house. The sitting room curtains were pulled back, those of the master bedroom were still drawn: all that meant, probably, was that he hadn't been upstairs again since getting back home. It was easy to read sinister inferences into normal, everyday occurrences: DCI Gorman described it as a detective's occupational hazard.

Hazel was out of the car first, trotting determinedly up the steps to the front door. She rang the bell but no one came.

She set off down the side path that led to the garage and, via a gate that Ash kept shut even though Patience could hurdle it with ease, to the kitchen door. It was locked. She shaded her eyes to peer through the window.

She could see him, on the leather sofa at the far end of the kitchen, with his head tilted against the back, not moving. There was no sign of Patience. Hazel rattled her knuckles on the glass and shouted his name. Still no response.

Alarm started to tighten its grip on her throat. He kept a spare key buried in a plastic box in the flowerbed, because she'd told him not to keep it under a flowerpot on the patio where any burglar worth his salt would look first. It had been good advice, and if he'd lost his key it wouldn't have taken him five minutes to dig up a replacement. But he was in there and he wasn't moving, and if something had happened to him he might not have five minutes to spare. Hazel snatched up a lump of granite from the rockery and took aim on a corner of the glass above the lock. 'Stand back,' she warned as Rachel came to join her.

A split second before the blow became unstoppable, Patience reared up against the inside of the door, looking at her in surprise; and Ash yawned and stretched and opened his eyes. Then he blinked. 'Hazel?'

'Didn't you hear me?' she demanded, querulous with relief, when he'd let them in. 'I rang at the front, then I knocked on the back door and shouted your name. I thought you were dead!'

'Why?' asked Ash.

'Because somebody burned your shop down last night! Because we were worried they might have come here and beaten your silly head in!'

'I suppose they might,' he agreed placatingly. 'But they didn't.'

'And I couldn't see Patience, and you weren't moving . . .'

'I must have fallen asleep. I had a broken night, as you know. And Patience likes the draught under the door in hot weather.'

Making sinister inferences from everyday occurrences: the detective's occupational hazard. Hazel sighed and let go of her sense of grievance. 'I was worried about you. We both were.'

'That was kind of you,' he said, without a trace of irony. 'Hazel – do you know you've got soot on your face?'

'I was making a start on the shop,' she said with restraint. His smile spread slowly, his deep eyes warm with regard. 'Which is what I should have been doing, instead of snoring on the kitchen sofa. Give me a minute to get into some old clothes and we'll blitz it together. We'll drop you off on the way, Rachel.'

'Can I help?' she asked shyly. 'I don't have any old clothes' – she looked down at herself doubtfully – 'but these certainly aren't new.'

Ash was in a quandary. He'd annoyed her mother enough already without sending her home looking like a chimney sweep. But one of his shirts would drown her, and one of Gilbert's wouldn't be big enough.

Predictably, Hazel had the answer. 'I've got a forensic onesie in the car: that'll keep you clean.' She caught Ash's look and bristled. 'Well? You never know your luck.'

'You mean, you never know when you'll be lucky enough to stumble on a crime scene and need a way of keeping your DNA from contaminating it?'

'Exactly.' She turned back to Rachel. 'Does your mother know where you are?'

The girl had the grace to look embarrassed. 'Well, no. I heard about the fire on local radio while I was having breakfast. Mum had already left for work, so I called a taxi.'

'You didn't call her?'

'I suppose I should have.'

Hazel rolled her eyes. 'Call her now. She needs to know where you are. If she wants you to go home, we'll take you. Though DCI Gorman wasn't keen on you being there alone. Are there some friends you could go to?'

'Not really.' Rachel went out to the patio to make the call.

Ash came back downstairs looking, Hazel thought, not very different to when he'd gone up. He didn't have much in the way of casual clothes. He did gardening and DIY jobs in what, a few weeks earlier, he'd been buying and selling books in. The basic principle seemed to be that when things were new he wore them for best; then as they became worn they served to knock around the house and garden in; finally he wore them for cleaning the grate and painting the fence. But, and this was somehow fundamental to who he was, *they were always the same clothes.* He bought the same styles in the same colours from the same shops, usually two at a time. His idea of following fashion was to buy checks one year, stripes another. So he never looked any different, just slightly more or less weathered.

Rachel came back, putting her phone away. 'I can help, as long as I look after my hands.'

Ash shook his head, bemused. The way he and Pru Somers had parted, he'd expected her to demand her daughter's immediate return on pain of . . . well, pain. Perhaps a night's sleep had helped her get things into perspective.

'I'll leave Patience here,' he decided. 'There's broken glass among the debris.'

I have to look after my hands too, said the white lurcher smugly.

TWELVE

A long with the white forensic suit, Rachel pulled on two pairs of latex gloves, one over the other. Then she looked up, embarrassed. 'I expect you think I'm a bit of a diva.'

In fact Hazel hadn't been thinking about Rachel at all. She'd been wondering if it made more sense to dump the entire stock in a skip rather than trying to sort through it. The shelves were worth more than the second-hand books they held. She looked round vaguely. 'Sorry?'

'Me. All this.' Rachel held up her gloved hands. 'I'm not Ashkenazy. I'm never going to *be* Ashkenazy. I'm not even Liberace. I'm just a girl who plays piano a bit better than most girls who play piano. And even that's probably less to do with natural talent and more to do with having a seriously pushy mother.'

'She wants what's best for you,' said Hazel mildly. 'What's wrong with that?'

'Nothing, I suppose.' She might have left it at that. But after a moment, she expanded on the subject with a certain doggedness, as if now she'd started she was going to finish. 'Not much wrong with a cage, either, except for the bars. There's a whole world out there that I know nothing about. Things I'd have liked to try, that I might have enjoyed, that I might even have been good at, but I wasn't allowed to because I had to look after my hands. I had to concentrate on my music.'

'Music is a gift,' said Ash. It wasn't a very contentious statement, or a very original one, and in the circumstances it wasn't particularly helpful either.

'It's not a gift when it's thrust down your throat,' muttered Rachel rebelliously. 'When I was younger, a lot of girls did gymnastics. It looked like fun. I did extra piano practice because I could have hurt my hands doing gymnastics. I could have hurt my hands pony-trekking. I could even have got hurt dancing. Anything at all active, at all interesting, came into the category of Dangerous Pursuits, and I wasn't allowed to do them. I was told I'd thank her later. I'm still waiting for the gratitude to show up.'

Hazel frowned, not sure if the girl deserved sympathy or a boot up the backside. 'Rachel, you're seventeen years old. You're not a child any more. If you don't want to play the piano, don't play it. Go pony-trekking. Take what you want from life, and pay for it. If you damage your hands – and there's no surer way of damaging any bit of you than playing around with horses – you can forget about the concert hall and get a job serving in a shop, but if the risk seems worth it to you, take it. But don't blame your mother for giving you chances that lots of people would kill for.'

The girl looked away. 'You don't understand.'

'Maybe I don't. I never had any particular talent that needed nurturing, any gifts that needed protecting. I *did* go pony-trekking. It was fun, but I can't say it was a gateway into a whole new way of life. I gave up riding when I went to university. It's pretty hard to keep a pony in student accommodation.'

'What do you think about a fire sale?' asked Ash, diplomatically changing the subject.

Both young women looked at him. 'What?'

'A fire sale. If we cleaned up the least damaged books, we could set them out on the long table – if we could clean up the long table – and sell them off at a reduced price.'

'Gabriel,' Hazel said levelly, 'if you reduce the prices any more you'll be paying people to take them away. Bin the lot. Go to a couple of house clearances and get some new ones.'

'I don't like giving up on them without even trying to salvage them,' murmured Ash. 'Some of these books are like old friends. You don't take old friends to the dump just because they've had a hard time and aren't as smart as they once were.'

'And that's the basic problem with your business model, right there,' declared Hazel. 'Your stock isn't meant to hang around long enough to become old friends. It's supposed to come in, attract a buyer, be exchanged for money and leave. It's never meant to be a long-term relationship.'

He knew she was right. But Gabriel Ash was more a

conserver than a consumer – which is why he was still driving a car that was already old when he inherited it. 'We could make three piles: save, dump, and not sure.'

'We could make four piles,' countered Hazel. 'Save, dump, not sure, and throw at Gabriel's head if he keeps moving things from pile two into pile three when he thinks Hazel isn't looking.'

Rachel was watching them with a tiny puzzled frown, as if she couldn't quite figure them out. They bickered like an old married couple, but they seemed not to be a couple at all. They didn't live together, yet at the first sign of a problem they rushed to one another's side. Ash had two sons: whoever their mother was, clearly it wasn't Hazel. Then there was the age difference: fourteen, fifteen years? She couldn't work it out.

'Earth to Rachel Somers,' said Hazel with a friendly grin.

Rachel gave a guilty start, as if her mind had been read. 'Sorry. I was picturing you keeping a pony in halls of residence.'

When it became obvious that there was more detritus than there was room to store detritus, Ash conceded defeat and Hazel phoned for wheelbarrows and a skip. The operator started talking about Sunday rates; Hazel showed a professional interest in his waste carrier's licence; the question of double-time was quietly shelved.

She let Ash sneak a few old favourites into the kitchen, but most of the charred volumes went straight into the barrows. They worked out a routine whereby the girls shovelled burnt books and broken glass into a barrow and Ash ran it up a plank into the skip. The merry tinkle as the contents crashed to the bottom was like tiny daggers in his heart, but an hour's work broke the back of the task and they took a breather to assess their progress.

The long table had survived almost intact under its cloak of soot. It was old and worn even before the fire, and its wood was hard. Even the polish went deeper than the damage in most places, and anyway, what were a few more honourable scars on the body of an old warrior? The same applied to the shelves. They'd been stained and battered before, they were more stained and battered now, but they were still tall and broad and strong, and when new books went in – well, new *old* books – they would look much as they always had.

Ash stretched his aching back. 'I think we're done. The glazier will be here later, I'll go shopping for some more stock over the next few days, and then we'll be back in business. Thank you for your help, ladies.'

'Don't thank me,' muttered Rachel. 'This wouldn't have happened if I hadn't given my mother an excuse to go ape in public.'

'You don't know that,' said Ash. 'Even if it's true, neither of you is to blame. This was the work of a stupid thug, and neither you nor your mother is either of those things. Rachel, don't underestimate what you've both been through – are still going through. It's a minor miracle that you can get out of bed in the morning. And it would help if your friends weren't quite so clumsy in their attempts to support you,' he added ruefully.

'Oh, you weren't,' Rachel said quickly, one double-gloved hand darting out to touch his. 'I know you mean well – I knew it at the time. It was probably a very good idea, and I'm sorry I didn't take the suggestion in the spirit in which it was offered. Can I give it some more thought when my head's settled down a bit?'

'Of course you can. It's for you to decide how far and how fast you want to go. No one's going to pressure you into anything. We just want to be sure that you get anything you need.'

'Er – guys,' said Hazel, nodding significantly at the gap where the window used to be.

Pru Somers didn't so much park her car as abandon it where it screeched to a halt, and the door was still open as she stormed across the pavement, the water that put the fire out dried to dirty streaks across the flags, and flung open the door to Rambles With Books in a gesture that might have seemed more dramatic if it hadn't resulted in the last few remnants of glass dropping with a sad clink at her feet.

Ash steeled himself for another attack; Hazel moved into position to intervene; but this time Pru had Rachel in her sights.

'Are you determined to make a fool of me?' she demanded, almost panting with fury. 'Do you think that making me look stupid makes you look smart? I think he was probably right after all.' A brief sideways glance at Ash, with no warmth in it, only knives. 'You do need your head examining.'

Rachel only flushed and looked down and said nothing.

Blessed are the peacemakers, thought Hazel stoically, as ready to protect the girl from her mother's venom as she had been to defend Ash. 'Mrs Somers, Rachel's fine. She's been with us all morning. Has something happened to upset you?'

The way Pru rounded on her, she may have forgotten that bit of the Sermon on the Mount. 'Upset me? Good heavens no, whatever would give you that idea? The man I loved has been murdered, I found out I was carrying his child just too late to tell him, and my daughter is hell-bent on making me appear unhinged. But upset? No. Slightly vexed, perhaps.' By now she was shouting loudly enough to make the pigeons shuffle uneasily on the rooftops opposite.

'No one thinks you're unhinged,' Ash ventured carefully. 'No one thinks Rachel's unhinged. If I gave that impression, I'm truly sorry. It was never my intention. I wanted to help, but I fully accept that what I said was inept and impertinent. I am deeply sorry that I offended you.'

Now, as Pru stared at him, the knives in her gaze were just a little blunted. 'Mr Ash, I'm not sure what I think of your involvement in this. I thought I did. Now, I'm wondering if I've been naïve. If I should have treated what I was told a little more circumspectly. If, in short, we are both the victims of a spiteful, manipulative girl who can't bear not being the centre of attention.'

Hurt fell through Rachel's face like a small avalanche, and she gave a broken sob. 'That's not fair!'

Automatically, Hazel reached out an arm to her. 'Listen, people, we can't do this in the middle of the street, and right now the shop doesn't have an inside we can go into. My house is only a couple of streets away: can we adjourn there, make some strong coffee, and figure out what everyone said, what they actually meant, and who owes who an apology?'

Pru seemed only marginally mollified by the suggestion, but at least she wasn't shouting any more. 'Does it ever occur to you two,' she asked coldly, 'that perhaps you drink too *much* strong coffee?'

Nevertheless, that's what they did, travelling in Ash's car because, after eighteen years of being a Volvo estate, two of them transporting a dog and two young boys, a little soot would probably improve the upholstery.

'I don't understand why you were so anxious,' ventured Ash while Hazel filled the kettle. 'Rachel told you where she was.'

'She *did* tell me,' agreed Pru Somers tersely. 'What she did not do was speak to me. If she had, I'd have told her to come home immediately. Which is undoubtedly why she sent me a text instead.'

Both of them looked at Rachel, who gave a haughty sniff and looked away.

Ash gave an apologetic shrug. 'I thought you knew what we were doing and were comfortable with it. She really hasn't come to any harm.'

'I see that.' Still tight-lipped, Pru was making an effort to calm down. 'Mr Ash, I'm not sure if you owe me an apology or if I owe you one – but I'm damn sure that Rachel owes us both. She gave me to understand that your visit yesterday was unwelcome, your suggestion offensive, and that she was left feeling distressed if not violated. I believed that you were taking an unhealthy interest in my daughter, and that after all she'd been through she shouldn't have to fend off the unwanted attentions of a middle-aged man with a curious history and dubious motives. That's what I came to your house to tell you. I thought I had made my feelings clear.'

'Oh, you did,' murmured Ash.

'Only the following morning I discovered that, far from avoiding your attentions, she had sought out your company, was blaming me for what had happened to your shop, and was helping to clear up the mess. This, a girl who will happily walk round a pile of clothes on her bedroom floor rather than put them in the laundry!'

Rachel took a deep breath. 'You misunderstood. I wasn't upset with Gabriel – I was just upset. I knew he was trying to help. I was a bit stunned that he thought I might need that kind of help, that's all. I needed you to sit down with me, give me a hug and tell me everything was going to be all right. That *we* were going to be all right. That maybe Gabriel was right and maybe he was wrong, but we'd figure it out and if we needed help we'd know where to find it. I did *not* need you to go off the deep end, storm out of the house, and go shouting abuse at a decent man in a quiet street.

'And when it comes to middle-aged people with curious histories, take a look in a mirror sometime. You're a woman of forty-two who's been made pregnant by her live-in boyfriend.'

If they'd been standing up, there was no question in Hazel's mind that Pru would have slapped her daughter's face. The low table, taking up much of the centre of the small room, saved both of them from that indignity. Pru fumed silently for a moment. Then she said, 'That's the man I loved you're talking about. The man who died protecting you. If you can't show some gratitude, at least show some respect.'

'I have nothing but gratitude and respect for Gethin,' insisted Rachel. 'I know what he did for me. He was a good man who cared about me. I think he cared more for me than you ever have.' She took a deep breath. 'There's something else you misunderstood. That text I sent you. I didn't phone because I didn't want another argument. I wasn't asking permission to help out at the bookshop. I was letting you know where I was, so you wouldn't worry. I'm not a child any more. I'll take my own decisions, even if that means making my own mistakes. Even if that means giving up the piano and going pony-trekking!'

Pru stared at her as if one of them had gone mad, and she wasn't quite sure which. 'Pony-trekking?'

It was time for the peacemaker to wave the olive branch again. 'I think that might be a metaphorical pony,' murmured Hazel. 'The kind you can keep in student lodgings.' Immediately she wished she'd kept her mouth shut. The way this was going, they'd have to make a block-booking with Laura Fry.

Pru squeezed her eyes shut, as if that might make the last few moments go away. Then she fixed her gaze on Rachel. 'You're serious? You want to give up the piano? After all your work? Everything you've achieved?'

Rachel considered before responding, which was progress of a kind. 'That's actually the wrong question, Mum. What you mean is, do I *intend* to give up the piano. I don't need your permission. I don't even need your approval.

'I know how much effort, and how much money, you've invested in my future. And I do appreciate it – really, I do. I'm just not sure that I'm prepared to be as single-minded about it as you need me to be. To give up everything else in order to do this. It's not that I've taken against the piano. It's just that I'm pretty sure there's more to life than knowing which key to hit when.'

'How can you betray your gift like this?' cried Pru. It was almost, thought Hazel, as if she was facing another bereavement.

'My gift?' echoed Rachel. 'Or you? You've always wanted this more than I have. It's true I have a certain talent. Well, lots of people have a talent. They don't all let it dictate what they do with the rest of their lives. You can enjoy dancing, painting, playing tennis – and yes, playing piano – without it being the centre of your existence!'

'Certainly – as an amateur.' Pru made the word the grossest of insults. 'If you want to make your mark in any of those fields, you have to apply yourself. You have to be disciplined, dedicated.'

'No, I don't,' said Rachel firmly. 'I can finish school next year, and go to university to study French or social work or astrophysics.' She darted Hazel a sideways glance and said out of the corner of her mouth, 'That's rockets and stuff, yes?' Hazel nodded, and Rachel went on. 'Or I can visit the jobcentre and start earning a living, and play the piano for pleasure. I might even decide to go on with my studies and try to make a career of it: I don't know. But it's going to be my decision, Mum. You can't pursue your dreams through me any longer.'

Pru continued to stare at her, dumbfounded. 'That isn't what I've been doing.'

'Yes. It really is.'

Pru turned an accusing eye on Ash. 'This is your fault. You put her up to this.'

'No,' protested Ash, 'I didn't—'

Before he could finish the sentence, Rachel shot back, interrupting. 'Nobody put me up to anything! I'm not a puppet – not Gabriel's, and not yours! And I'm not having my strings jerked any longer. You need to get used to the idea.'

'And you need to remember all the sacrifices that have been made for you,' snarled Pru. 'All your life, the people around you have put their own wishes on hold so Rachel could have what was best for her. After your father left, I was alone for four years, because that was the only way I could be sure of giving you what you needed.

'Then I found Gethin. And that was some kind of a miracle, because Gethin was that rarest of creatures, a natural family man. He felt almost as strongly about your talent as I do. He wanted to help you succeed. That's more than most men do for their own children, let alone someone else's. But he believed in you and he cared for you – and it cost him his life, Rachel. Before you start whining about people pulling your strings, you should acknowledge what bringing you this far, keeping you safe to exercise your precious freedom of choice, has cost. A good man died for you. If he'd known you'd be stamping your foot like a spoilt brat this soon afterwards, he might have thought better of it.'

That broke Rachel's self-possession, the veneer of calm control behind which she was not a rational adult engaging her mother in an adult debate but a traumatised teenager hanging onto the exploding fragments of her world by her fingernails. Her face cracked and thick slow tears spilled from her eyes. Her voice cracked as well. 'I loved Gethin too! He was there for me when you were way too busy. Gethin knew how much I appreciated that. If you don't, it's because you're never around when people are talking about the stuff that matters.'

'I wasn't around because I was working! Good piano tutors don't come cheap!'

'Maybe you should have asked which I wanted more: piano lessons or a mother!'

Hazel tried again. 'Guys, guys – what are you doing? You're tearing one another apart. Does either of you think this is what Mr Phillips would have wanted? His last generous act in a generous life was to stand between Rachel and a man who meant her harm. And he did that because he cared for her – but Pru, mainly he did it because he cared for you. He loved you enough to keep safe the thing that mattered to you most in the world. Please don't let that be tainted with bitterness.'

Pru stared at her as if she'd said something impertinent. 'What the hell do you suppose you know about it?'

Despite her best intentions, Hazel bristled. 'I probably know as much about loss as most people. It's part of the human condition. Nothing is for ever: you love, and sooner or later either you lose your loved one or your loved one loses you. And life goes on. I don't suppose you want to hear that right now, but it's true. You won't always feel as you feel today. You won't always hurt as much as you hurt today. The loss will remain, the grief and the anger will remain, but you'll learn how to deal with them. The grief will turn to sorrow, and you'll incorporate that sorrow into yourself. The scar will remain; the pain will seep away.

'Right now you can't see any further back than what happened in Highfield Spinney a fortnight ago. All the good times that went before seem dream-like, unreal. But that will change. When it does, it'll be these weeks that seem like a dream – like a nightmare – and the years you had together, the happiness you gave one another, will be what you remember. Hold onto that. And don't do anything, don't say anything, don't strike out at one another in ways that you'll regret when the dust has finally settled. You are each now all that the other one has.'

Both women – the one more than ten years younger than her, the other more than ten years older – stared at her: Rachel wide-eyed, Pru with suspicion. Ash was regarding her with deep respect.

Finally Pru said, 'What is it with you two and the psychobabble? Do you get commission for drumming up business for this shrink?'

Hazel laughed out loud. 'It isn't psychobabble. Or if it is, it's also honestly held belief, distilled from years of experience. Look, I can't tell you when you'll start feeling that life's worth living again. But I can promise that you will. It'll be a different life, not the one you chose, but it will get better. A time will come when you'll think about Mr Phillips and your heart will fill, and not break.'

Pru shook her head, and Hazel couldn't tell if it was in disagreement or wonder. It didn't really matter: she was entitled to all the emotions bubbling under her breastbone. The sad fact was that if she'd been the sort of woman who collapsed in helpless tears, she'd have won the sympathy of all of them; but since she was intelligent, articulate and a fighter, everyone – Hazel included – was struggling to make allowances. It wasn't fair; she vowed to try harder to like Pru Somers.

Pru stood up. 'I think we've said all that can usefully be said. I think some of us have possibly said too much. In any event, I believe I shall go home now.' She looked directly at Rachel. 'Are you coming?'

The girl hesitated. It was almost as if she wanted either Hazel or Ash to make the decision for her. Both knew better. Eventually Rachel put down her mug. 'I suppose so.'

'Don't do me any favours,' said Pru.

Ash got up too. 'I'll drive you back to the shop, shall I?'

'Thank you,' said Pru coolly, 'but I believe we can manage to walk that far.' And with that she was gone, Rachel trailing in her wake like a pram dinghy towed behind a schooner.

Hazel shut the door behind them and turned to Ash in exasperation. 'I have no idea how I managed not to bang their heads together!'

Ash lifted his shoulders in a compassionate shrug. 'They're hurting.'

'I know. But even when you're hurting, there are standards of behaviour that civilised people do not sink below.'

After a moment Ash said, 'Do you suppose Rachel *will* give up the piano?'

Hazel shook her head. 'Not a chance. That would be like tearing up the compromising photographs – she'd have nothing left to hold her mother to ransom with.'

Ash blinked. 'Isn't that a little cynical?'

'She's a teenage girl, a species you have minimal experience of. The only difference between a teenage girl and a viper is eye-shadow. They are all ruthless, self-obsessed and manipulative. Their hormones are more toxic than strong drink.'

'All? I don't believe you were like that.'

Hazel reflected. 'No, actually I don't think I was. I was a very boring teenager: a bit of a swot and a bit of a prig. What were you like when you were seventeen?'

He thought for a moment. Then he said wryly, 'Pretty much like I am now.'

From Gilbert:

I knelt on the board today. The instructor says I'm a natural. Guy fell in.

THIRTEEN

As the kind of boy who had distinguished himself, insofar as he had distinguished himself at all, more at sports than any of the academic subjects dear to head teachers' hearts, the young Dave Gorman had been summoned to the principal's office on more than one occasion. It hadn't bothered him unduly at the time, and in the years since he'd come to see it as useful training for working in the police. The expression of attentive neutrality he had acquired had got him through any number of interviews which would otherwise have ended in tears.

Monday morning presented him with another such. In the CID offices on the second floor of Meadowvale Police Station, they referred to it as being Up In Front Of Miss, an expression which caused a certain amount of juvenile sniggering in the largely male preserve.

Superintendent Grace Maybourne may or may not have been aware of this – the smart money was on the former: not much happened at Meadowvale that escaped her notice. Either way, and even when she was under pressure from Division, she avoided the temptation to treat her officers like errant schoolboys who Could Do Better, and would Never Amount To Anything Until They Learned To Apply Themselves.

She welcomed Detective Chief Inspector Gorman with a smile and gestured him to a chair. He noticed with dismay that space had been cleared on her desk for a tea-tray. Her china tea set terrified him: the cup handles were too small for his thick fingers, and he never knew if he was allowed to dunk his biscuit.

'I shan't keep you long, David.' She called him David, possibly because of her genteel upbringing, possibly to annoy him. 'I know you're busy. I thought we should speak about the Phillips inquiry.'

Gorman nodded, waited for her to start. But it seemed

she meant him to speak, which she indicated with an encouraging look.

'I don't know what to tell you, ma'am. We're not making much progress. Forensics haven't come back with anything useful. We have no blood except for the victim's, no fibres at the immediate scene except for those from Phillips' clothes or the girl's, no footprints good enough to take casts from, no tyre-tracks fresh enough to be relevant. I don't know if the attacker was careful or just lucky, but so far we have no physical evidence to indicate who he was or help convict him if we find him by other means. And time is passing. Anything we haven't found already, I doubt we're going to find now. I hate to say it, but it's beginning to look as if our best chance of finding this man is if he attacks another girl.'

'The other girl who said she'd been attacked . . .'

'. . . Was lying,' said Gorman plainly. 'She was scared of what her dad would do if he found out she'd been making whoopee with her boyfriend.'

'Yes,' murmured Superintendent Maybourne. It might have meant anything; it probably didn't mean she knew how that felt. Although looks, as Gorman knew very well, could be deceptive. As a forty-something senior police officer and a single woman who lived with her widowed mother, it was hard to imagine the superintendent ever sneaking home after lights-out with straw in her hair and grass-stains on her back. But presumably she'd been a teenager once. 'And the incidents down by the canal?'

'The jury's still out, but probably one and possibly the other may have been misunderstandings. Nervous people overreacting to random events.'

'And the fire at Gabriel Ash's bookshop?'

'Also a case of mistaken identity. People have noticed a similarity between Ash and descriptions given of the supposed attacker.'

'Hm.' Superintendent Maybourne topped up his cup. She had a habit of doing this every time he'd nearly drained the damned thing. 'Rachel Somers, of course, gave no description.'

Gorman shook his head. 'She never saw her attacker. He jumped her from behind, held her face against a tree. When she broke free, she ran and never looked back.'

'Was she able to say anything about him?'

'Only that he was a lot stronger than her.' He shrugged. 'Rachel Somers is a seventeen-year-old music student – every man in Norbold is stronger than her.'

'Was the post mortem helpful?'

'Not really. Gethin Phillips died of bleeding to the brain caused by blunt-force trauma which fractured his skull. Two blows, from left and right, probably a right-handed assailant standing behind him. We're not going to find the murder weapon – there was bark in the abrasion so it was a bit of a fallen branch, probably snatched up on the spot and thrown away into the undergrowth.'

'We've done a fingertip search?'

'We have. But a knife or a gun is one thing: expecting people to spot one bit of wood among the other bits of wood in a wood is asking a lot.'

'Dogs?'

'Apparently it's asking a lot of a dog as well.'

Superintendent Maybourne sipped her tea. 'I suppose you've considered the possibility that it was Gethin Phillips, not Rachel Somers, who was the intended target?'

Neat, thought Gorman. That was the word that best described her: neat. Neat in appearance, neat in manner, neat in her mental processes. There was nothing burly or mannish about her, one of the first generation of women officers who'd won their promotions not by emulating their male colleagues but by bringing something different to the table. Even as a uniformed constable, trained and equipped and experienced in street policing, Grace Maybourne would never have won a stand-up fight with a sixteen-stone skinhead. But she would have been able to think rings around him, managing the situation to neutralise his physical advantages. She was as different a superintendent as it was possible to imagine from the man who preceded her. Gorman had been an admirer of Johnny Fountain, until he realised how the chief superintendent had racked up his successes.

'It did occur to us. There's no evidence one way or the other, so we're keeping an open mind. When we find the bugger – beggar – we'll have to ask him.'

Maybourne smiled. 'So the next question is, how do we find this man, so that Norbold can relax and go back to being the small, dull, unenterprising town that we know and love?'

That was irony. Gorman was getting quite good at recognising it. It was one of the tools she used instead of shouting. But he didn't have a good answer for her. 'I don't know, ma'am. No one's back-pedalling on this—'

'I didn't think they were,' murmured Maybourne.

'. . . Everyone's doing their job, we're asking lots of questions, we're just not learning anything useful. No reason – except the obvious – why someone should attack the girl, no reason someone would want to brain her stepfather. We'll keep looking. But I don't know where a breakthrough's going to come from.'

Superintendent Maybourne smiled at him again. 'If your job was easy, David, anyone could do it. Perhaps . . .' And there she stopped.

Gorman waited for the other shoe to drop. Perhaps it's time to call in Scotland Yard? Perhaps it's time you went on gardening leave while someone keener, smarter, more celebrated, more experienced gives it a shot?

'Perhaps,' Maybourne said again, slowly, 'if we can't marshal any more facts, we need to look at those we have from a fresh perspective.'

Gorman didn't know what she meant. He waited to be told.

The superintendent seemed uncharacteristically reticent. 'I don't know, maybe this is a non-starter. Maybe you've already considered it, and dismissed it as implausible. But . . .' Again, the hiatus.

'But what, ma'am?'

Maybourne's pale narrow brows drew together in an alabaster frown. 'If the only people we can definitely place in the spinney that evening are Gethin Phillips and Rachel Somers, is it conceivable that they were in fact the only people there?'

Detective Chief Inspector Gorman hadn't already considered it. He considered it now. 'You're suggesting that Rachel brained her stepfather?'

Across her desk, Maybourne gave a faintly disappointed sigh.

'I'm suggesting – on no evidence whatsoever, only a rejigging of the parameters – that Gethin Phillips may have been the one who attacked Rachel. That he did not, as we all assumed, die protecting her, but had in fact ambushed her in that wood.'

Gorman was staring at her. He'd always thought he had a nasty suspicious mind. He saw now that he was a mere beginner. 'So who decked him? Ash was half a mile away, and as far as we know, no one was closer.'

'We know Rachel fought him off. Could she have pushed him with enough force that he fell, and landed badly enough to fracture his own skull?'

Gorman tried to see what she was seeing. Slowly he began to. 'So . . . Phillips followed Rachel outside when she went to get the cat in. He followed her into the spinney, grabbed her from behind and pushed her face into the tree so she wouldn't see him. But she fought back more vigorously than he was expecting, and struggling to hold onto her he lost his footing among the tangle of roots and fell backwards, hitting his head.' There, coming up against the spoiler, he stopped. 'Twice?'

'Ah.' Superintendent Maybourne pursed her lips. 'Yes, that is something of a problem. We'll have to come back to that. Hopefully, we'll understand that when we know exactly what happened. In the meantime, Rachel was running as fast as she could, trying to lose him in the spinney, not realising he was no longer a threat to her. She doesn't know to this day either who attacked her or that she owes her deliverance to no one but herself.'

She waited, but Gorman offered no comment. 'David?' she prompted gently. 'Does that seem feasible to you?'

Gorman had no difficulty picturing the scene right up to the point where Phillips sustained the second injury. But he could see no plausible way that could have been accidental. 'I'm sorry, ma'am, but no. Not until we can explain how he hit his head not once but twice.'

'You're right, of course,' conceded the superintendent. 'There must *be* an explanation. Could he have run into an overhanging branch, then rebounded into the tree-trunk, causing the fracture to the back of his head?'

'Anything's possible,' murmured Gorman diplomatically.

'I'll talk to Rachel again, see if the idea of Phillips as her attacker makes sense to her.'

'Talk to Mrs Somers too. If Phillips had inappropriate feelings for his stepdaughter, his partner may have suspected.'

'People are good at seeing only what they want to see.' Gorman nearly said *women*, but stopped himself in time. He made another manful attempt on his tea cup.

Before talking to either Rachel or Pru, Gorman wanted to talk to Hazel. As the family's liaison officer, she knew the parties involved better than anyone in CID.

She heard him out in silence, her eyes widening at certain predictable junctures. When he'd finished she gasped, 'That's some theory!'

He thought so too. He'd have liked to pass it off as his own, but honesty forbade. 'Maybourne's. But the more I think about it, the more plausible it seems. For one thing, it would explain the lack of forensics.'

Hazel did as he asked and thought about it. Considered the firm facts at their disposal in the light of what she had learned of the people involved. Gorman watched closely but made no attempt to hurry her.

Finally she said carefully, 'Gethin Phillips was not Rachel's father. They were family of a kind, but they were not blood relatives. According to Pru, she and Phillips were in a settled relationship, and her pregnancy tends to support that. But Rachel said things had gone cold between them – that they were still together mostly out of habit. If she's right, it's possible that Phillips' eye was starting to rove. It would be pretty tacky if it only roved as far as the teenage daughter of his current partner, but it's credible. Men – sorry, Dave – can be incredibly lazy sometimes. She's an attractive girl, he was seeing her every day, he might have started thinking about her in a different way.'

'Wouldn't Pru Somers have noticed?'

Hazel gave a rueful shrug, said exactly what Gorman had stopped himself from saying to Superintendent Maybourne for fear of sounding like a chauvinist. 'Women can be amazingly blind to things they don't want to see.'

She thought a little longer. 'Gabriel was talking with his shrink about this – about modern families. With divorce so common and other people not bothering to marry at all, it's almost the norm for children to be raised by adults who are not their biological parents. But if you shuffle the deck so that a man takes on the father's role without being related to the children, you can confuse everyone's instincts. If the relationship starts going stale, you can see how a man's hormones might get a bit uppity. Of course he knows it's wrong. But where hormones are concerned, we've all done things we knew were wrong.'

Gorman said nothing. He knew, and she knew he knew, Hazel was speaking from experience.

'The problem I have,' she went on after a moment, 'is that I've heard nothing to suggest he was that sort of man. Pru describes him as a natural family man; Rachel seems to think he was kind if a bit boring. But everyone under the age of twenty thinks everyone over the age of thirty is a bit boring, so if that's the worst she has to say about him, I don't think she can have been aware of any unhealthy interest in her.'

'Maybe he was good at hiding it.'

'Maybe he was. It's surprising what we can keep secret if the stakes are high enough.'

'We need to talk to more people about Phillips,' decided the DCI. 'Get a better picture of who he was, if he was generally liked and trusted or if people had their reservations. It won't prove anything, but it might give us a reason to take Miss's theory seriously.'

Hazel laughed out loud. 'Miss?'

Gorman actually blushed. 'You've got to admit, it's a bit like being back at school.'

'Oh yes,' agreed Hazel. 'Blood on the lino, stab vests in the locker room, sago pudding in the canteen: exactly like every school I ever taught in.'

DS Presley travelled to Coventry to interview Gethin Phillips' partners and colleagues. DC Friend talked to people at his golf club, and DC Lassiter drew the short straw and spent the evening chatting with regulars in the snug at the Royal Oak in Whitley Vale. On nothing more than a hunch, Hazel enquired of the local classic-car club if Phillips had been a member and, finding that he had, went round to see the secretary.

They got together again in the DCI's office the following morning. Hazel was the last to arrive; the actual members of Meadowvale CID waited for her. It didn't seem to occur to anyone that she might not come.

The first thing she noticed was that no one was itching to speak. Which probably meant that no one had any information that showed Gethin Phillips, professional man, expectant father and pillar of the community, in a new, unflattering light.

The staff at his architects' practice, from the senior partners to the receptionists, all thought of him as Mr Reliable. A clever man, a successful man, but also a kind man; someone you could approach with problems that had nothing to do with building regulations.

Fellow-golfers knew more about his handicap than the man, partly because they were golfers but also because he didn't spend much time in the clubhouse. Enough that he didn't seem unfriendly, but he rarely made a night of it. 'Rushing back to that hotty at home, I suppose,' the assistant treasurer had said, leering in Emma Friend's face.

'His partner – Pru Somers?' asked Friend, just to be sure.

'Is that what we're supposed to call them now?' leered the assistant treasurer.

The regulars in the Royal Oak were a little more helpful, but only a little. Phillips had usually dropped in alone, around midweek, for a pint and a game of darts, and then again on a Saturday for a meal with Pru. He was well liked; better liked, Lassiter gathered, than Pru Somers was. No one had noticed any tension growing between them. No one had noticed Phillips, on the nights when he was in the pub alone, chatting up other women.

The members of the Morgan owners' club, Hazel reported, knew Phillips' engine to the last valve and sprocket, but didn't know he had a partner and teenage stepdaughter at home. They never saw him chatting up other women either, possibly because all the other club members were men.

DCI Gorman was disappointed but not surprised. 'So what

you're telling me is, Gethin Phillips was exactly what he seemed to be – an all-round decent guy, no hint of a secret life, no evidence that he was unhappy with his domestic arrangements. Exactly the kind of guy to rush to her defence in his slippers if he heard his stepdaughter scream.'

There was a silent chorus of glum nods.

Hazel was a little wary of speaking up in this company, where she had no claim to equality and only squatters' rights to justify her presence at all. But if no one else was going to say it, she thought she should. 'Almost seems too good to be true, doesn't he?'

Meadowvale CID stared at her: with curiosity, with disapprobation and, in the case of Dave Gorman, with grim approval. 'Do you know, that's just what I was thinking?'

Emma Friend frowned. She was a tall young woman, a little younger than Hazel, and though she was still on the lowest rung of CID, the general feeling was she'd be a detective sergeant by the end of the year, and after that Gorman had better superglue his name-plate to his office door. 'That's a bit cynical, isn't it? We're not hearing anything bad about the guy, so we suspect him of being sneaky? There are a lot of perfectly decent men out there, just doing their jobs and looking after their families and not bothering us. All the evidence is that Gethin Phillips was one of them.'

'He's bothering us now,' grunted Tom Presley.

'Not from choice! He didn't ask to be murdered.'

'No-o,' said Gorman slowly. 'All the same, allowing for all the exceptions, what is the general rule for murder victims? Most of them know their attackers. And lots of murderers are on our radar for something.'

'But Phillips wasn't,' Friend pointed out.

'That might mean he was a perfectly decent guy,' allowed Gorman. 'Or it might just mean that he was smarter than our general run of cell-surfers.'

Again, Hazel felt obliged to stick her oar in. 'Aren't we getting our wires crossed a bit here? The theory is that he might have jumped Rachel's bones in the spinney while Pru was working late. Whether he did or not, that's not the sort of thing that will show up in the records. Unless he had form, and there's nothing in the files to suggest that he did.'

'People who break the law in big ways often have a history of breaking it in small ways first,' offered Mark Lassiter. 'Often unrelated ways. People who don't respect other people's rights, steal or vandalise property before they graduate to rape.'

'That's a bit sweeping!' complained Friend.

'It's certainly a generalisation,' said Gorman, 'but there's some truth in it. We know, for instance, that if we have a case of cruelty to animals, we need to consider the safety of any children in the household. Law-abiding people may feel the same urges as people who thumb their noses at it: the difference is that they don't act on them.'

'Phillips has no record of any kind,' said Lassiter. 'Not so much as a motoring offence. Mr Clean.'

'Jesus,' growled Gorman, 'was the guy running for pope or what? It's enough to make you wonder if he was a real person, or just an ID dreamt up by the witness protection people.'

They exchanged thoughtful glances over the litter of nasty cardboard cups.

Emma Friend said, 'What about his slippers?'

DS Presley scowled at her. 'What *about* his slippers?'

'In this alternative scenario we're considering, Gethin Phillips followed his stepdaughter outside, down the garden and into the spinney. She was there to get her cat in, his purpose was to attack her. For anything else – to ask how her day went, to complain that she'd finished the milk – he'd have waited until she came back inside. Wouldn't he?'

'Probably,' conceded Presley. 'So?'

'So if he knew what he was going to do, why didn't he put his shoes on first? He must have known she might fight back, she might give him the slip, he might end up running after her. Over rough and broken ground littered with stones and thorns and tree roots. Even if he was acting on impulse, surely he'd have taken a few seconds to put on suitable footwear?'

Gorman was nodding his approval. 'Whereas a scream at the bottom of the garden, you'd dash out just as you were, in slippers – or barefoot, come to that. She's right. It's not proof, but it is suggestive.' He turned his head, fixing Hazel with his gaze. 'You know who's most likely to have noticed if there was something dodgy developing between Gethin Phillips and Rachel Somers?'

Hazel felt her heart sink. 'You want me to ask Pru if her partner of four years, the father of her unborn baby, the man who's been hailed as a hero for saving Rachel from her attacker, may in fact have been trying to rape her?'

Gorman took pity on her and shook his head. 'No. It'd destroy any hope of a relationship with the family, and they still need that and so do we. I'll talk to her. She'll go ape and call me names that'd make even Detective Sergeant Presley blush, but I doubt she'll come up with anything I haven't heard before. Give her a call, ask her when she can see me and where.'

FOURTEEN

Pru made him drive out to Westbroke, and had a uniformed porter show him to her office in the conference centre of The King's Head. She could as easily have come home and seen him there, but seemed to be making the point that her job was also important and she too was still working at eight o'clock in the evening. In a faintly mollifying gesture, she ordered tea. Gorman just knew her china would be as delicate as Superintendent Maybourne's, and he was right. It still wasn't as delicate as his mission.

He should probably have had DC Friend accompany him. He'd decided against because, if this went the way he fully expected, the fewer witnesses there were, the better. He could cope with an unhappy woman's vitriol. It would be easier for both of them to forgive and forget if there was no one taking notes.

'This was a good idea,' he began, casting an admiring glance around her office. It was four times the size of his, with not just a desk but comfortable chairs arranged around a coffee table. Of course, she entertained important clients here. The King's Head was not only a smart hotel with a busy conference centre, it was the hub of a chain of similar businesses spread across the Midlands. 'I've some difficult questions to ask you, and we're not going to want Rachel wandering in while we're talking.'

'All right,' said Pru composedly. 'Ask away.'

Gorman still found her hard to read. The way they'd last parted, he'd expected her to be on her guard. But she poured his tea and sat back in her comfortable chair and waited for him to begin as if none of that had happened; as if the situation was now entirely different. Yes, he thought, that was it – as if, because this was her office, she was the one in control. She might have been interviewing him for a job.

'I need to understand more about the family dynamic,' he

said. 'For instance, how well did Mr Phillips get on with Rachel? Would you say they were friends? It can be an awkward relationship, between a teenager and the parent's new partner.'

'Gethin wasn't my new partner,' Pru pointed out. 'We were together for four years. Rachel was thirteen when we met.'

'I notice she never refers to him as either her father or her stepfather.'

'That's because he wasn't either of those things. We might have married at some point – but actually, I don't think we would. We were fine as we were.'

Gorman nodded. 'Were Gethin and Rachel fine too?'

Pru pursed her lips in thought. 'Gethin was very fond of Rachel. Well – obviously, you don't give your life for someone who doesn't matter to you. Rachel was – is – a typical teenager: all their friends are in their own age-group, the most you can hope for as an adult is tolerance and reasonable courtesy. She wasn't rude to him. But they didn't have much in common.'

'Except you.'

'Well, yes,' said Pru. 'That's the deal. If you're the mother of a thirteen-year-old child, anyone who wants a relationship with you has to accept that you come as a boxed set. Most men aren't looking for that degree of commitment, but Gethin never made an issue of it. He said that Rachel wasn't the price he had to pay for me, she was the bonus.' She smiled, a cool, corporate smile outlined in dark red lipstick. 'I don't expect he really thought that, but it was a nice thing to say.'

Or it's just possible that's exactly what he thought, mused Gorman. Out loud he said, 'Did they have any interests in common? Sports? Birdwatching, bike riding? Did he play a musical instrument too?'

Pru was beginning to watch him a little more keenly, wondering where this was going. 'Not really. Rachel doesn't do sports – anything that could put her hands at risk – and Gethin had Van Gogh's ear for music. You don't have children, do you, Detective Chief Inspector?'

Taken by surprise, Gorman had answered before deciding if he should. 'No.'

'They don't really want to do things with their parents,

let alone their parents' partners. They think of us as a separate species. They think that anything which interests us must by definition be boring. All they want of us is to feed them, clothe them and keep them in iTunes, to house them in a manner they'll be middle-aged before they can afford for themselves, and keep out of the way when they have friends round. The Bank of Mum and Dad, with an open-all-hours café attached.

'Now, Detective Chief Inspector,' she said briskly, 'what's this all about? I don't see how the relationship between my daughter and my partner can be of more than academic interest in the search for Gethin's killer.'

OK, thought Gorman, here we go. 'We've scoured that spinney with every tool at our disposal. We haven't turned up anything we can positively link to a third person in the woods that evening.' He waited for the explosion.

Pru seemed to be expecting something more. 'And?'

Slightly deflated, Gorman tried to make himself clearer. 'It's pretty unusual to have a crime scene with no forensic evidence of the criminal. Very often, it's *how* we identify a crime scene. Forensic experts like to say that every contact leaves a trace – blood, sweat, hair, fibres, fingerprints, footprints. When you haven't got any of those, you have to ask yourself if what happened is what's supposed to have happened. If you're looking for someone who, actually, was never there.'

Pru still wasn't angry. She was confused. 'You think Gethin beat his own head in?'

Gorman drew a deep breath. 'This is the difficult bit I warned you about. I have to consider the possibility – I wouldn't be doing my job if I didn't – that Gethin Phillips was the one who attacked Rachel in the spinney. That she got away from him, and in giving chase he fell heavily and that's how he died. That there's no evidence of a third party because there were only the two of them.'

'Steak,' said Tom Presley judiciously. 'My mum swore by it when we were kids.'

'Witch hazel,' said Emma Friend.

Gorman frowned. 'Don't call her . . . Oh, I see what you mean. Yes. Thanks.'

As the detective sergeant, it was Presley's job to find out. The rest of CID waited expectantly.

'So what happened?'

Gorman rounded on him. 'I walked into a door. All right? It was a glass door, and it was edge on, and I walked into it because I was talking to someone over my shoulder. OK? Everyone satisfied?' He continued on to his office, leaving silence and significant glances behind him.

DS Presley was not a naturally tactful man. In fact, the expression 'a bit of an oik' had been applied to him so often it was hard to go on taking it as a compliment. But he'd worked with Dave Gorman for years, and though they weren't close friends they had earned one another's respect. So Presley squashed any discussion of the DCI's shiner by means of a pre-emptive glare, and made no attempt to follow Gorman to his office until he had a plausible excuse in the form of paperwork needing his approval.

'So, this door,' he said, putting the papers in front of his boss. 'Do we charge it with assault?'

Gorman looked up quickly, expecting to catch him in a smirk. But Presley wasn't smirking.

Gorman gave a lugubrious sniff. 'Yeah, right. Then I can explain to a magistrate how I asked a newly bereaved – door – if her dead partner, the father of her unborn child, might have tried to rape her teenage daughter. What's he going to do, send her to the Old Bailey? I suppose he might bind her over to keep the peace. Or he might just tell me I got nothing more than I deserved – and do you know, I'd find it hard to argue. So it was a door, and my own fault for being clumsy, yes?'

Presley nodded. 'This door. It might have seen red because you were casting nasturtiums at its dead partner. But it might have taken a swing at you precisely because you touched a raw nerve. Maybe it had been thinking along the same lines itself. In which case, with Phillips dead and no further risk to anyone, she – this door, I mean – might have felt that her priority was to protect Rachel. Better that everyone went on thinking there was a third person in the spinney that evening, and the Keystone Cops were just too slow to catch him.'

This was fairly sophisticated thinking for a man as uncomplicated as Tom Presley. If Gorman had got the sense that Pru had lashed out because he'd put into words a suspicion she'd been desperate to avoid confronting, he'd have considered his black eye cheap at the price. But he hadn't. She had been outraged, and she was far too handy with that right hook, but there had been no hollow place in the depths of her eyes where the suggestion might have met belief coming the other way. To the best of his judgement, Pru had flared up in righteous indignation, not to distract attention from an unpalatable truth.

'I'm not ruling it out,' he said, 'but I don't think that's what it was about. I think she was genuinely startled by what I said, and then she was furious. After my ears stopped ringing I asked her again, and made her look at me while she answered. She said I was wrong. That Phillips would never in a hundred years have attacked Rachel or anyone else. I think that's what she believes. Which doesn't necessarily mean she's right. But if he was starting to see Rachel as fair game, could he have hidden it from Pru? Wouldn't she have known, at least at some level?'

But Presley didn't know either. 'Keep it on the long finger?'

'For the moment.' Gorman scowled. 'I still like Miss's theory. It ties up the loose ends – well, most of them – pretty neatly. Plus, if it's not going to fly, where do we go next?'

'Down the butcher's for half a pound of frying steak,' said Presley firmly. 'My mum used to use witch hazel too – I've got three brothers, there was always one of us in the wars. But the thing about a steak is, that's your dinner sorted as well.'

After the skip had gone, and the glazier had been, again, and Hazel had helped him wash the soot off everything worth keeping, Ash set about the shop with pots of paint. Hazel had brought in some colour charts, and talked knowledgably about contemplative shades that would encourage people to linger and energising wavelengths that would encourage them to buy. But Ash's heart wasn't in it. He bought off-white for the woodwork and cream for the walls, on the basis that they were going cheap at the hardware shop. He wasn't confident he wouldn't have the whole thing to do again quite soon.

In spite of which, he felt his mood lifting as the new paint covered not only the sight of the damage but also the smell. In any catalogue of personal disasters, a small fire set by frightened men who couldn't focus on a real target came nowhere near the top. The boys were safe on a Cornish beach; he was unhurt; and a couple of days' work had put right most of the damage. He was tired, but not in a bad way.

A small red van pulled up at the kerb and a small, shaggy youth stepped out. 'Got a delivery for you.'

Puzzled, Ash frowned. 'I'm not expecting anything.'

The passenger door opened and it was Rachel Somers, smiling. 'This is Buzz. He cuts our lawn. He's been helping me get a few books together.'

A few books. When Buzz – Buzz? – opened the cargo door, the load-bay was full of cardboard boxes, and the boxes were full of books. Beautiful books, many of them, coffee-table volumes bought to stack with studied nonchalance in well-to-do drawing rooms, and hardly ever – to judge by the pristine pages – read.

Ash looked at Rachel in astonishment. 'Whose are they? Where have they come from?'

'Some of them were ours,' said the girl, 'but most belonged to friends. Friends of mine, friends of Mum's, neighbours, people at school, people in Whitley Vale. Everyone's really sorry about what happened and wants to help.'

'This' – Ash glanced back at the shop – 'wasn't your fault. Or your mother's. I appreciate the thought, but I can't accept these.' He looked at the books with longing. 'They're better than the ones that got burnt.'

'You have to,' Rachel said breezily, 'I can't take them back. I can't remember who half of them came from – and even if I could, they were glad to be rid of them. They weren't anyone's treasures, they were just décor. Next time minimalism is in fashion, most of them would have gone in the bin.'

'And if the chap with the cigarette-lighter comes back tonight?'

'Then tomorrow we'll do the rounds of Westbroke,' said Rachel. 'You're not busy tomorrow, are you, Buzz?'

The shaggy youth shook his head. Grass clippings flew out of his hair.

'I know what you're thinking,' Rachel said before Ash could refuse again. 'You're thinking you should probably have a word with Mum, to make sure I haven't taken anything I shouldn't. She said you would. Here.' She passed him her phone, already ringing.

'Mrs Somers, it's Gabriel Ash . . .'

'I've been expecting your call.' There was no warmth that he could detect in her tone. 'The answer to your question is, this was Rachel's idea but I have no objection. In the circumstances, it's the least we can do. I hope it'll be helpful.'

'Enormously,' he admitted. 'But—'

'Good,' said Pru Somers, and rang off.

Ash turned round, bemused, to see Rachel and Buzz carrying the heavy boxes across the pavement into the shop. Rachel stumbled on the doorstep and Ash hurried to take her burden. She rewarded him with a smile.

'Where do you want them?' asked Buzz.

'The paint'll need time to dry. I suggest we stack them on the long table for now. Then we can see what we've got, and organise the shelves accordingly. I really . . . I don't know how to thank you.'

He began decanting the boxes. Every one was a treasure-trove. He couldn't believe people were prepared to part with books like these, to help someone they didn't even know.

'Where do you normally get your stock?' asked Rachel.

'House clearances, mostly. Auctions sometimes. Junk shops, jumble sales. Sometimes people bring half a dozen in to exchange for a couple of new ones. Well – new to them. Oooh,' he added, sounding even to himself like a child in a sweet shop, 'this is from *National Geographic*! The photography in these is superb.'

'Me da found you a couple, too,' said Buzz; adding, a little shame-facedly, 'They're only old poetry books, but maybe someone'll want them.'

Ash dug them out. One was from the Oxford University Press. The other was a leather-bound volume of nineteenth-century romantics. 'Tell your da he has great taste,' said Ash, and the youth grinned again, relieved.

Rachel was looking from the table, stacked high as it was, to the newly painted shelves which were even higher. 'There aren't enough,' she said, disappointed.

'It's a wonderful start,' Ash said firmly. 'It would have taken me a week to get this many together, and even then they wouldn't have been as good as these.'

'Are there any auctions coming up?'

Ash shook his head. 'But a dealer I know gave me the heads-up on a house clearance he's doing on Friday. He said there were a lot of books, though he hadn't done any kind of an inventory. I thought I'd go with him, buy anything I can use. Right now, almost anything that will fill some shelf-space would be worth having. No one comes into an empty shop. But with your books laid out on the table, and some makeweights filling out the shelves, we'll look as if we're back in business. Oh look,' he added, peering into a box, 'that's an early A.A. Milne!'

'Can I come?' asked Rachel.

'Hm? Sorry?'

'On Friday. To the house clearance. Can I come? I can help you load the car.'

'What about your—?'

'Hands?' finished Rachel. 'Don't you start: I get enough of that at home. I'll be careful, all right? It's books – it isn't edged weapons and assorted rat-traps!'

Ash couldn't think of a reason why not. He'd have taken Gilbert, if he'd been at home. Guy wouldn't have thanked him for a morning spent poking through someone else's library. 'Yes, all right. I'll pick you up about ten. You will tell your mother, won't you?'

''Course I will.'

'How about you, Buzz? Are you coming too?'

'Mum wants him to weed the patio,' Rachel interjected swiftly. The youth gave her an odd look, but Ash didn't notice. 'Look – Hemingway, *A Farewell to Arms*! I think that's a first edition.'

From Guy:

Frankie took us to a castle. Its called Tint Hairgel, which is a funny name for a castle. Then we went surfing again, and I fell in.

'Has anyone asked Rachel if Phillips could have been her attacker? If anyone's going to know, she should,' said Hazel. 'Maybe she *does* know. Maybe she's just not saying for fear of upsetting her mother. If someone asked her directly, maybe it would be a relief to have it out in the open.'

There was a studied silence in the big room that housed most of CID. Well-trained and experienced detectives suddenly discovered an interest in lost dogs, in Dunnit Duncan's latest improbable confession, and in their own fingernails. Since Yes is a short word and easy to say, Hazel inferred that the answer was No.

She gave them the withering stare she'd perfected in the classroom. 'What, frightened of getting your faces slapped?'

Emma Friend refused to be intimidated by the prospect of the Naughty Corner. 'If the chief wanted us to talk to her, he'd have said so. I imagine he wants to talk to her himself.'

'If he gets another black eye, he'll look like a giant panda!'

'Constable Best,' said DS Presley deliberately, 'if Sergeant Murchison doesn't need you downstairs, there's nothing to stop you finishing your leave.'

Hazel knew when she wasn't wanted. She'd had a certain amount of practice. And she knew she had no right of tenancy in the CID offices. She was tolerated, sometimes, for her IT skills and a knack of making herself useful. There was nothing to be gained by antagonising those who were entitled to be here.

She gave a disparaging sniff. 'It's not as if a black eye would come between any of you and a career as a supermodel.' She was out in the corridor before anyone could think of a suitable retort.

FIFTEEN

DCI Gorman hadn't wanted her to risk her relationship with the Somers family. Thinking about that now, Hazel decided that if the relationship couldn't survive her raising something that was becoming increasingly pivotal every day the inquiry was stalled, probably it wasn't worth preserving. Meadowvale could appoint another family liaison officer. Or the family could be their own mouthpiece: Pru in particular seemed to have no difficulty expressing her wants and needs.

Plus, Hazel was almost certain she could broach the subject more delicately than Gorman had. She didn't feel any overweening pride in this: there were rhinoceroses with more delicacy than Dave Gorman. Some things, and she thought this was one of them, were better handled by women. She believed she could put the question without upsetting Rachel unduly, and also judge how far her answer should be relied on.

She told Sergeant Murchison where she was going without explaining why, and he didn't ask. He'd given her the job of family liaison: it seemed obvious to him that spending time with the victim's family was fundamental to that.

Turning into the Somerses' long gravel drive, Hazel was glad to see that Pru's car was absent from its usual spot in front of the house. If Rachel was editing her memories to protect her mother's feelings, the conversation would be easier without Pru present.

But it did require Rachel to be present, and when Hazel first rang the bell and then rapped her knuckles on the glass of the front door, there was no response. She tried again. Then, reasoning that it was a big house and the sound of someone at the front door might not reach all the way to the back, she walked through the side garden to the kitchen door. There was no bell, but she rapped again and called out.

Still there was no sign that the house was occupied. Indeed, the presence of the black and white cat on the kitchen step, yowling softly and weaving its sinuous body around her ankles, suggested it was not.

Pondering whether to wait or come back later, absent-mindedly she bent to stroke it. At which point a small red van passed on the other side of the hedge, turning with a chatter of gravel in front of the house. Hazel walked back along the side path and met Rachel coming the other way.

'I hope you don't mind. I thought you might be in the garden.'

'We were in town,' said Rachel. The van was moving again, tooting its horn as it headed down the drive.

'I was just wondering how you're feeling now?'

'Oh, you know,' sighed Rachel. 'Good days and bad days. We do a lot of skirting around what's happened in the hope that, if we ignore it for long enough, we'll find it was all a terrible mistake.' She ventured a shy smile. 'That must sound pretty pathetic.'

Hazel shook her head emphatically. 'It sounds like two people who've been badly hurt looking for a way forward. You're not trying to ignore what happened – it's just too big to deal with all at once. Your mind would break trying. So it bundles it up and pushes it into a corner so you can step round it for a while. It'll take the bundle out and deal with it, bit by bit, in due course. Every bit you deal with will leave the bundle slightly smaller and you slightly stronger.'

The girl was eyeing her cautiously. 'Are you some kind of a shrink too?'

'No – just someone who's seen the process before. The thing to remember, the thing to hold onto, is that we heal. Cut fingers heal; broken bones heal; and minds heal too. They want to. They come up with all kinds of strategies to help themselves, and none of them is wrong. If your mind needs time to come to terms with what's happened, there's no reason to hurry it. You don't have to confront the tragedy every minute of every day.'

'It feels as if we're in denial.' Rachel's voice was so low Hazel strained to hear. 'As if we're betraying Gethin by not admitting how much he meant to us, how much it hurts to have lost him.'

'I didn't know him,' said Hazel softly, 'but you did. Don't you think he'd understand that this is just what you have to do for now, to get from one day to the next? Don't you think he'd want you to be gentle on yourselves?'

'I suppose.' The girl didn't sound convinced.

'He cared about you, didn't he? Was fond of you?'

'I thought so . . .'

And that wasn't the right answer, and Hazel knew it immediately. She felt a kind of adrenalin rush behind her breast-bone. She knows! she thought. Or at least, she suspects. This man's supposed to have died saving her from a rapist. Why would she even wonder if he cared for her?

She made herself move slowly, speak carefully. It would be so easy to get this wrong, and there'd never be another chance as good as this one. 'Rachel, I need you to think about something and give me your honest opinion. I know it was confusing in the spinney that night, and I know you never saw the man who attacked you. Just for the moment I want you to put aside what we think happened, because without any physical evidence it's always possible that we've got it wrong. Just for the moment, I want you to forget what you told us that night, and anything your mother might have said, and focus purely on what you remember. What happened, not what you figured out afterwards. Not what you want to be true, only what is.

'And tell me if there's any chance that it was Gethin Phillips who grabbed you in Highfield Spinney that night.'

The silence that followed was not, somehow, the silence of absolute shock. Hazel was as sure as she could be that this was not the first time Rachel had considered the possibility.

As the silence stretched, Hazel wanted to prompt the girl for an answer. She resisted the temptation. She was on uncertain ground, ethically and legally: she was questioning a witness, not a suspect, but Rachel was both underage and vulnerable. Even more to the point, she didn't want Rachel to think, or anyone analysing the exchange later to think, that Hazel had pushed her into a corner and she'd said the first thing that had come into her head to end the questioning. So she waited.

Rachel had been looking at her shoes. Or not looking, because her eyes were out of focus, seeing another place, another time. Now, hesitantly, but with a kind of flayed courage, she made herself meet Hazel's gaze. When the words came, they were thin and breathy, but they were her own. They said what she wanted to say, not what she believed was expected of her. The wait had been worth it.

'I thought I must have imagined it. I thought, how could *anybody* think that? Gethin was my mother's partner for four years. He was as much part of our family as any of us. He was kind, and I liked him. How could I even ask myself if he'd tried . . . tried to . . . rape me? And what I told you was true: I never saw the man, never heard his voice. Only there was something . . . familiar . . . about him. I don't know what, but something. There must have been, or why would I even wonder?'

She swallowed painfully. 'I hoped desperately that I was wrong. I thought you'd find the man who really did it – who grabbed me and killed Gethin – and then I could mourn him properly, the way he deserved. I could forget the crazy, *wicked* thoughts that had been going through my mind. And I'd be so grateful I'd never shared them with anyone. Not even with Mum – *especially* not with Mum. Not even with you.'

Hazel was nodding sympathetically. 'I understand. And we both understand, don't we, that suspicion isn't the same as knowing? That this is a possibility we need to look at, but considering a possibility isn't the same as making an accusation. We may still find that someone else was responsible.'

'Please keep looking,' Rachel begged her. 'Not just for Mum's sake. If it *was* Gethin, you know what that means, don't you? It means I'm the one who killed him.'

Hazel took the girl by both arms, felt her trembling. She spoke directly into her anguished face. 'Rachel, none of what happened – whatever happened – was your fault. If we come to the conclusion that it probably was Mr Phillips, that still doesn't make you guilty of anything. At the very worst, if you did knock him down, it was self-defence. But he may have fallen and hit his head after you got away, when he was chasing after you. When you were already twenty metres away. It really doesn't matter. There are no variations on the theme that make you responsible for his death. If anyone tries to make you feel differently, refer them to me.'

'But . . . what am I going to tell Mum?'

Hazel bit her lip. There was no easy way of telling Pru Somers, and no way that would get easier with time. 'What you tell her, or if you tell her anything, is up to you. I'll support you whatever you decide. If you want me to be there, I will. If you want to tell her the suggestion came from me, that's the truth; if you don't want to say it had already occurred to you, that's fine too. All I would say is that things – difficult things, things we'd rather not talk about – have a habit of coming out in the end. And when they do, people are usually more hurt about being kept in the dark than if they'd been told earlier on.

'I don't know if we can prove that Mr Phillips attacked you. It may be the closest we'll get will be failing to show that anyone else did. But your mother's no fool: she'll know what that means. Sooner rather than later, she will put it together. She won't blame you for what happened in the spinney. She might blame you for trying to keep it from her.'

Rachel was crying now. Hazel thought it was more relief than anything, that she'd finally been able to share her fears, to exorcise the demon that had been clawing at her. If she could find a way of dealing with this last ordeal, the burden on her would be halved and more than halved: she would be able to see her way clear into the future.

'Hazel – will you tell her?' she sobbed, her eyes pleading.

Hazel nodded. 'If that's what you want.'

She was going to phone Pru at work, ask her to come home; find some pretext that would seem important enough for her to leave The King's Head early without worrying her unnecessarily. Every minute that passed, anxiety was putting Rachel through the wringer. Hazel wasn't sure she'd be able to go through with it if her mother didn't get home until the middle of the evening.

As luck would have it, though, before she could make the call she heard again the crunch of wheels on gravel, and a moment later the sound of the front door.

Pru Somers didn't often leave work in the middle of the afternoon, and when she did it wasn't because she wanted to talk to a well-meaning police constable. The pregnancy was weighing on her, sapping her energy; she'd intended to put her feet up in peace and quiet. Finding Hazel's car on the drive was discouraging, and Pru greeted her without much enthusiasm. 'I don't suppose you've any news for us?'

'Well,' Hazel said slowly, 'in a sort of a way I have. Do you want to come and sit down so we can talk?'

It was in Pru's expression that she resented being offered a seat in her own house. But perhaps she sensed that what was coming would put good manners in the shade. She threw the linen jacket she was wearing over the newel post at the foot of the stairs and followed Hazel into the drawing room.

'All right. So what is it you have to tell me?'

Breaking bad news is an inseparable part of a police officer's job; and if that officer happens to be a woman, she's likely to get more than her fair share. Not because her male colleagues will refuse to do it, but because of the general feeling that 'women are better at it'. Undoubtedly some women *are* better at it than some men; and some men are better at it than some women; and perhaps the fact that more senior officers are male, and they're the ones who decide who to send, has something to do with it too. Whatever the reasons, Hazel was not new to the task of delivering news that the recipient was desperate not to hear. It was never an enjoyable part of her duty, but doing it well – neither dumping the bald facts on unprepared ears, nor pussy-footing around for so long that the agony of uncertainty outweighed the grief of hearing – gave her a certain professional satisfaction.

She talked quietly, sombrely, about how the forensic search of the spinney had drawn a blank; about the different ways the few sure facts could be interpreted; and then about the scenario she'd put to Rachel, and how Rachel had been unable to dismiss it.

Halfway through she saw understanding beginning to

dawn in Pru's face, in tandem with incredulity at first, then with anger. Hazel wasn't sure if the anger was directed at her, at Rachel, at the shade of Gethin Phillips, or even at herself for not suspecting. She kept talking, quietly, calmly, giving the woman time to get a grip on her emotions. Of all the ways she might have thought to spend her afternoon, this was probably the least welcome; she was entitled to some compassion.

When Hazel had finished there was a long moment of silence. Even the air in the room was still. Rachel was watching her mother covertly between the half-drawn curtains of her hair. Then Pru stood up: not abruptly, but not hesitantly either, a woman still in full command in her own house. Hazel stood up too.

'How dare you?' said Pru Somers, almost conversationally. The dark red lipstick sketched a haughty half-smile as she carefully sidestepped the coffee table and slapped Hazel's face.

Hazel slapped her right back.

Pru's hand flew to her cheek. Rachel let out a gasp of astonishment.

Hazel said, still in the same quiet tone, 'That's the third time you've struck someone who's been trying to help you. Well, Gabriel Ash and Detective Chief Inspector Gorman are both gentlemen and wouldn't dream of repaying you in kind. But I'm not a gentleman, Mrs Somers. I'm much more like you. I've always felt that the first time someone sticks a knife in your back that's their fault, but the second time it's yours.

'Now you have my career in your hands. If you tell my superintendent that I struck you, regardless of the circumstances it'll mean immediate suspension, and probably I'll be dismissed. We aren't allowed to react to provocation with violence. If that's what you want to do, I shan't call you a liar. I won't even say I reacted instinctively because, in all honesty, I didn't. I knew what you were likely to do, and I knew what I'd do if you did. Because it needed doing, and neither Gabriel nor Dave Gorman could do it and I could.

'So it's your call. Do you want to talk to Superintendent Maybourne? I have her number on speed-dial.'

Pru Somers went on looking at her for a very long time. Hazel continued to hold out her phone. Rachel went on holding her breath.

Finally Pru gave a weary sigh and a dismissive gesture. 'Just, go away. Keep your job, and do it. Stop chasing phantasms and find the man who attacked my daughter and killed my partner. Until you have, leave us alone.'

SIXTEEN

Superintendent Maybourne heard her out in a silence so absolute it was not remotely reassuring. Hazel stood to attention before her desk, hands clasped behind her back, and reported everything that had happened: everything that had been said, everything that had been done.

Overnight, she'd tried to persuade herself there was no need. She didn't think Pru Somers would make a complaint, if only because the episode cast her in no very flattering light either; and that being so, it should be possible to keep Meadowvale's senior officer officially in the dark. (In the same way that the Queen has two birthdays, an official and an actual one, senior police officers have two sorts of hearing. What they hear officially must be acted on. What they hear unofficially may, in certain circumstances, be enjoyed in private.)

But in the early hours of Wednesday morning, she came reluctantly to the conclusion that she would have to 'fess up. The incident was part of an ongoing inquiry into a man's death: it was inevitable that at some point in the days ahead any attempt to tap-dance around the truth would turn into an outright lie. And she wasn't prepared to lie to Superintendent Maybourne, whatever the cost might be.

So she had asked for this interview at the earliest opportunity; and asked if Detective Chief Inspector Gorman might sit in on it; and turned up in the uniform she hadn't had on for weeks, which she'd hoped to be able to moth-ball indefinitely before too long, and which she was now desperately anxious to keep wearing.

Hazel finished her report but the silence continued. She didn't dare look at either of them: Superintendent Maybourne seated on the other side of the desk or the DCI hunched in the armchair behind Hazel's shoulder. So she didn't see the series of wordless messages, conveyed by a raised eyebrow here and a sucked tooth there, that passed between them.

Finally Grace Maybourne said quietly, 'Mrs Somers struck you first.'

Hazel nodded. 'Yes.'

'Did you believe it might be the start of a protracted attack?'

'No, ma'am.'

'Could you have been momentarily stunned by the blow?'

Again Hazel shook her head. 'No.'

Maybourne sighed. 'Are you *sure*?'

Hazel knew what she was trying to do. She was trying to offer a way out: a plausible defence. But even if it got her off the hook, it would be dishonest. 'Pretty sure, ma'am. It wasn't a knee-jerk reaction. I knew what she was going to do – she'd already done it twice before – and I knew what I was going to do when she did it. I knew it was unprofessional and could cost me my career. I did it anyway.'

Maybourne leaned forward slightly, studying her. 'Why?'

Hazel thought for a moment. 'Because it's pretty despicable to hit someone who can't hit back. She slapped Gabriel when he was trying to help her and Rachel, and someone saw that or heard about it, misread the situation, and torched his shop because of it. She slapped DCI Gorman because she was offended by his questions, and she knew he couldn't – or at least wouldn't – do anything about it. Well, I could, so I did. That's the truth. I'm not proud of it. But I think it needed doing.'

The superintendent considered. 'Do you think Mrs Somers will make an official complaint?'

'I doubt it. I think she'll feel it's beneath her. But I could be wrong.'

'You realise you've compromised yourself? That – depending on how this inquiry shapes up – it could appear that she is now in a position to hold this over you. Over *us*. That we might be less rigorous in our examination of her role in all this than if she had not been capable of ending a promising officer's career.'

'Blackmail? I really don't think it's her style, ma'am. And it's hard to see how she stands to benefit anyway. As far as I know, she's not a person of interest in that sense.'

'Detective Chief Inspector?'

Gorman hadn't said a word yet. Now he rumbled, 'As things stand, I have no reason to suspect Pru Somers of any criminal offence. So I can't see how she'd gain from having Constable Best's indiscretion in her back pocket.'

Maybourne returned to Hazel. 'So what am I supposed to do about this? What did you come in here expecting I was going to do?'

Hazel took a deep breath. 'Honestly, ma'am? I'm expecting to be dismissed.'

'I see.' Maybourne considered some more. 'And if you walk out of here with your P45, will you still think it was the right thing to do?'

'Right, no,' said Hazel immediately. 'Regrettable, certainly. Necessary? – I thought so at the time. Actually, I still think so. But I am sorry to have put you in this position.'

Maybourne and Gorman exchanged an unfathomable look. The superintendent shook her head, puzzlement, exasperation and despair chasing one another through her expression. 'Seriously, Hazel, what am I to *do* with you? You have the makings of an outstanding police officer. But every time you get your career back on track, you do something like this – something that, however much I might sympathise, I cannot possibly condone. Something that makes me wonder if I'm wrong, and your lack of self-discipline – your readiness to throw the book out of the window whenever it suits you – makes you fundamentally incapable of doing the job.'

'Sometimes,' Hazel began, and then she stopped. She was aware that her future was on a knife's edge, making this a really bad moment to be spitting on the whetstone.

'Sometimes?' prompted Maybourne.

Oh well: she probably didn't have anything left to lose. 'Sometimes, the book is no help. Sometimes, the best we can do – as police officers and as individuals – is to go by what we feel in our hearts to be just. I know' – and she did know: Maybourne's mouth was already open to remind her – 'you're going to tell me that policing is a matter of law, not justice. But surely it has to be both. Law without justice is tyranny, and none of us signed up for that.

'You're right, I find it hard to accept that there are some

occasions when we have to turn the other cheek. Literally, in this case.' She didn't dare risk even a very small grin. 'My first instinct is always to get stuck in and try to put things right. Maybe that's naïve. Maybe I'll get better at exercising discretion when I've been longer in the job. If,' she added with a worried emphasis, 'that's still an option. But ma'am, if I've anything to offer in my defence, it's this: that excessive zeal may be a nuisance, an embarrassment and a sign of professional immaturity, but maybe it's still better than no zeal at all?'

Another of those long silences. Then Maybourne said simply, 'I don't know, Hazel. I'll have to give it some thought. Of course, the decision will be out of my hands if Mrs Somers decides to make a formal complaint. Then we'll be into Police Conduct territory – again,' she added grimly. 'In the meantime, I think you should change out of that uniform and take the rest of your leave. And do *try* to stay out of trouble.'

Subdued, Hazel nodded. 'Ma'am.' She left, closing the office door quietly behind her.

Having been brought up almost as nicely as Grace Maybourne, it didn't occur to her to check that the corridor was empty and then listen at the keyhole. If she had, she'd have heard the silence persist a little longer, and then Dave Gorman ask gruffly, 'Will it do any good, do you think?'

'Bawling her out? I shouldn't think so,' said Superintendent Maybourne resignedly. 'It never has before.'

'You could sack her. She's given you reason enough.'

'And have all that enthusiasm go to waste? You've been around police stations as long as I have, David, you know how rare a commodity it is. I was absolutely serious: I don't know what to do with her. I don't know if she's going to end up as chief constable or doing time in Styal. I don't doubt her goodwill, not for a moment. I have serious reservations about her judgement. What did she think she was doing, quizzing the Somers girl like that?'

'We made her the family's liaison officer,' Gorman reminded her. 'I think she thought that meant helping them get at the truth.'

'Well – yes, of course, but . . .'

And that was the problem in a nutshell. It was hard ever to say that what Hazel Best did was wrong. It was how she set about doing what was right that caused such problems.

'How about . . .?' Maybourne stopped again, reflecting.

Gorman waited.

'Maybe she needs more structure, closer supervision. Working in a smaller unit might provide her with both, and save me having to write her marching orders.'

The DCI's heavy brows lowered further. 'What do you have in mind?'

'You know, of course, that she's desperate to join CID. This is a case in point: she's supposed to be on leave, but all she's actually done is move upstairs. And I presume, from the fact that you keep finding things for her to do, you're not wholly opposed to the idea?'

'I suppose,' admitted Gorman warily.

'If I gave her to you on secondment, do you feel you could knock her into shape? Not literally, of course,' she added hurriedly, 'although the temptation might be there.'

'It's not . . . procedure,' Gorman felt obliged to point out.

'No. Frankly, it's a bit of a last resort. If this doesn't bring her into line, I may have to let her go. And I think we'd both regret that.'

'With immediate effect?'

'No-o-o,' said Maybourne slowly. 'No, that might look too much like a reward, and we really shouldn't be seen rewarding officers for assaulting members of the public. No, we'll let the dust settle, then I'll get her in here again. Read the Riot Act, and warn her that this is the Last Chance Saloon.'

Dave Gorman had never seen his superintendent as a reader of cowboy fiction. He wiped the image from his mind. 'In the meantime, you have to admit that the information she obtained from the Somers girl moves the inquiry forward.'

'I can see that it does,' agreed Maybourne. She gave him a cat-like smile. 'I imagine that means you'll be interviewing both Pru and Rachel Somers again yourself.'

Gorman did the wooden expression that had served him so often in the past. 'I imagine so, ma'am.'

*   *   *

'Well, I've done it this time,' said Hazel, resignation in her tone, desolation in her eyes. 'It's down the jobcentre on Monday for me.'

Ash regarded her over the day's accounts that he was preparing at his kitchen table. It wasn't a demanding task: he could afford to give her his full attention. 'You don't know that.'

'Yes, I do. We're not allowed to deck members of the public, however tiresome they're being. If we were, we'd get nothing else done.'

'She slapped you first.'

'She slapped you first before she slapped me first,' Hazel pointed out. 'You didn't slap her back. Neither did Dave. Self-restraint is possible, it's just that I'm not very good at it. Maybe Division is right and I've no business being a police officer. If it was my decision, I'd sack me too.'

'What will you do?'

'Long term? I have no idea. See what jobs I'm qualified for. Something in IT, maybe. Short term, I'll tender my resignation to save Maybourne the trouble of sacking me.'

Ash frowned. 'Are you sure that's a good idea? I have a lot of confidence in Superintendent Maybourne. I'd lay odds that right now she's looking for a way of keeping you on.'

'I have a lot of confidence in her too,' said Hazel. 'I just don't think she has any choice. The facts don't allow for much creative interpretation. I was appointed family liaison officer to a woman whose world had been torn to shreds, and I ended up slapping her face. How can my senior officers ever trust me again?'

'Possibly, by acknowledging that perfection is a rare commodity, and most of the time all we can hope is that people will do their best and try to put things right when they make a mistake. You could start by apologising to Pru Somers.'

'I don't think I can,' said Hazel regretfully. 'I'm not sorry I did it.'

'You'll be sorry if it costs you your job.'

'Yes. But I don't think that's much of an apology, do you?'

'Is it worth reminding you that it's the tree that bends which survives the storm?' said Ash.

He wasn't making things any better. But his friendship, his support, his genuine and unqualified concern never lost their value to Hazel. 'Oh Gabriel,' she sighed, 'I've never been much good at keeping my head down.'

He chuckled ruefully at that. It was absolutely true, and he was alive today because of it. 'I could have a word with Dave Gorman.'

I could have a word with Dave Gorman. It wouldn't do any good. Not because he wouldn't want to help, and not because he wouldn't stick his neck out to try and help, but because I've put myself beyond the reach of any help he can offer. Superintendent Maybourne will sack me because it's her duty to do so. If it was Dave's call, he'd sack me too. He'd be sorry, but he'd do it anyway. He'd have to.'

Ash thought a little longer. 'You're a constable, yes?'

'You know I am.'

'And Dave Gorman's a detective chief inspector? And Grace Maybourne is a superintendent.'

Hazel waited in vain. 'And your point is?'

'That perhaps a superintendent and a detective chief inspector have ways and means – weapons in their armoury, if you like, possibly even unlicensed weapons – which a lowly constable might wot not of.'

'What not what?'

'Wot not of,' Ash repeated solemnly. 'Look, I don't know, I could be wrong. But you're in the fortunate position of having your future decided by two people who wish you well. I can't believe it's a good idea to take matters out of their hands when they might at this very moment be drawing up a plan to save you from yourself. What's to be gained by jumping the gun? What's to be lost by waiting to see what they come up with?'

Hazel eyed him dubiously. 'I'm not sure that my career prospects are important enough to keep Superintendent Maybourne awake at night.'

'Exactly. You're not sure. Until you are sure, don't do anything precipitate.' He saw the puzzlement in her eyes, and her lips rounding on the word 'Rain?' and he breathed heavily and rephrased it. 'Anything that can't be undone.'

Hazel thought he was clutching at straws. She thought there was more dignity in jumping than waiting to be pushed. But she had always trusted Ash's judgement – well, almost always – and she couldn't quite dismiss the hope that he might be right this time. 'I suppose I could give it twenty-four hours.'

'Forty-eight. In fact, wait till after the weekend.'

He was right about that too. Nothing was accomplished in a police station in twenty-four hours. Putting all Meadowvale's clocks forward an hour in spring and back an hour in the autumn commonly took three days. 'The weekend,' she agreed. 'Then I'll empty my locker.'

DCI Gorman telephoned an instruction – not an invitation – to Pru Somers to be at home at seven o'clock that evening, when he intended to interview her and her daughter together. This time he took DC Friend.

Mrs Somers met them at the door. Her manner was, for her, subdued. As soon as they were over the threshold she began, 'Mr Gorman, I owe you an apology.'

Gorman was both surprised and encouraged. 'Well, maybe,' he agreed. 'Try to remember that I'm not here to upset you, only to find out what happened. I'm sorry if sometimes that means hitting raw nerves, but it's important we get to the truth. If we don't, Rachel could still be in danger.'

Pru dipped her gaze and nodded. 'I appreciate that. I'll try not to go off half-cocked again.'

'Is Rachel in the lounge?'

She couldn't help herself. 'The drawing-room, yes. Come on through.'

Rachel was waiting for them, perched on the edge of one of the big sofas, washed and brushed and dressed as if for a formal occasion – a piano recital, perhaps, or a prize-giving. She started to her feet when they came in, then bumped back down awkwardly at an irritable gesture from her mother.

Pru saw the visitors seated before taking the big armchair for herself. She said a little hesitantly, 'I'd rather hoped to see Constable Best again this evening.'

Gorman bit back the obvious retort. 'Yes? I didn't think you would. Anyway, she's on leave.'

'Just leave?'

The DCI squinted at her. 'Yes, just leave. Mrs Somers, you're probably wondering how much I know about what happened here yesterday. The answer is, everything. She thought we ought to – me and Superintendent Maybourne both. She didn't want us to hear about it from someone else.'

Pru's voice was low. 'I wasn't going to report it, you know.'

'She didn't think you were. She still thought we ought to know.'

'Is she in trouble?'

'Trouble is Hazel Best's natural habitat,' growled Dave Gorman. 'So far, she's always managed to find her way out of it. Hopefully she will again.'

Pru nodded. She seemed relieved. 'Well, you wanted to talk to us, Chief Inspector, and here we are. It would be naïve to pretend not to know what you want to talk about.'

Gorman nodded. 'Mr Phillips.'

'Gethin Phillips was a good man,' said Pru, laying out her stall immediately. 'He was the kindest man I ever knew. He loved me, and he cared for my daughter. And I know what you're thinking, and you're wrong. He cared for Rachel the way her own father should have done and didn't: not just for high days and holidays, but all the times when she was tired and fractious and sullen and spiteful too.

'I'm sorry, Rachel,' she said, cutting the girl's protest off at the pass, 'I don't mean to be unkind, but that's what having children is about. Loving them when they're lovable, and also when they're not. Anyone can love a cute little four-year-old in ringlets and a party frock. Loving a hormonal teenager who thinks the world's her enemy and hopes to make herself feel better by making those around her feel worse, that's the test. And Gethin passed with flying colours, again and again. I was incredibly lucky to find him. We were both – me and my daughter – lucky to know him.'

DC Friend was taking notes. 'Is that how you felt?' Gorman asked Rachel.

'Yes.'

He gave a ghost of a grin. 'Even when you were feeling tired and fractious?'

She didn't return his smile. 'Yes, even then. I know I'm not perfect. Fortunately, Gethin was.'

'Nobody's perfect,' suggested Gorman, watching for her response.

'You're wrong, Chief Inspector. Ask my mother.'

There was an awkward silence. Gorman waited to see if someone else would break it; when they didn't, he said, 'Then why would you suspect him of doing something so very far from perfect as following you into the spinney and attacking you?'

Her first instinct was to deny it. 'I never said that! Never.'

'But you thought it. At least, you thought it was possible. Or did Hazel make it up?'

'I'm sure she didn't make it up,' said Pru tersely. 'I think she put two and two together and got five, and instead of telling her to do her sums again, Rachel went along for the ride. I don't know why. It must have made her feel better in some way. Perhaps because, if Gethin created the situation, there was no need for her to feel guilty about his death. Or perhaps it's mainly about this.' She patted her stomach, not yet straining her clothes. 'She's never going to be able to compete with either his ghost or his legacy. All she can do now is soil his memory.'

Emma Friend was an experienced detective constable. Even so, she couldn't keep the astonishment off her face. Her biro came to a halt, hovering above her notebook, and she stared at Pru as if the woman had kicked a Yorkshire terrier.

Dave Gorman had been doing the job for fifteen years longer than his DC, could have coached the sphinx in keeping a straight face. He just said, 'Is that what you're doing, Rachel?'

'Of course not.' The girl's eyes were brimming with tears. 'I liked Gethin. I didn't believe he was capable of . . . you know. That's why I didn't say anything. I didn't *want* to believe it. But when Hazel said it was a possibility, I thought maybe it wasn't just me being paranoid. Maybe suspecting him didn't mean I was a horrible person; maybe there was a reason to think that. I don't know what the reason was, Mr Gorman. I truly never saw his face or heard his voice. But there was something familiar about him. I don't know what.'

'His aftershave?' suggested DC Friend softly.

DCI Gorman turned slowly to look at her. She reddened slightly, but stuck to her guns. 'The part of the brain that deals with the sense of smell is close to the part that deals with memories. That's why nothing evokes a memory like a scent. If she didn't see him and didn't hear him, it's possible that he smelled familiar.'

Dave Gorman was not an avid consumer of male toiletries. He privately thought that the most appropriate perfume for a working copper was a blend of boot leather, spilt beer and diesel fumes *à la* lock-up garage. 'Did Mr Phillips use after-shave?' Pru nodded, reluctantly. 'Show me.'

There was a half-used bottle in the bathroom cabinet. A time would come when Pru would dispose of his things, but it hadn't come yet. Gorman pulled on a plastic glove and extracted the bottle carefully, straight into an evidence bag. They went back to the sitting room.

'Rachel.' Still using the glove, he unscrewed the top, held it a little distance from her. 'Sniff.'

She did as she was bid. Immediately her face creased up in panic; one hand flew to her mouth.

'Is that what you smelled in Highfield Spinney when you were attacked?'

'Yes! Oh God, yes.'

'Are you sure?'

'Yes! Oh Mum, I'm sorry, but yes. That's what seemed familiar. I'd forgotten. It all happened so quickly – I knew there was something, but I couldn't get a hold on what it was. But it was that. The smell of his aftershave.'

Pru Somers looked as if half the sky had fallen on her. Her white cheeks were sucked hollow, her eyes deep and bruised. Under the power-pack lipstick her lips were pale, parted; she was panting slightly. Any half-trained first aider would have diagnosed shock.

Finally she found a voice, low and breathy though it was. 'That's a popular high street brand. There'll be a bottle in every second household.'

'Possibly,' agreed Gorman.

'It doesn't prove anything.'

'No. But it is suggestive. We know Mr Phillips was in the spinney. We can't find any evidence that another man was there as well. And whoever attacked Rachel was wearing Mr Phillips' aftershave.'

'It could still be a coincidence!'

'Yes, it could. Mrs Somers, I wish I could tell you what you want to hear. Or failing that, tell you what you *don't* want to hear, because even that might be better than not knowing. I can't. If Mr Phillips was still here, the evidence we have would be strong enough to question him: it wouldn't be enough to charge him. He may have been entirely innocent. But a point comes where circumstantial evidence mounts up and you start to think that what it's telling you is the truth. Whether or not it would stand up in court, where a jury has to be satisfied beyond reasonable doubt before they call a man a rapist and take away ten years of his life.'

Gorman took a deep breath. 'We're getting close to that point now. Not because of what Rachel's saying – at least, not only because of what Rachel's saying. We don't have any other suspects. There's no evidence that anyone else was involved. That may not sound like grounds enough to accuse someone – especially when he's dead and can't defend himself – but modern forensic techniques are so good it would be pretty remarkable if someone else was there and we couldn't find *any* trace of him. If Rachel was grabbed by a stalker, and the stalker was tackled by Gethin Phillips, I should have found some kind of corroborative evidence by now.

'So when Rachel says she recognises the aftershave her attacker was wearing as the same one Mr Phillips left in your bathroom cabinet, I wouldn't be doing my job if I didn't take a long hard look at where that takes us. You're right, it isn't proof. But it is significant.'

'I don't believe it,' said Pru, as if that really ought to be the end of the discussion.

'I'm sure you don't. I'm sure that, if you'd had any reason to suspect that your partner was a danger to your daughter, you'd have taken steps to protect her.'

'Gethin wasn't a danger to anyone! You've got this wrong. I don't know why you haven't been able to find any cigarette butts, or chewing gum, or hairs caught on twigs in the spinney. Perhaps because the attacker was a bald non-smoker with a spearmint allergy! – I don't know. But I know Gethin didn't do this. I know it.'

SEVENTEEN

Walking back to his car, Gorman gave DC Friend a sideways look. 'What do you think? Is she defending Phillips because she thinks he's innocent or because she's afraid he's guilty?'

But Friend didn't know. 'I find her incredibly hard to read, sir. It's almost as if she blames Rachel for what happened; and even if what happened is that Phillips tried to rape her, she still blames Rachel. I mean, not many of us are finalists in the mother-of-the-year competition, but surely that's not normal.'

Gorman was staring at her. 'You have a kid?'

She met his gaze unflinchingly. 'You didn't know? I have a daughter too – Poppy, she's eight.'

The DCI didn't know what to say next – what he was allowed to say next, and what would see him up in front of an Equal Opportunities Tribunal. 'You must have been very . . .'

'Young? Yes, I was. Eighteen. I was still at school.'

'You didn't . . .?'

'Marry Poppy's father? Good God, no. He was pretty, I was hormonal, but even at eighteen I knew better than to hitch my wagon to a guy with a Sex Pistols tattoo. He said he was going to be a pop star. He's a brickie now.'

'It *is* a good trade. The world will always need houses,' Gorman said levelly.

'It *is* a good trade,' agreed Friend. 'He pays his child support, and takes Poppy out most Sundays. It's a long time since we were close, but he's a decent enough dad.'

'So who looks after Poppy when . . .?'

'When we're burning the midnight oil because you've had a tip-off about a lorry-load of smuggled cigarettes? My mother. She looked after her when I went to university, and she still does. I've been very lucky.'

'You've worked hard.'

She thanked him with a smile. 'That too.'

'University,' mused Gorman, who'd never been. 'Is that where you learned that stuff about memory and the sense of smell?'

Friend shook her head. 'I saw it on TV.'

Gorman cleared his throat. He'd worked hard too, and he'd done well, but he still had the uncomfortable feeling that the world was moving on slightly faster than he was keeping pace. 'Going back to Pru Somers. Faced with a choice between supporting her boyfriend and her child, surely a woman would choose her child?'

'You'd expect so,' agreed Friend. 'But they don't always, do they? We have cases every year where a man brutalises his partner's child, and she knows, and all she has to do is grab the kid and leave, and she doesn't do it. Finally it ends up on a ventilator, with X-rays that look as if it was thrown from a fourth-floor window. And when we ask her why she let it happen, she says she couldn't face being alone. As if a man who would do that to her child was still better than no man at all.' Her expression was bemused.

Friend wasn't telling him anything he didn't know, hadn't had to deal with in person. Gorman still didn't think it was a good analogy. 'But it's already too late for Pru to have that choice. Phillips is dead. If he hadn't had his brains bashed out, maybe she would be crazy enough to protect him. But Rachel is now the only family she has left. Why is she so angry with her?'

'For being young enough and pretty enough to appeal to the man she loved? Because if she hadn't had a teenage daughter she'd still have her partner?'

That made a kind of sense. Dave Gorman didn't claim to be an authority on the female heart – he'd seen too much of what happens when relationships go wrong and not enough of when they go right – and he didn't pretend to understand Pru Somers well enough to judge her role in all this. For instance . . .

They'd reached Gorman's car a couple of minutes ago. He made no attempt to unlock it, was peering over the roof into the leafy middle distance.

DC Friend waited patiently; but at length, feeling they were becoming conspicuous, she prompted him. 'Chief?'

The DCI blinked, and looked at her as if he'd forgotten he wasn't alone. 'Emma – are we being stupid here? Not seeing the wood for the trees?'

The language changes year by year: it was an idiom more familiar to his generation than to hers. 'The spinney?' she hazarded, perplexed.

'What? No. Look. Suppose we're right about Phillips taking a shine to Rachel. Following her out into the spinney and trying to jump her bones. And Rachel got away, and ended up throwing herself into Gabriel Ash's arms. But what if Phillips didn't fall and somehow contrive to bang his head twice in the process? What if someone really did bang it for him, which is what we assumed at the start?'

'There's nothing to indicate there was another man at the scene,' Friend reminded him. She was surprised that he'd forgotten.

'No, I know. Well, maybe that's because there was no one waiting in the spinney, smoking roll-ups and chewing gum. Maybe, after Phillips followed Rachel into the wood, the killer followed Phillips.'

Friend frowned. 'From their back garden? Oh . . .!'

'Yes. Suppose Pru got home early. Suppose it was her, not Phillips, who heard Rachel scream. She'd run out into the spinney – of course she would. When she saw Rachel struggling free, she'd know exactly what was going on. And she'd be bloody furious. Shocked, and hurt, and incredibly angry.

'This is a woman who strikes out, verbally and physically, in response to fairly minor irritations. If she saw her partner – the man she'd thought she was going to spend the rest of her life with – attempting to rape her teenage daughter, do we really believe she'd have settled for calling us? Or would she have grabbed the first thing that came to hand and beat his head in with it?'

'I thought he hit his head when he fell,' Friend objected faintly.

'Me too. But what we *know* is that he sustained not one

but two fractures, one each side of his skull, and there was bark residue in his scalp.'

Emma Friend was catching up fast. 'If it was Pru who hit him, she probably had the same residue on her hands. If we'd thought to swab her that night . . .'

'Well, it's too late now,' grunted Gorman. 'And there's no point doing another sweep of the wood. We were looking for men's footprints, and assumed that any smaller ones were Rachel's. Maybe some of them were Pru's, but we're two and a half weeks too late to use them as evidence of anything. If we ask her, she'll say she was in the spinney before that night, or since. We can't prove anything different.'

'We could take another look at the photos,' suggested Friend. 'They were taken that night and the next morning. Lord knows there are enough of them. We may be able to identify two kinds of women's shoes. Pru would be in heels, I bet, and Rachel was in trainers. Heels would leave pretty distinctive holes in the leaf-litter.'

'Good – do it,' said Gorman. 'Get SOCO to help. Sergeant Wilson reads a crime scene better than any of us.'

Friend nodded, making a note. 'If we can put her in the spinney that evening, Pru will tell us what happened. Tell us, and dare us to charge her. She'll claim she was protecting Rachel. That it was justifiable homicide.'

'It's a good defence. It might even be an honest one. It comes down to the timing. If Pru hit him to get Phillips off her daughter, there's no charge to answer. But if Rachel had already got away, Pru was acting out of vengeance and that makes it murder. In my book, anyway.'

They were talking as if they'd solved the case, as if they knew something now that they hadn't half an hour before. But both of them knew they were still just speculating.

'How can we establish if Rachel was already safe?' asked Friend.

Gorman gave it some thought. 'If she'd still been pinned to the tree when Pru floored her attacker, she wouldn't have run. And they'd have told us what happened – there'd have been no reason not to. But Rachel has no idea her mother was there. I think she was already out of danger when Pru arrived.'

Emma Friend returned to that aspect of the case which still seemed to her the hardest to explain. 'Then why is Pru so angry with Rachel? Why is she still defending Phillips, why is she willing to hurt Rachel even more, if she knows exactly what happened and who was to blame?'

They were back to why women do what they do, which was the murky ditch round Gorman's field of expertise. 'Because the one she's really angry with isn't here to be yelled at any more?' he hazarded. 'Or maybe she thinks Rachel was the author of her own misfortune – that she was too casual with him, too cosy, so it wasn't altogether Phillips' fault if he misunderstood. Or maybe she's just generally livid at how her life's going to change. A month ago she had a long-term partner, a talented daughter, a good job and a nice house. Now she's got no partner, a baby on the way, she may not be able to keep the job and could end up losing the house. Plus, if we figure out who did what, she's going to find herself in court, explaining how her partner wasn't satisfied with her but lusted after her daughter as well. The papers will have a field day. She'll be pitied and she'll be mocked. Imagine what that will do to a woman as proud as Pru Somers.'

Friend had no difficulty imagining it. She had no difficulty imagining what the woman would be prepared to do rather than face public humiliation.

'Half the time she thinks Rachel ought to be sharing the burden,' Gorman went on, finding his own argument increasingly persuasive, 'and half the time she knows she can't afford to trust anyone with the truth. She's angry at Rachel for going into the spinney, for being young and pretty, and because right now anger is the only thing she dares feel. Anything else would tear her apart, but anger keeps her strong.'

Emma Friend was regarding him with undisguised admiration. 'It makes sense, doesn't it? Hellfire, chief, I think you've got it! Should we go back in there – put it to her, arrest her on suspicion?'

Tempted as he was, Gorman shook his head. 'Not yet. Pru's not going anywhere, there's time to think this through. Before I accuse her of murder, I want to have another look at those photographs. And I want to talk to Hazel.'

'Hazel?' There was no missing the surprise in Friend's voice, nor the edge of disapproval. 'Hazel Best, who isn't actually a member of CID?'

Gorman blinked at her owlishly. 'I know she isn't. But she *is* the family's liaison officer: she knows Pru and Rachel better than any of us. I want to know if the idea chimes with her.'

'You're going to ask Constable Best's permission to treat Pru Somers as a suspect in the murder of her partner?' This time there was no room for doubt: it was professional jealousy.

DCI Gorman raised an eyebrow at her. 'Don't get precious with me, Emma. I'd ask the tea lady if I thought she knew what a person of interest was and wasn't likely to have done. Besides . . .' And there he stopped, rather wishing he'd never begun.

A skill shared by many detectives, and probably all the best ones, is the ability to hear what hasn't actually been said. 'You're *kidding* . . .' hissed Friend, startled and appalled.

Gorman found himself making excuses. 'It wasn't my idea. Miss wants me to take her on secondment, try and instil some discipline into her. What's the problem? I thought you liked Hazel.'

'I *do* like Hazel,' said Friend darkly. 'The way you like having your sister's kids for the weekend. You like it because you know they're going home on Sunday night. You'd feel differently about it if you knew they were moving in with you.'

At ten o'clock the next morning he found Hazel in the bookshop, trying to make sixty books fill fifty metres of shelving. She looked up as the opening door set the old-fashioned bell jangling on its spring.

'This is ridiculous,' she said, gesturing at the yawning gaps. 'Whatever they've got at this house clearance tomorrow, Gabriel had better buy the lot. Cricketing yearbooks, *Boys' Own* annuals, handbooks on how to service a Vauxhall Viva and *A Smallholder's Guide to Farrowing Sows*: anything that'll take up a bit of shelf-space.'

'Where is Gabriel?'

'Gone to the junk shop in Mincing Lane to buy some chairs. We couldn't get the soot out of the ones he had. Every time you sat on one, you stood up with a black bullseye on your backside.'

'Good,' said Gorman absently. 'It was you I wanted to see.'

She'd bought a new kettle, a set of mugs and a jar of coffee on her way here. She brewed up while he talked. She didn't interrupt, even to agree or seek clarification; all she contributed at this point was a quiet space, a listening ear, and the coffee. Gorman found it a little unnerving. He hadn't been a DCI so long that he was used to people hanging on his every word. He was still expecting to be challenged on any imprecision in his deductive processes, any wishful thinking masquerading as a theory. He wasn't sure if Hazel's silence indicated consent, or if she was marshalling arguments to confound him, or if she'd quietly fallen asleep.

Last night, talking it through with DC Friend, he had all but convinced himself that they'd finally got their ducks in a row. This morning, explaining it to Hazel, he was a little less comfortable with his premise. He was aware that he'd solved one puzzle – the two blows that killed Gethin Phillips – at the cost of creating another one. Why *had* the man gone into the spinney in his slippers?

Gorman squinted at Hazel, holding his mug out for a refill. 'You've seen more of Pru Somers than any of us. What's your gut feeling? Can you see her beating the crap out of Phillips if she caught him interfering with her daughter?'

Hazel was careful not to smile. 'I'm not sure gut feelings are admissible in court.'

The squint turned into a glare. 'I know they're not. If that's what happened, we'll need either a confession or some evidence that *will* stand up in court. SOCO is going over the crime-scene photos again with his biggest magnifying glass, to see if there's anything there that we missed first time round. What I want from you is your considered opinion of Pru as a suspect. Is this something she could have done? If that was the situation she was confronted with, is it credible that she reacted that way?'

Considered he wanted, considered he got. Hazel topped up

her own mug before she answered. 'Pru Somers is a fiercely
ambitious individual. She's been successful in her own
career, and she's put the same kind of focus into Rachel's.
She doesn't accept the possibility of defeat. She'll be a hard
woman to work for, maybe even harder to live with. She's
driven Rachel to her wits' end: she's talked about giving up
the piano because she can't take the pressure any more.

'Gut feeling? That Pru Somers knows what she wants and
is willing to do what it takes to get it. I suppose the word for
that is "ruthless". Which isn't the same as calling her a
murderer. There are a lot of ruthless people in the world, and
lots of them never murder anyone.' She paused, thinking still.
'But if she *did* discover that Phillips had gone after Rachel,
she would be incandescent with rage. Not even so much for
Rachel's sake as for her own: she couldn't endure that kind
of disrespect. In the heat of the moment, she might well have
felt that throwing his belongings onto the drive wouldn't be
enough. That even setting fire to his car wouldn't be enough.'

'She could have called us. What she witnessed was a crime.'

'Calling us would mean people knowing that the man she
loved fancied her daughter more. A woman with much less
pride than Pru Somers would struggle with that.'

Although Hazel's conclusion agreed with his own,
Gorman's voice rose incredulously. 'So she beat his head in
with a branch?'

'Conceivably. This is a woman who hits people for crossing
her in quite trivial ways. This wasn't trivial. If that's what
she saw, she might use any weapon that came to hand. We've
both seen enough of Pru Somers to know that, in any
fight-or-flight situation, flight would never be her first choice.'

Gorman was feeling happier with the theory again. 'So
– still speaking hypothetically – Rachel went into the wood
looking for her cat, and Phillips followed her. Maybe he
simply forgot that he'd got his slippers on – there's been no
rain, his feet weren't getting wet. Anyway, he grabbed her
from behind and held her face against a tree so she couldn't
see him. But she could scream, and Pru, coming home earlier
than expected, heard her and rushed down the garden to see
what was happening.'

Now the DCI could see these events playing out before his inner eye. He knew that didn't prove he had the scenario right this time; but he was confident in his ability to recognise if a working hypothesis came up against an insurmountable obstacle, and he knew it hadn't yet.

'What she saw made her reach into the undergrowth for something hard and heavy,' he went on. 'If she acted out of fear, because Rachel was still pinned to the tree, Pru has a good defence. If Rachel had thrown Phillips off and was already on her way to safety, then Pru's primary motivation was furious indignation and she hasn't.'

Hazel frowned. 'But if Pru was protecting her daughter, why not say so? Why let Rachel run off through the spinney? If that's what happened, neither of them had done anything wrong. She'd have taken Rachel back to the house, locked the door in case Phillips got up again, and called us. Wouldn't she?'

Gorman couldn't see any reason for her to do anything else. 'I suppose it might all have happened at much the same time – that Rachel broke free as Pru swung. Maybe Phillips was distracted enough at being confronted by Pru to lose his grip; and Rachel ran like hell without looking back. She never saw her mother floor the man who was trying to rape her.'

Hazel took no issue with that. 'But what are you suggesting that Pru did next? Leave the house for half an hour, and come back only after Gabriel had brought Rachel home? Why would she do that – pretend she'd only just got in from work, knew nothing about what had happened in the spinney – unless she was concealing a crime?'

'So Pru knew that Rachel was safe,' rumbled Gorman. 'She brained Phillips out of anger and injured pride rather than because he needed stopping. Even if he was still on top of Rachel, the first injury he sustained would have floored him. The second was nothing but retribution.'

Hazel blew out her cheeks despairingly. 'I don't see how else we can read it. But proving it'll be a bugger if Pru sticks to her story. Rachel can't be a witness against her mother even if she's willing to be. Phillips' death was only a crime if Rachel wasn't there to see it.'

'I'll do a formal interview with Pru down at Meadowvale.'
The DCI didn't sound as if he was looking forward to it. 'I
wanted your take on whether it was feasible first. Whether, as
the family's liaison officer, you thought it was credible for
Pru Somers to do what was done.'

'Credible, yes. Do I think she did? – hell, Dave, you may
be asking the wrong person. I'm the go-to girl for unjamming
computer glitches, giving road safety talks to under-tens and
reminding old ladies not to sign over their life savings to
plausible conmen. You should be talking this through with
another detective.'

She was puzzled by the expression that crossed his square,
unlovely face then. A mixture of distaste and rueful amusement: the expression of a man who's just swallowed a goldfish.
She frowned. 'What?'

'There's something else I have to run by you. Now, don't
think this is my idea because it isn't. It's Miss's. She was
going to tell you herself, but events have rather overtaken us.
And it's not necessarily to be seen as a compliment . . .'

He was surprised at how calmly she took the news. She
repeated it back to him, to make sure she'd understood
correctly; and she thanked him, and asked him to thank
Superintendent Maybourne; and promised to do all in her
power to justify their decision. She asked when he'd like
her to start; and Gorman asked if she wanted to finish her
leave first, and Hazel said she didn't, and that made sense
because she'd be doing pretty much the same things anyway
so she might as well save her leave for another time.

She saw him out to his car. 'I'll see you tomorrow then,'
he said. Still the model of professional calm, Hazel nodded
and returned to the shop.

But Gorman didn't start his car. He sat and waited. Thirty
seconds; a minute. Then, muffled by the new glass, he heard
the unmistakable whoop of triumph. Smiling to himself, he
drove away.

EIGHTEEN

For the first time in years, Hazel agonised over what to wear. It hadn't been an issue since she was a teacher. For work she wore uniform, for most other occasions she wore jeans with a shirt or sweater or jacket, as the weather dictated. Ordinarily, she gave about as much thought to her wardrobe as Ash did.

Now she was a detective, if only a semi-official one, she was going to have to make decisions again. Jeans were practical but too casual when she wouldn't know at the beginning of each day who she would need to see about what. A skirt suit would be professional and authoritative, but a major drawback if she found herself having to run down a suspect.

Also, there was the question of what her new colleagues favoured. The men were no problem – they all, including DCI Gorman, appeared to frequent charity shops, and thought knotting some donkey-chewed string of a tie under their collar equipped them to appear in any company. Emma Friend was more of a challenge. She managed to be one of the CID crew without trying to be one of the boys, and she hit the right sartorial note too, combining style with practicality. No one else would care or even notice what the new detective wore, but Friend would. Instinct warned Hazel that, of all the new relationships she was going to have to create with these people that she'd known for years, the one with Emma Friend could be the most difficult and also the most important.

Stylish and practical; but not – and this was important – *quite* as stylish as the more experienced officer. Hazel poked through her wardrobe that afternoon and came up with some dark tailored trousers – with a bit of stretch to the fabric, in case athleticism was required – a blue and white striped shirt and a linen jacket. But she stuck with her uniform shoes, because they were comfortable and she knew she could run in them. She dashed the iron over the clothes to take out the creases they'd acquired hanging at the back of the wardrobe. Then she decided that looked like trying too hard, and carefully ironed a few of the creases back in. Finally she told herself to stop being such a silly mare, left the outfit hanging behind the bedroom door and went over to Highfield Road.

She found Ash at the kitchen table, poring over his insurance documents. He gave her a harassed look. 'When they drew up this business policy, I don't think they had businesses like mine in mind. They want to know how many people I employ, and whether I have security staff on the premises overnight.'

Hazel chuckled. 'They'll get the picture when you tell them a couple of thousand pounds will replace your entire stock.'

He regarded her severely. 'Insurance fraud is a serious crime. I should know: I used to investigate it.'

'All right, so what did you value your contents at?'

He had the grace to look faintly embarrassed. 'Twelve hundred quid,' he mumbled. Then, brightening, 'But replacing the window again will be expensive.'

Hazel pushed Patience up to one end of the kitchen sofa, threw herself down on the other. 'Is this what you were doing all morning? I thought you were staying out of the way until I had the bookshelves organised.'

Ash blinked. 'You were down at the shop? I'm sorry, I got held up. You should have called.'

'That's all right,' said Hazel generously, 'I probably got on quicker on my own.'

'No, really,' Ash said with a slightly odd emphasis, 'you should have called.'

'Why? What held you up?'

He sighed. 'Rachel was here again. I'm not sure if she thinks she's safer sticking close to me or I'm safer sticking close to her. Either way, it's getting a bit tiresome.'

Hazel grinned. 'What was the excuse this time?'

'She asked if she could take Patience for a walk. She thought it would free me up to sort out my insurance.'

'What did Patience think about that?'

Ash gave her a startled rabbit-in-the-headlights look. Though he'd trembled on the brink of indiscretion a couple of times, in the two years they'd been friends he'd managed to keep even Hazel from knowing that his dog talked to him. Whether Patience was a freak or he was, he had enough insight to know that once *that* genie was out of the bottle, one of them was going to end up with electrodes attached to their brain. 'She – er – didn't look very keen.'

Actually she'd said, You go. Tell her I've got a sore leg. I'm tired of playing gooseberry.

In the end they had all gone for a walk. At the gate, where Rachel looked edgily right towards the fields and the spinney, Ash turned firmly left towards the park. Patience showed no signs of having a sore leg, but she did sulk because they'd left home without her new Spiky Ball.

Apparently apropos of nothing, Ash asked: 'What's gooseberry?'

Hazel tilted her head, birdlike, to one side. 'I'm guessing you already know about the small green fruit.'

Ash scowled. 'I think it must be a game people play.'

Hazel contrived to keep a straight face. 'Playing gooseberry is when a third party joins a couple to make it look as though there's nothing going on between them. Like a chaperone.'

'Not a ball game, then?'

'No. Why do you ask?'

'Oh – something I overheard,' he said vaguely. 'Hazel, should I discourage Rachel from coming round? I don't want her mother to get the wrong idea. Or anyone else, for that matter.'

'She's got a bit of a crush on you, Gabriel, that's all. It's not a criminal offence. She's seventeen years old – in lots of ways she's young for seventeen – she's been through some serious trauma, and you were kind to her when she needed it most. Now she thinks the sun shines out of your left ear. It won't last. Next week or the week after, some nineteen-year-old who plays air guitar and washes on alternate days is going to offer her a ride on his motorbike, and you, my friend, will be history.

'Talking of making history . . .' Hazel told him her news. She'd had a couple of hours to absorb it, and she thought she could report Dave Gorman's bombshell now with a degree of composure. But nothing short of a sack would have hidden the thrill of happiness in her face and her eyes, and even a sack wouldn't have disguised it in her voice.

'Hazel, I'm delighted for you,' said Ash with genuine pleasure. 'I know this is what you've wanted.'

'I'd just about given up,' she admitted. 'And to be fair, it isn't a done deal yet. It's kind of like a trial marriage, to see how we get on together. Dave's been given the job of whipping me into shape.'

'And if it doesn't work, you'll be back in uniform?'

'If it doesn't work, I think I'll be out on my ear,' Hazel said honestly. 'So it's got to work. You might remind me of that, if you catch me showing undue initiative.'

Ash was chewing his lip.

'What?' said Hazel.

'The problem isn't you,' he said reluctantly. 'The problem is me. I get you into these situations. I don't mean to, but I do. When I first knew you, you were the perfect police recruit – respectful, smart but not *too* smart, kind and thoughtful and dedicated. The things that make senior officers wary of you – the fearless determination, the refusal to submit to pressure, the willingness to do what you believe to be right regardless of the consequences – they came later. They're the result of the things we've done together. If you hadn't met me, you'd never have been accused of showing undue initiative, and you'd have made CID years ago.

'I'm afraid that, because of our friendship, you're perceived as damaged goods. And much as it grieves me to say this, I wonder if the time hasn't come to put your career first. Continuing our association could cost you everything you've worked for and will be bloody good at.' He never swore, however mildly, unless he felt intensely passionate about something.

Hazel stared at him. 'What are you suggesting?'

Ash sucked in a deep breath. 'I think you should look for support among your new colleagues. People who can help you and won't harm your prospects.'

She blinked. 'You're breaking up with me?'

Gabriel Ash didn't have much of a sense of humour, and

didn't realise she wasn't entirely serious. He also didn't have much experience of breaking up with someone. His first girl-friend had become his wife; and eventually she had broken up with him. He didn't know how to answer. 'It's not that. After all, we're not . . . I mean, we both know how much I owe you, and I'll always be grateful – more than grateful. But we've never . . . been . . .'

Hazel arched an eyebrow, waiting for him to stumble into deep water. 'Been what, Gabriel?'

But Ash retreated onto safer ground. 'We've been friends. Really good friends, special friends, but there was never any question of a romantic dimension. Was there? I'm married, and you're fourteen years younger than me and can do a damn sight better than the proprietor of a second-hand bookshop with no books and a lift that doesn't go all the way to the top floor.' He flicked her a sombre little grin. His mental breakdown had become easier to talk about, even to joke about, with the passage of time.

'You should do something about that,' Hazel said quietly.

Ash frowned, surprised and even mildly offended. 'I see my therapist when the need arises. Unless you think it arises more often than I do?'

'That isn't what I meant. Your mental processes may be a bit off-the-wall sometimes, but I'm pretty sure you're sane. I mean your marriage. You should do something about that. You don't need to be legally tied to a woman who tried to kill you.'

It was more shock than resentment that rocked Ash in his chair – it was something they never talked about, the elephant in the room that they walked around and never acknowledged – but it was resentment too. It wasn't just that he hadn't got round to starting divorce proceedings: somewhere deep in his psyche he was as married today as he had ever been. His sons were daily proof of it. It was a state of mind as much as a legal status, and the fact that he didn't expect to see his wife again was almost irrelevant.

If he'd been single, he'd have done something about Hazel long ago. He believed that, despite their differences, he could have made her happy; he knew she would have made him happy. He thought it possible she might have given a proposal some consideration. But he was a married man whose wife was, to the best of his knowledge, still alive, and how he felt about that wasn't going to change. Perhaps it wasn't rational, but the feeling was in him at a bone-deep level and he couldn't get past it.

Hazel gave up waiting for an intelligent response. 'Oh, I know, it's none of my business,' she said shortly. 'But it's unfinished business, and it needs dealing with – for your sake. You're in a kind of limbo until it is. If Cathy comes back tomorrow, she could try to take her sons away from you.'

His eyes widened, astonished and appalled. 'She's wanted for murder!'

'She wouldn't be the first person to beat a murder charge. If she managed to persuade a jury that she was a dupe rather than a criminal, she could then insist on her parental rights, and it wouldn't be a foregone conclusion that the boys should stay with you. If you get a divorce, it'll include custody of the children – and since no one even knows where Cathy is, that would be you. That piece of paper would be priceless to you. Stop clinging onto the past, Gabriel. Tidy up the present, and you'll be ready for whatever the future throws at you. If you wait until you think it matters, it may already be too late.'

His stare had lost none of its intensity. 'You think I ought to marry again?'

Hazel's green-gold eyes snapped with impatience. 'Hell, Gabriel, I wouldn't presume to advise you about that! But it doesn't seem unlikely that you'll want to, at some point. You're not totally decrepit, you've got a nice house and a comfortable income, and if the right person came along it's just possible you might manage to make your mind up before she got bored enough to try her luck elsewhere.

'But you're not going to do that while you're still married, are you? Most men would, and most people would look at the circumstances and say good luck to them, but we both know you're not most men. That's neither a compliment nor a criticism, just a statement of fact. While you're tied to Cathy, you'll never have a relationship with anyone else.'

'I didn't know it was compulsory,' he muttered rebelliously. She laughed out loud, a brittle, jangling laugh so unlike her usual bubble of mirth. 'You really do live in a binary world, don't you? Everything which is not compulsory is forbidden. Forget I mentioned it. Lord knows it's nothing to do with me. If you want to shackle yourself for eternity to a woman who broke you in a million pieces, why should I care? I just don't like to see you keep volunteering for a kick in the teeth.'

Ash watched her miserably and didn't know what to say. He hated arguing with Hazel; actually, he hated arguing with anyone, but particularly with Hazel. He found it painful, thought she did too. Every time it happened, he swore to himself it would be the last time: that next time they disagreed about something, he'd find a better way of resolving it. Somehow he never quite succeeded. He never saw it coming in time.

He wasn't sure how this argument had started. She'd told him about her career move, he'd been worried about the corrosive effects of his friendship, and they'd ended up arguing about his marriage. How had that happened? It was less that he thought she was wrong, more that there were areas of his life – quite big areas, actually – that Ash felt were private, into which he didn't want to admit even very good friends, even Hazel. Perhaps – probably – he was being unreasonable; still, it was dangerous ground for even a very good friend to trespass on. She must have known she was hurting him.

He got as far as, 'Hazel . . .'

Apology or justification, she didn't want to hear it. She brushed it away with an irritable flick of her corn-coloured hair. 'Let's just forget it, shall we? Tell me about this sale you're going to tomorrow.'

Glad as he was to have something safe to discuss, he suspected it was a mistake to leave the dispute unsettled. He could have said so. Cowardice, masquerading as a sensible desire to avoid further acrimony, won out. 'It's not so much a sale as a house clearance. Robin Venables – you know Robin, he has the antiques shop in Windham Lane – offered me the books if I'd help him load his van with the furniture.'

'Are there a lot of books?' Hazel didn't entirely trust his ability not to be taken advantage of.

'Supposedly. It's a rambling old place in the country on the far side of Wittering – in the same family for generations; the last survivor's just gone into a nursing home. Robin says the inhabitants can't have thrown anything away for decades. He says there are bookcases and bookshelves in every room.'

'Probably more pig-breeding manuals than first folios, though.'

'Oh, certainly. But then, sooner or later someone who wants to breed pigs will turn up in my shop. Will you come? We could get some lunch afterwards.'

'I said I'd clock in with Dave in the morning,' said Hazel. It was true, but she heard the coolness in her own voice and regretted it.

'Never mind,' Ash said, rebuffed. 'It was just a thought.'

A transitory malice made Hazel say, 'If you're looking for company, I bet Rachel would go.'

Ash looked uncomfortable. 'As a matter of fact, she's already invited herself. I couldn't think of a reason to say no.'

'So *that's* why you asked me along. To safeguard your virtue! To play gooseberry.'

His cheek flushed hotly. 'Of course not. Anyway, Robin'll be there. If she wants to help, she can pack the books into boxes. That should keep her out of trouble. She'd better not manhandle any of Robin's furniture: she might—'

'Damage her hands,' finished Hazel, with a bit of a grin that suggested their argument was probably over.

For a moment she was on the point of telling him about Gorman's latest theory. As recently as yesterday she would have done. But if she was now on DCI Gorman's staff, she had no right discussing CID business with outsiders, even with Ash. For the first time it struck her that there was a price to be paid for achieving her goal.

Instead she said, 'When will you be finished?'

'I'm not sure. It rather depends on Robin, on how much of the stuff he thinks he can sell. What about you?'

Hazel shrugged. 'I don't know either. When Dave says so, I suppose.'

That was when Ash realised that things between them would not be the same in the future as they had been in the past. 'Well, if you're free, come round for supper,' he offered lamely.

'Can I let you know?'

From Gilbert:
I stood up today. The instructor says I'll be Hanging Five by the weekend. I don't know what that means, but it sounds cool. Guy fell in again.

'I miss them so much,' said Ash, holding the card to his chest and stroking Patience thoughtfully with his other hand. 'They've only been gone ten days, and it feels like weeks. Do you think it would be safe enough to bring them back now?'

Patience didn't venture an opinion.

'I think it would be safe enough now,' said Ash. 'Don't you?'

NINETEEN

Pru Somers did not have to be brought to Meadowvale in handcuffs. She arrived for her interview ten minutes early, with her solicitor in tow. Gorman knew better than to read anything into that beside what he already knew, that she was a woman who liked to be in control of things. Events, and people. He kept her waiting for five of those minutes before conducting her to Interview Room 1 and introducing everyone present to the tape.

He had never met Mr Willis of Willis, Willis & Peabody before, but he could tell by the cut of his suit that he didn't come cheap. None of the car thieves, drug pushers and convenience store blaggers who were Norbold CID's usual suspects would have been able to afford him, and he probably wouldn't have turned out for them if they could. By contrast, Mrs Somers was a valuable client. He represented her in her capacity as a prominent local businesswoman, a senior manager in a hotel franchise whose account had put his children through college and bought him a small yacht, and he was clearly astonished to find himself safeguarding her interests in a murder inquiry.

In a rare moment of sensitivity, the DCI had asked DC Friend to assist with the interview. She nodded and seemed pleased; but Gorman caught the unspoken question in her eyes. She was wondering what Hazel was doing that was more important than interviewing Mrs Somers.

And in fact, Hazel had been given a task to carry out – not more important, but important enough. 'Find out what time she left the office that night. We know when she got home – the same time I got there, about half past eight. The incident in the spinney began maybe half an hour earlier: there was time for Rachel to run as far as the fields behind Highfield Road, for Gabriel to take her to his place and calm her down, and then for him to drive her home. What I need to know is, could Pru have got home half an hour earlier, then gone away

and come back? Talk to people at The King's Head, see if
you can establish what time she left. And drive the route
yourself: I need to know how long it takes from Westbroke to
the Somerses' house.'

Hazel had nodded her understanding and left immediately,
arriving at The King's Head at about the same time Gorman
started the tape running in Interview Room 1.

Predictably, Pru Somers took the initiative. 'So what can I
tell you that I haven't told you before, Mr Gorman?'

Gorman let the question hang in the air for a few moments
before answering. 'I don't know, Mrs Somers, what *can* you
tell me that you haven't told me before?'

Pru stared at him combatively, her chin raised. 'Perhaps
that's the problem here, Detective Chief Inspector. Perhaps if
you knew what you wanted to ask me, I could be more helpful.'

'We're trying to find out who attacked your daughter and
murdered your partner,' said Emma Friend quietly. 'Why
would you not want to tell us everything you know without
waiting to be asked?'

Pru breathed heavily at her. 'Because I've already done that,
and it hasn't had the desired effect. I've told you' – looking
at Gorman – 'everything I know. I'm sorry it isn't more, but
I wasn't there. You know that. You arrived at my house the
same time I did. You know that everything was over and
the culprit was halfway to Droitwich by then.'

'Droitwich?'

She gave an angry shrug. 'Or Birmingham, or Ashby-de-
la-Zouch, or wherever he came from. He'd have been on the
motorway long before you had your cordon round the spinney.'

'Assuming,' said Gorman, 'the perpetrator was a stranger.'

Pru's flawless, china-hard features cracked a frown.
'Someone from round here? You have a suspect?' The creases
smoothed out abruptly as her eyes widened. 'You don't mean
Gabriel Ash?'

'No, I don't,' said Gorman sharply. 'It would have been
materially impossible for Mr Ash to fight with Mr Phillips
and still get to where Rachel found him before she did.
Gabriel Ash has never been a suspect, and he isn't one now.'

'So who is?' she demanded.

Gorman raised an eyebrow. 'You *know* I'm not going to answer that! Mrs Somers, in view of what's been done to your family, DC Friend isn't the only one wondering why you're making this so hard. Why you're not bending over backwards to co-operate. All I need – from you, from anyone I interview, about this or anything else – is honest answers to my questions.'

'Then ask me some questions!'

'All right.' He paused, let her think he was pondering where to start. 'What time did you leave your office that evening?'

'Same as usual – about twenty minutes before I got home.'

'So, around ten past eight. Isn't that rather late to be finishing work?'

She stared at him insolently. 'When's the last time *you* went home at five o'clock, Mr Gorman? I manage an hotel: it's an open-all-hours business. I finish work when there's nothing more I can usefully do. Sometimes it's earlier than that, occasionally it's later.'

'Can anyone confirm what time you left that evening?'

Her eyes flayed him. 'You want me to produce an alibi? *Me?*'

'It's standard procedure,' Gorman said tersely, 'to establish where everyone was at the material time. It helps us check the accuracy of everyone else's statements. Figure out if somebody's lying, or just not very good at remembering.'

'It's a reasonable question,' murmured Mr Willis of Willis, Willis & Peabody.

'Then, I suppose so,' said Pru shortly. 'My secretary usually leaves before I do, but you could try the staff in the Grenadier Bar. It overlooks the car park; someone may have seen me go out to my car. Ditto any of the customers, of course. Any of the regular clientele would know me.'

'Good,' said Gorman, nodding to Friend who made a note. 'That's helpful. And it takes you twenty minutes to drive from Westbroke to Norbold?' He looked disapproving. 'I think most people would take longer.'

'Perhaps it's the V-8 that makes the difference,' Pru Somers said with iron satisfaction. 'Mr Gorman, am I here about my partner's murder or a possible speeding ticket?'

'Tell me about the relationship between your daughter and Mr Phillips.'

The frown was back. 'What do you mean? There *was* no relationship.'

'They lived in the same house for four years – there must have been a relationship of some kind, friendly or otherwise. Were they on good terms? Did they make an effort to get along for your sake, or was the situation difficult?'

'My daughter is seventeen, Chief Inspector,' said Pru. 'She has no interest in making friends outside her own circle of school and musical contemporaries. And she has never shown any inclination to make an effort for my sake.'

'You're saying that things were strained between them?'

'No. I'm saying they had nothing in common. Gethin extended the hand of friendship. Rachel didn't exactly take it, but she didn't bite it either. Mostly they stayed out of one another's way.'

Which, based on what he knew of teenage girls, sounded perfectly normal. Gorman nodded. 'Any recent arguments between them?'

'No.'

'When there were arguments, whose side did you take?'

'I can't remember any arguments. Gethin wasn't an argumentative man. He was aware that Rachel would have been happier if he and I hadn't got together, and he cut her some slack because of it. And to be fair, Rachel doesn't go round picking fights. It really wasn't an issue, Chief Inspector.'

'Had *you* argued with either of them in the previous few days?'

Pru's eyebrows arched but she answered without demur. 'With Gethin, not at all. Rachel and I always argue, at a routine mother-and-daughter level. There was nothing specific that I remember. Even if there was' – now her tone sharpened – 'what possible bearing could it have on what happened?'

Gorman ignored that. 'Was Rachel in the habit of going into the spinney at night?'

'It wasn't night, it was early evening. And she didn't go into the spinney, she just opened the garden gate and stepped through. Yes, two or three times a week she'll have to go hunting for that damn cat. If she takes his food bowl, he'll come out of hiding and follow her inside.'

'And I'm assuming that, if you knew that, Mr Phillips did too.'

'Of course.'

'You knew he would be home early that day?'

'He said something at breakfast.'

'But Rachel didn't know.'

'Rachel doesn't eat breakfast with us.'

It was like pulling teeth. Gorman persevered. 'So you weren't surprised that Rachel didn't know Mr Phillips was at home.'

Pru shrugged. 'He'd put the Morgan in the garage. If he'd gone into his study, she might well have thought she was the first one home.'

Gorman nodded mechanically. 'Why do you suppose she thinks Gethin Phillips attacked her?'

The fairly innocuous nature of the previous questions had lowered Pru's defences. But she never stood them down: the most she ever did was let the garrison put their weapons aside long enough for a brew-up. The guns were always close enough to snatch and point. 'I don't think she does think that. I think Constable Best suggested it to her in a vulnerable moment and she didn't know how to refute it. It was very unprofessional, you know, putting words in the mouth of a traumatised girl. You really should keep your officers on a tighter leash.'

The DCI ignored that. 'You don't think it's credible?'

'I think it's a fantasy.' She laid an emphatic hand on her belly. 'You think Gethin was losing interest in me? Really?'

Emma Friend said quietly, 'We don't always know people as well as we think we do.'

Down the corridor, almost out of hearing, a phone rang. Then it stopped.

DCI Gorman said, 'The problem we're having with this is that the facts can be interpreted in different ways. There isn't enough hard evidence to say which is right. There could have been a stranger in the wood that night, an opportunist who attacked Rachel and killed Mr Phillips when he intervened, and then disappeared without leaving anything for Forensics to get their teeth into. That's possible. We can't rule it out.

'Or Gethin Phillips may have been the one who attacked Rachel. I know' – he raised a hand to deflect her immediate, angry protest – 'you want us to concentrate on the random stranger hypothesis. But I have to tell you, there are fewer problems if it was Phillips. We know he was there; we know Rachel was there; we don't have any physical evidence that anyone else was; and Rachel remembers the smell of his after-shave. Yes,' he added, forestalling her objection, 'it's a common brand. But you must see why this seems a valid line of inquiry to us. Our scenes of crime officer is going over all the photos again this morning – he may spot something we missed before.'

He watched carefully for any sign that this was not what Pru Somers wanted to hear. He saw nothing. But she was never an easy woman to read. Some people's faces are an open book. Pru's was a closed fist.

There was a tap at the door, and someone passed in a slip of paper. DC Friend handed it to Gorman. He read it, read it again, and gave a grim smile.

He pushed his chair back far enough to look under the table. 'You wear high heels, Mrs Somers.'

She looked at him as if he was mad. 'So?'

'Always?'

'Pretty much. Trainers look fairly silly with a business suit.'

'But Rachel doesn't.'

'Sometimes, if she's going out in the evening.'

'That evening, she was wearing trainers.' One red and white trainer had arrived in the evidence bag with the rest of her clothes; the other had been picked up in the spinney the next morning.

'I expect she was. She'd been at a music class, then she went home. No reason to dress up.'

'So if my people find the imprint of high-heeled shoes around the crime scene?'

It was a critical moment. If she said, 'I was out there that morning, I wanted to see how the blackberries were coming along,' all his warning bells would sound at once because she'd know she had to explain her presence in the spinney.

But she only shrugged and said, 'Maybe you're looking for a transvestite, Chief Inspector.'

He treated that to the silence it deserved. Then: 'What time did you tell me you left your office?'

'What time did we meet at my house? About half past eight? Twenty minutes before that, then.'

Gorman looked at the sheet of paper in front of him. 'So why is your secretary telling us that you left before she did, and she left at six?'

From Guy:

Frankie thinks surfing isn't really my thing. We left Gilbert at the Surf School and played crazy golf instead. There was a little pond in front of the windmill. I fell in that.

Ash hadn't intended to take his car to the house clearance. He picked Rachel up at ten and drove to Windham Lane, where Robin Venables was waiting with his van. But the antiques dealer had also enlisted the help of his twenty-year-old son, who was christened Gordon but had been known as Godzilla since he was thirteen. The bench seat at the front of the van wouldn't have taken four of them, even if one of them hadn't been the human equivalent of a fork-lift truck.

'Bring your own car and follow us,' said Venables; and, looking critically at the elderly Volvo, 'She should make it. A lot of it's downhill.'

It was too late to make his excuses, either to Venables or Rachel, so Ash did as he was bid and tried not to show his discomfort. He would have been happier if Patience had been there too: a chaperone in his mind if no other. But he'd thought she might get trodden on, or someone carrying a Ming vase might trip over her, so he'd settled her down on the kitchen sofa with Spiky Ball and access to the biggest cat-flap he'd been able to find.

'I'm afraid you're going to find this rather boring,' he said, heading off in the van's wake.

'More boring than piano practice?' Rachel flashed him a smile. 'Anyway, it doesn't matter. We owe you. *I* owe you. More than a day spent sorting books.'

He knew he should try to make conversation. But he had no idea what to say to her. His own children were both boys, and both sub-teens: with a seventeen-year-old girl he was out of his depth. The only thing they had in common was the one thing he was fairly sure she wouldn't want to talk about; or, if she did, he had to let her pick the moment. He managed a few wholly predictable remarks about the weather (still hot, still dry) and the traffic (quite light; likely to be heavier later) before lapsing into an uneasy silence.

He was pondering the nature of silence – what made some silences uncomfortable when others were like an old cardigan you could lounge around in for hours; why you felt the need to make conversation with people you didn't know or care about when you were perfectly content to be quiet with good friends whom you did – when Rachel said out of the blue, 'I've given up on the pony-trekking.'

Something akin to relief made Ash laugh out loud. A conversation that began like that, he could cope with. 'Well, perhaps that's a good idea. If you want to try some dangerous pursuits, perhaps you should start with something a bit less ambitious than an animal that's lethal at both ends and untenable in the middle.'

'A rocking horse, maybe.' She smiled.

'I don't know,' Ash said doubtfully, 'Victorian children used to break their fingers under errant rockers all the time. I don't think your mother would be happy with a rocking horse.'

'No.' The girl gave it some thought. 'I could start with a skateboard with the wheels taken off; move up to rubber-soled skis; and finally graduate to scuba-diving in a paddling pool.'

'How deep a paddling pool?'

Rachel looked pensive. 'How about scuba-diving on a wet pavement?'

They chuckled together in a way that was almost like being with Hazel. The stupid jokes. The precious, inconsequential exchange of random thoughts.

As if she'd read his mind, Rachel said, 'I thought Hazel might come too.'

'She's busy,' said Ash, realising as he said it that he was admitting he'd asked her, and wondering if it mattered. 'She's got a transfer into CID, starting today.'

'A promotion?'

'I'm not sure,' he said honestly. 'I know it's something she wanted.'

There was a pause. Then Rachel said, 'I'm glad. She works hard.'

'She *does* work hard,' agreed Ash. 'She doesn't always work wisely.' As soon as the words were out he felt a little disloyal.

'She slapped my mother's face,' said Rachel.

'I heard.'

'She deserved promotion for that alone.' There was a lengthy pause. Then Rachel said diffidently, 'Can I ask you something?'

'Of course.' It was what people always said, what convention required them to say. It didn't mean he would answer. It *did* mean he'd probably waived the right to be offended by whatever came next.

'I can't figure it out between you and Hazel. Are you a couple? You behave like a couple, only maybe not quite.'

Perhaps it was a little impertinent; and Ash could have refused to answer, although he was afraid that would be taken as an answer, and not necessarily the correct one. Somehow he felt that making a mystery of it would be unfair to Hazel – would suggest there was something surreptitious about it. 'No, we're not a couple. Hazel is a very dear friend of mine, but that's all. I'm married – I thought you knew that. Anyway, I'm far too old for Hazel. When she's ready to settle down, it'll be with a doctor or a lawyer of her own age, not a second-hand bookseller who remembers the Berlin Wall coming down.'

Rachel gave him an uncomprehending look that made him feel even more ancient than usual. Then she said in a low voice, 'Age isn't everything. If people care about one another, I don't think an age gap ought to matter.'

'A fourteen-year age gap?'

'Whatever,' Rachel said stubbornly.

Ash thought for a moment. 'When I was seventeen, I was so sick of people telling me I'd understand things better when I was older. I understood things perfectly well. I understood that the people who said things like that were stupid and narrow-minded and knew nothing about the really important things in life.'

Rachel waited politely, but eventually she had to prompt him. 'And?'

'Ten years later, it amazed me how much those stupid, narrow-minded people had learned. It turned out they were right: I *did* understand things better. It turned out that all the things I thought didn't matter actually did; and lots of the things I thought *did* matter, didn't matter much at all. It's called growing up. Even without trying very hard, you pack a lot of experience into ten years, and it colours how you see the world. That's not to say that I made bad decisions at seventeen. I didn't. I made age-appropriate decisions. But this long after, I'm still unpicking some of them in order to move on with my life as an adult.'

The girl looked at him askance. 'You were a teenage rebel?'

Ash sighed. 'Actually, no. I was about as stuffy as it's possible to be when you're seventeen. I didn't like beer, I didn't like sports or fast cars, I was terrified of girls, and I quite fancied being an accountant.'

Rachel laughed. 'All right, give me the benefit of your great age and experience.'

'When you're seventeen, you think it doesn't matter what other people think. You think that right is more powerful than might, that love conquers all, and that sincerity is a valid substitute for common sense. What you learn in the next ten years is that lots of things which are not wrong in themselves are still capable of making your life, or the lives of those around you, more difficult than they need to be. Sometimes, what you want is important enough to know that and do it anyway. But usually it isn't.'

'And this relates to pony-trekking, how?'

Ash blinked. He thought they'd moved on from there. 'Pony-trekking? Not at all. To hitching your wagon to someone old enough to be carrying baggage, quite a bit. Choosing a partner is always a gamble. My mother used to say that marriage meant having someone to share the problems you wouldn't have had if you'd stayed single. You don't need to make it riskier still by choosing someone you have nothing in common with. Not on a whim, or to startle your friends and upset your family, or because you're bored or think you're running out of options. It's the surest way yet discovered of making two people miserable.'

'What if you're in love?' asked Rachel, barely audibly.

Ash snorted. 'Hazel isn't in love with me!'

'Hypothetically speaking.'

He frowned. The conversation was going places that were not only personal but borderline inappropriate. He wondered if he should choke it off right there. What stopped him was the knowledge that this wasn't just a teenage girl with hormones fizzing in her blood. This was a teenage girl who was still trying to process what had happened to her, and trusted him enough to seek his help.

So he didn't signal his disapproval with a sniff, or pointedly change the subject. He thought for a minute longer before attempting an answer. 'You're not really asking the right man. I didn't make a conspicuous success of the only relationship I was ever in. And we had everything going for us. I thought we were forever, and I was wrong.'

'But lots of relationships *are* forever,' insisted Rachel in a low voice. 'Including some that start off with the odds stacked against them.'

Ash flicked her a smile. 'You're right, of course. There are lots of ways of being happy in this world. All you have to do is find someone who can be happy in the same way you can.'

Ahead of them, the van slowed and turned between crumbling gateposts into a drive that had seen a lot of cows since it last saw a load of gravel.

'I think we're here,' said Ash.

TWENTY

Pru Somers' hands, long-fingered like her daughter's, flew to her face. Above them her eyes flared wide with horror. 'What? You really *did* check up on my story? Oh no! Then I am undone. I haven't a leg left to stand on. Arrest me now, Chief Inspector, I'm ready to confess.'

Dave Gorman regarded her woodenly. He'd heard a lot of confessions in his time, to everything from shoplifting to murder, but he'd never heard *anybody* say 'I am undone' before. Any moment now she was going to add, 'You've got me bang to rights . . .'

'I can't keep up this pretence any longer,' moaned Pru, 'I'll tell you everything. You've got me bang to rights.'

Mr Willis of Willis, Willis & Peabody was also staring at her, silently appalled. Nothing in his previous dealings with the manager of The King's Head had prepared him for this abject and most unwise collapse. Already he was mentally striking out all the possible defences that his client had just scuppered.

Gorman said nothing. It had been his experience that when things made no sense, someone was pulling his chain. He was waiting to see what Pru Somers would say next.

And indeed, after a long moment, her eyes lost the stretched look of shock and her quivering lips pursed on a small crimson smile. 'Oh wait,' she said, much more normally, 'maybe you haven't. Maybe there's been a little misunderstanding. Maybe my secretary was telling the literal truth, and I did leave the office before she did – but maybe, just maybe, if you'd stretched your ingenuity a little further and asked some of the evening staff, *they'd* have told you that I returned to the office at about six thirty and worked on until finally leaving for home sometime after eight.'

Still Gorman betrayed no emotion. 'And if they did tell us that, how would you explain it?'

'Let me think.' The woman was positively enjoying herself now. 'I might have fancied a wander round the shops, but there aren't many shops in Westbroke and it would have taken too long to head into Norbold or Coventry and then go back to the hotel. Besides, a proper alibi should be a matter of record or verifiable by some disinterested party. A dentist's appointment, for instance.'

They regarded one another across the Formica table-top, the detective giving little outward sign of the disappointment that lay like a rock in his belly, the suspect making no attempt to disguise her satisfaction.

'You were at the dentist's?' said Gorman.

'Miss Roy, in Wittering,' said Pru. 'Nothing grim, just a routine check-up – I made the appointment six months earlier. For five forty-five, but she was running a little late and it was six before I got in. I got out around six twenty and went back to The King's Head to finish some projections I was working on. My secretary had indeed left the office by then.'

'Miss Roy will be able to confirm this, of course,' said Gorman, deadpan.

'Of course. Miss Roy, her nurse, her receptionist, *my* receptionist, the bar staff . . . oh, lots of people, Chief Inspector. As many as you could possibly hope for.'

Gorman let the silence return until he was sure he wasn't going to shout. 'You could have told me this before.'

Her head came up coolly. 'It wasn't remotely relevant, *before*. That I saw my dentist a couple of hours before my partner was murdered, in a village four miles away? How could I *possibly* have been expected to know you'd want to hear about that?'

DI Gorman stood up, carefully, so as not to bang the chair. 'Excuse me.' He told the tape he was leaving the room.

DS Presley was waiting outside. Gorman said through gritted teeth, 'Get me Hazel on the phone, *right now*.' He still wasn't shouting. It might have been less alarming if he had been.

'I take it we believe her,' said Presley. He'd been observing through the one-way glass.

'Of course we bloody believe her,' snarled Gorman. 'Nobody makes up a story that easy to disprove!'

'So . . .' The detective sergeant was trying to do sums in his head and dial Hazel's number at the same time. 'Does that mean she couldn't have been there when Phillips was killed?'

'If people saw her leave Westbroke after eight, then yes, she's pretty well off the hook for braining Gethin Phillips in Whitley Vale at around ten past. That's a fast car she drives. It isn't a time machine.'

The house clearance proceeded apace for approximately forty minutes. Rachel boxed up books, Venables & Son loaded furniture, and Ash tried to be in two places at once, helping with the heavy lifting *and* making sure Rachel took care of her hands.

Then Godzilla, having manoeuvred a massive secretaire downstairs almost single-handed and entirely without incident, twisted awkwardly in reaching for a reading lamp and let out a groan of agony. The men on either side of him stopped what they were doing and looked at him in concern.

'Are you all right?' asked his father.

Godzilla shook his head. 'No.'

'Back?'

'Knee . . .'

'Not that damn cruciate again?'

Godzilla nodded. His eyes were squeezed shut, tears leaking out between the lashes.

'Well, that's us stymied for the day,' Venables told Ash. 'I'll have to run him in to A&E and get it strapped up.'

'I take it he's done it before?' said Ash. Godzilla nodded wordlessly. 'Shifting furniture?'

'Bouncy castle,' grunted Robin Venables, rolling his eyes.

He left Ash the keys of the house so he could finish packing the books. It only took another half-hour. By dropping the back seats, Ash managed to squeeze four of the big cardboard cartons into the rear of the Volvo; there was nothing he could do about the other three, except leave them lined up in the hall for when Venables should return with his van. It was a little past midday.

If Hazel had been there he'd have taken them for lunch at some pleasant local hostelry as thanks for the morning's work.

But he was wary of turning up alone with a teenage girl. He thought it might invite misunderstandings, and no one with Gabriel Ash's history could afford misunderstandings.

He was still looking for a tea-room – somewhere nice enough to take Rachel but not too smart for people who'd spent the morning clearing the dust of ages off bookshelves – when the girl spotted the sign tacked to a roadside tree. She turned a luminous face to him. 'Can we? I haven't been to a funfair since I was a little girl.'

Had he been alone, it would never in a hundred years have occurred to Ash to take the side-road indicated. Crowds, noise and organised jollity held no appeal for him. His pleasures had always been quiet ones, usually bookish and often solitary; they had hardly ever involved balloons and piped music. But Rachel's expression was more animated than he had ever seen it. The simple childish longing that had displaced the habitual unhappiness touched his heart, and he could no more have disappointed her than he could have refused his sons.

As funfairs go, it was a modest affair: a couple of carousels, a red and white helter-skelter, a witch's hat that whirled its shrieking passengers almost as high into the air as the top of a double-decker bus, a swinging boat that soared and plunged, a number of hoopla and shooting stalls. Rachel bought five rings and almost captured a genuine leopard-print plastic handbag. She pressed Ash to try the shooting gallery, and he won an inexplicably purple teddy bear which he passed on to her as soon as he decently could.

Her pleasure in the thing was almost as odd as its colour. 'You've done this before,' she said, hugging it.

'Beginner's luck,' said Ash.

There was also a burger van, which solved the problem of lunch. He bought burgers and drinks – cola for her, a cardboard cup of stewed tea for himself – and they found some straw bales behind the helter-skelter where they could sit and eat.

'Thank you for your help this morning,' Ash said formally.

Rachel smiled over her burger. 'I enjoyed it. Getting out of the house, doing something useful. It was a good day. The best since . . .' Her gaze dipped abruptly. 'You know.'

He nodded. 'How are you feeling now, Rachel? Any . . .

steadier?' He wasn't sure it was the right word but couldn't find a better.

The girl freed a hand and rocked it. 'Some days are better than others. Which is a kind of progress. To start with, all of them were pretty unbearable.'

'It's only to be expected,' said Ash. 'You won't get past this in a hurry. But you will get past it.'

She gave a helpless little shrug. 'People keep telling us that. A week ago I thought they were lying. Now, it seems just possible they know what they're talking about.'

Ash remembered that: being told that one day he'd be able to look back on the wreckage of his old life from the vantage of his new one, and not believing it. 'The primary drive of all living things is to find a way to go on living.'

'Right now,' said Rachel softly, 'it feels like we're going through the motions of living – moving around and eating and talking just because it's hard to break the habit. The way a chicken goes flapping round the yard after you've cut its head off. It's dead, but it hasn't realised it yet.'

'Do you and your mother talk about what happened?'

Rachel gave him an astonished glance. 'Good grief, no! We couldn't go on living together if we did. She blames me for Gethin's death. She hasn't exactly said so, but she does. She shows it every day. How can you talk with someone who thinks that?'

'Sometime,' Ash said patiently, 'you're going to have to find a way. Or you'll lose one another forever. And you'll both regret that for the rest of your lives. Have you given any more thought to talking things through with a therapist?'

Rachel shook her head. 'Mum won't. Not now, not ever – I know that. I might, at some point, but I wouldn't want to go alone.'

'Alone is how it works,' said Ash. 'You and the therapist, no distractions, nothing to get in the way. It's not something to be frightened of, Rachel. There are no trappings, no rituals – it's just two people talking. Like talking your worries over with your best friend, if your best friend was clever enough to understand what you were going through and help you to find the way out.'

'Do you still see your therapist?' she asked, watching his face for his reaction.

'Occasionally,' he admitted. 'If I feel things are getting on top of me, that I'm not coping as well as I should be. Mostly, it's just nice knowing there *is* somewhere I can get a bit of insight if I'm feeling low. Most of the time, knowing she's there is enough – I don't actually have to go and see her.'

'Is she – I don't know – sympathetic, your therapist?'

Ash laughed out loud. 'Laura? Not a bit. She's really quite spiky. Doesn't take a lot of nonsense; doesn't take a lot of prisoners. But she treads a fine line between understanding what's going on in my head and prodding me to pick myself up and move on to a better place. Carrot and stick. I don't know if that's how she is with all her clients. I know it worked for me.'

'Yes?' Rachel didn't sound convinced.

Ash hesitated, unsure how far he should push her. 'Is there someone else you talk to? Grandparents, cousins, friends? Everyone needs someone.'

She didn't answer directly. 'What about you? Who do you talk to? That you don't pay to listen.'

Again there was that slight jarring note, as if more had passed between them than Ash was aware of. It was the sort of thing Hazel might have said, not a girl young enough to be his daughter who was little more than a casual acquaintance. Again he put it down to fall-out from her ongoing battle with her demons.

'Hazel,' he said immediately. 'She's the one whose door is always open. The one who'll always listen, even when she has more important things to do; who'll always take my side, even when I'm wrong; who'll *tell* me that I'm wrong, but have my back anyway. She's the very best of friends. Not everyone can find a friend that good, but perhaps everyone should look for one.'

Rachel had gone quiet again. Ash finished his burger. His tea had gone cold.

The small trophies – Divisional Team Target-Shooting (2nd place), the Meadowvale Pot White snooker cup – rattled on top of the CID bookshelf for six and a half minutes. In the

Radio Room beneath DCI Gorman's office, the Queen's portrait acquired a rakish angle on the vibrating wall. Then silence fell.

A minute after that, Hazel Best emerged onto the upstairs corridor, white-faced and visibly trembling, and closed Gorman's door carefully behind her.

No one said anything. There was nothing anyone could say that wouldn't make matters worse. She went down the stairs cautiously, feeling her way as if she didn't trust her footing, left Meadowvale Police Station by the back door and went to her car.

But she didn't go home. She drove first to the canal basin, and sat blindly looking at the water until the palpitations stopped and she was able to review events with at least a semblance of calm.

The exercise brought her no comfort, however. Now the thrill of the chase had subsided, she could see with brutal clarity how unconscionably stupid she had been. *Of course* she should have cross-checked what Pru Somers' secretary had told her. There could be any number of reasons why it should not be relied on, from honest mistake to downright malice. And it was a big hotel: *dozens* of people worked there, dozens more would have been within sight of the car park or lobby at the relevant times. When Hazel obeyed Gorman's instructions to go back and check, she immediately found two people who had seen the manager return to her office at around six thirty, and three who had seen her leave again around ten past eight.

If she'd asked first, instead of leaping on the secretary's accurate but still misleading account as the missing link in the chain of evidence which would solve a murder case and earn her plaudits wherever detectives met, Hazel would not have put her DCI in the toe-curling position of quizzing the dead man's partner about a crime she could not possibly have committed. *Of course* Dave Gorman was furious with her. She'd behaved like an excitable child playing 'Cluedo' instead of a professional police officer. She was ashamed of her performance, ashamed of herself.

At length, feeling steadier but no happier, she started the car again. But she still didn't go home. She drove to Rambles With Books; and then, finding the shop closed, to Highfield Road.

There was no sign of Ash's car, not in the drive and not in the street outside. She even checked the garage, although it had hardly been used for its intended purpose since Ash started driving again, and now most of the available space was taken up by a ping-pong table. She didn't expect to find the Volvo there, and she didn't.

She looked round to see the white lurcher watching from the kitchen steps. Absurdly, Hazel felt the need to explain herself. 'Gabriel not home yet, then?' She checked her watch and frowned. It was after four. He'd expected to be finished in time for a late lunch.

Rachel had gone with him, Hazel remembered, so he'd have come home via the Somerses' house to drop her off. Probably she'd asked him inside, and he'd been too slow to invent an excuse. He was a perennially ineffectual liar. Rachel would have made coffee, possibly something to eat. It was still hard to see why, three hours later, he hadn't yet made it home.

Not that he had any particular reason to hurry. Knowing nothing of her blunder, he couldn't know Hazel was looking for him. She didn't make a habit of crying on anyone's shoulder, even Ash's; but oh, the comfort of friends in the bitter times. If he'd known she needed him, he'd have been here, no matter who or what he had to leave. She thought about phoning him, had his number up on her screen before second thoughts stopped her. He might still have Rachel with him – perhaps they'd gone elsewhere in search of new stock – which would inhibit their conversation. Hazel was desperate to talk to him, but the phone wasn't how she wanted to do it. Another hour and he'd be home. She'd rather wait than try to explain what had happened over the phone.

She reached over the garden gate, lifted the latch and walked round the back of the house. There was a bench on the patio: Hazel lowered herself onto it. Perhaps by the time Ash got here she'd have figured out a way of telling him how she'd shot down the chandelier in the Last Chance Saloon.

After a minute Patience climbed up on the bench and lay down beside her, her long head on Hazel's knee. Hazel stroked her ears absently. So they waited.

TWENTY-ONE

'Maybe it's time we moved,' said Ash, gathering the debris of their meal and looking for a bin.

'Do we have to?' Rachel's voice was small; she stayed where she was on the straw bales.

'Your mother will be worried.'

'She's probably at work.'

Ash thought he understood. 'If you don't want to be in the house alone, I could drop you off at a friend's . . .?'

'I don't have any friends!' she cried in an angry rush. 'Everyone I know plays the piano, and they're not friends, they're the competition.'

Ash was out of his depth. 'So what do you want to do?'

'What do I want?' she demanded, eyes flaring. 'I want the last three weeks not to have happened! I want Gethin to be alive again. I want my mother not to hate me. I want somebody, just one person on this whole damn planet, to value me for something other than my fingertips!'

Ash wanted to fold his arms around her, knew he shouldn't. 'I'm sure that's not true. About your mother. We're not all perfect parents. I'm not, and perhaps she isn't either. Perhaps she has allowed herself to focus too much on your career. She thinks she's doing what's best for you. How can you think she doesn't love you?'

'I've seen happy families,' Rachel said to her kneecaps. 'They talk about things that don't matter. They laugh together. They don't set a price on everything.'

'A price?'

She parodied an adult's voice. '"Of course I love you, dear. Just win this little festival for me. Win the Leeds Piano Competition and I'll love you forever."'

Ash was pretty sure Pru Somers had never said anything so crass. But he could imagine how what she *had* said might have sounded uncomfortably like it.

'Remember this a few years from now, when you're a parent,' he suggested. 'It'll give you a laugh when the boot's on the other foot. I'll let you into a secret: parents get it wrong all the time. We push too hard, or we don't push hard enough. Whichever we do, we're pretty sure we should be doing the opposite. We're convinced other parents have a much better grip on the job, and can't believe our inadequacies. We think they get together in the bar of the Better Parents Club in order to poke fun at us.

'Like most jobs, some people are naturals and some have to work at it. I had to learn from the ground up – even the basics, even stuff you'd think *anyone* would know. I mean, how hard can it be? We've all been children, we should know how child-rearing works. Am I as good a father as I want to be? No, of course I'm not. Am I as good as most fathers? I don't know, but possibly not. I know I try hard. I know I love my children, and I think they love me, at least most of the time. And I have to hope that's enough.'

Rachel went to say something, but Ash wasn't done. 'The families you've seen and envied, the ones who seem to find it easy – I think maybe they're the minority. And maybe even they have their problems, they just don't air them when anyone is looking.

'Can I tell you three things I'm pretty sure of? One, that your mother *does* love you. Two, that she's proud of you. And three, that she wishes she was better at showing how much. Your mother's a strong woman, determined and successful. The traits that make her a successful businesswoman don't lend themselves to knitting mittens and baking birthday cakes and making Christmas cards at the kitchen table. That doesn't make her a better mother, or a worse one, just different. So maybe she doesn't do everything right. Appreciate her for what she *does* do better than just about anyone else.'

Ash wasn't much given to making speeches. He'd surprised himself with both the length and the vehemence of this one. It was, of course, a subject close to his heart; but he wasn't accustomed to revealing the contents of his heart, except sometimes to Hazel.

Rachel listened attentively, as if she was absorbing at least some of what he'd said. Then she said softly, 'You're a good man, Gabriel Ash. Your sons are lucky to have you.'

Brains work in peculiar ways. They don't take the shortest route from point A to point B. They take the scenic route. They visit a local beauty spot, and stop for a cream tea, and drop in to see Aunty Mavis and admire her petunias before getting back on the road and ending up at point B just as the pubs are closing. Because everything on a cellular level happens very fast, it isn't always apparent to the owner of the brain that this is how it works. Sometimes the only clue is the odd connections that we make. The smell of candyfloss that you find unsettling long after you've forgotten the first love you shared it with. The song that fills you with trepidation, though you never even noticed the car radio playing as the other car jumped the red light.

And maybe it was because she was already upset, and maybe it was because Ash wasn't there to hear why, and maybe it was because it was a summer's afternoon so she was waiting in his back garden instead of using the spare key whose location she and probably most of Highfield Road were familiar with . . .

. . . But what Hazel found herself thinking about was back doors. Patience sitting on the step at Ash's back door. Rachel Somers' cat waiting at the back door when Ash took the shaken girl home. How did she know that when she hadn't been there? Oh yes, it was in the witness statements, Ash's and Rachel's both. As if it mattered. As if a hungry cat had anything to say about a murder . . .

Two seconds later, Hazel was on her way back to her car. And she wasn't walking, she was running.

Arriving back at Meadowvale, she checked the statements first, in case she'd remembered wrong, but she hadn't. Then she checked the list of items recovered from Highfield Spinney. The interesting thing about that was what should have been listed and wasn't.

She raced upstairs, taking the steps two at a time. DCI Gorman didn't want to see her. He was still too angry. Hazel gave him no choice. She pushed his door open and shouldered her way inside. 'Sack me tomorrow. But right now you need to listen to me.'

He could have thrown her out unheard. He could even, thanks to his new status, have had other people throw her out. The problem was, he probably *did* need to listen to her. Hazel Best didn't have an exemplary record of being right about things, but she did tend to be right most often when everyone else thought she was wrong. Gorman gritted his teeth, and reminded himself that he could indeed sack her tomorrow, then nodded tersely to a chair and went to close his door.

There was an urgent whine and he looked down. 'What's that dog doing here?'

Hazel almost said, 'What dog?' She gazed at Patience for a moment as if she'd never seen her before. 'Oh – I was at Gabriel's. She must have come with me.'

'You didn't notice? You had a damn great dog in your car, and you didn't notice?'

'I was thinking about cats.'

He made a noise in his throat that was half a sigh and half a growl. 'Go on, then. *What* were you thinking about cats?'

'Gabriel said Rachel's cat was on the doorstep when he took Rachel home after the attack. Rachel mentioned it as well. It must have been pretty keen to get inside for them to have noticed it at such a time.'

'I saw it too,' said Gorman. 'So? It's a cat. It's what cats do.'

'It's what cats do when they want feeding,' said Hazel. 'All that weaving round your legs and tripping you up. The moment the food's gone, they go back to being selfish little bastards who'd pretend not to know you if you met in the street.'

That's right, Patience said smugly, unheard.

'So?'

Hazel sucked in a deep breath and took a moment to organise her evidence. 'Rachel went into the spinney with the cat's dinner in a bowl. Then somebody jumped her. That's what we've been told. But if that's what happened, she'd have dropped the bowl, and the cat would have polished off the contents while first Rachel and then Gethin Phillips were fighting with her attacker. So what was it doing on the back step half an hour later? Rachel says that's the only way she can get it in at night, by coaxing it in with food. And the guys searching the wood should have found the empty bowl. I can't see the murderer gathering up the cat's used crockery, can you?'

It was absurd. Dave Gorman knew it was absurd. Cats? Feed bowls? The resolution of major crimes did not hang on such things! Except that, actually, sometimes it did. Sometimes it was what the dog *didn't* do in the night. It was the tiny, trivial piece that didn't fit; that couldn't be made to fit, whatever angle you studied it from.

If Rachel had gone into the spinney to bring her cat in, the bowl should have been found in the undergrowth. She never returned to the house, fled through the spinney until she stumbled into Ash. Phillips never returned to the house either. The next people into the little wood were the police, and then it was a crime scene and nothing was moved without being logged. If Rachel had told the truth, the cat would have eaten its dinner and disappeared back into the spinney, prowling for naïve young birds not long out of their nests. It would not have been waiting on the doorstep, demanding to be fed.

Gorman stared at Hazel as if accusing her of something. Then he picked up his phone.

It was a brief conversation, but memorable in its way.

'Are you at home?'

The answer must have been yes.

'Don't even wonder why I want to know. Just tell me where the cat's bowl is.'

The answer may have been unprintable.

'Humour me. Go and look.'

Another brief response.

'Is it the same bowl? The one you've always fed it from?'

A one-word answer.

'Thank you.' He rang off.

He looked at Hazel again. 'The cat's bowl is under the sink, where it's always kept. It's the same bowl they've used for as long as they've had the cat.'

Hazel was nodding. 'Rachel lied.'

* * *

Rachel was staring at the toes of her trainers again, just visible past her thin knees. She mumbled, 'I want to tell you something. Can I tell you something?'

'Of course you can,' said Ash.

'You won't hate me?'

'I don't imagine so.' He smiled. 'I've managed not to hate much worse people than you.'

'I lied,' she whispered.

'Did you? What about?'

'About Gethin. He was a good man too. He didn't attack me. I don't know why I let people think he had. Hazel thought it explained some stuff, and I couldn't prove she was wrong, and somehow it seemed easier to go along with it than argue. But I should have stood up for him. Gethin would never have hurt me. Never.'

Ash was trying to remember exactly what she had said. 'Hazel has a habit of dragging people along in her wake. But you didn't say that it was him, did you, only that it could have been.'

'I let people think that was what I believed.' Her voice was a stubborn whine. 'And I didn't, and I should have said so. All the time I knew him he was kind to me, and I shouldn't have let anyone think differently.'

Ash appreciated her candour. 'The important thing now is to set the record straight. Chief Inspector Gorman will understand. People who've been through traumatic events get confused. That's why policemen keep asking the same questions, even after they've been answered – because sometimes the passage of a little time helps people remember more clearly. He won't think you were lying, only that you were a bit confused. He'll be pleased you were honest enough to admit it. Shall I call him?'

He began searching his pockets for his mobile phone. At some level he believed it was called a mobile because it wouldn't stay where he put it but wandered off in search of other, more interesting pockets.

Rachel stayed him with a light hand on his arm. 'Not yet. Please. I'm not ready to talk to him just yet.'

'We need to bring him up to date,' said Ash, aiming for the

sweet spot between persuasion and pressure. 'If you're right and it wasn't Mr Phillips who attacked you, the police need to be looking for someone else.'

'I know. I *will* talk to him. Just . . . It was hard enough saying it to you. Let me get my breath back before I have to say it to the police.'

After a moment Ash nodded. Nearly three weeks on, he couldn't see how a few minutes, or even a few hours, could matter.

TWENTY-TWO

'Why would anyone lie about feeding their cat?' demanded Hazel. 'Whether she'd fed it or she hadn't, why lie about it?'

Dave Gorman had to remind himself that lies, and the reasons for them, and the people that tell them, were not her stock-in-trade in the way that they were his. 'She wasn't lying about feeding the cat,' he explained with a kind of heavy patience. 'She was lying about why she went into the spinney. She didn't want us to know the actual reason.'

'Which is?'

'I don't know,' he growled. 'But I'm going to ask her.'

He had Rachel's number in the file on his desk. But the call went straight to voicemail, and he didn't want to leave a message. He raised an eyebrow at Hazel. 'Any idea where she might be?'

Hazel's eyes widened. 'Actually, yes. She's with Gabriel. At least, she was – she was helping him pick up some books at a house clearance. Shall I call him?'

Gorman nodded. 'Don't say anything to alarm her.'

She gave him a worried look. She wanted to ask what he was thinking – if he was treating Rachel as a suspect because he suspected her of something, and if so, what – but recognised that she'd barely repaid him for her earlier gaffe and shouldn't start presuming on their friendship again just yet. She rang Ash's number. He didn't answer; nor did it go to voicemail, but that didn't surprise her. He hated voicemail, expected people to call back later.

'No reply,' she said.

'Were they going far?'

'I don't think so. He expected to be finished around lunchtime, maybe a bit afterwards.'

Gorman glanced at his watch. 'It's gone four. Try the shop.'

Hazel phoned Rambles With Books but the result was the

same. 'Well, wherever they are, presumably they're there together. That's all right. Isn't it?'

Gorman drove. Hazel climbed in beside him. After a moment, with narrowed eyes, he opened the rear door for Patience. She sat on the leather seat, gazing round complacently, like the Queen Mother being driven up the home straight at Ascot.

Pru Somers met them at her front door, her face lined with tiredness and exasperation. 'In the name of all that's holy, Chief Inspector Gorman, whatever do you want now?'

'Is Rachel here?'

'No.'

'Do you know where she is?'

'No, I don't. I know where she *should* be. She should be here. She said she'd be back ages ago.'

'Have you tried calling her?'

'Of course I have,' said Pru tartly. 'She isn't answering. She went book-buying with Gabriel Ash. Try his number.'

'He isn't answering either,' said Hazel. 'Did Rachel say where they were going?'

'I don't think she knew. She said he needed a hand and she was going to help him. Absurdly enough, she feels responsible for what happened to his shop.' Her brows drew together. 'Is there a problem? Should I be worried?'

'If she's with Ash, she'll be fine,' Gorman said stoutly. 'I'd just like one of them to confirm it.'

Hazel said, 'I'll try Robin Venables. The antique dealer, he has a shop in Windham Lane. It was his clearance.' She didn't have his number, got it off the internet.

At least Venables was answering his phone. He was still at Norbold General, waiting while Godzilla had his knee immobilised.

He gave her the address and, possibly more helpful in view of the rural location, directions for finding it. 'But they won't still be there. A couple of hours should have packed up all the books – they must have been away before one.'

'Did Gabriel say anything about going on somewhere else?'

'Not to me. I assumed he was going back to the shop. Why, gone missing, has he?' he asked jovially.

'I'm sure it's nothing to worry about,' said Hazel, hoping she was right.

By now Pru had had time to marshal her thoughts. 'Why are you looking for Rachel, Mr Gorman? I'm sure she's already told you everything she can.'

Gorman eyed her speculatively for a moment. Then he said, 'We're puzzled about why she went into the spinney that night.'

So far as he could tell, Pru was genuinely surprised. 'She went to bring the cat in. You know that.'

'I know that's what she said,' Gorman said carefully. 'I don't understand why the cat was still hungry when we all met here half an hour later.'

Pru's perfectly shaped eyebrows rocketed. 'You don't think, maybe, with everything that was going on, Rachel never got the chance to feed the damn cat?'

Hazel glanced at Gorman, got a tacit approval. 'Being attacked would certainly have made her drop the bowl. But then the cat would have helped itself and vanished back into the spinney. I can't see it bringing the bowl inside, washing it and putting it away in your kitchen cupboard, can you? The search team scouring the spinney that night and all the next day should have found it, but they didn't. We don't think Rachel went out there for the cat. So she had another reason. Can you think what it might have been?'

It was the one part of the saga that had seemed entirely uncontentious, that they'd all taken at face value. The possibility that it might have been untrue hadn't occurred to anyone at Meadowvale in the course of nineteen days' investigation, and seemed not to have occurred to Pru Somers either. Hazel watched bewilderment chase irritation chase affront across the pale severity of her face.

When she managed to muster some words, they were – typically – an accusation. 'Are you telling me you've been working on a mistaken premise for two and a half weeks?'

Gorman breathed heavily, hanging onto his patience by a thread.

Hazel said quietly, 'What Rachel told us, which seemed to make perfect sense at the start, doesn't make sense any more. There has to be more to it – something she wants us not to know. Mrs Somers' – too much had passed between them to continue with first names – 'if you have any idea what that might be, please tell us. We need to understand what happened or we can't be sure Rachel is safe.'

'You really are shooting in the dark, aren't you?' Pru's tone was passing through icy to the red-hot anger on the other side. 'You've no more idea what happened to Gethin than you had when you stumbled over his body. You told me he tried to rape my daughter. You told me *that* was the only thing that made sense! I told you it wasn't true – everyone who knew him told you the same thing – except for Rachel. Poor, traumatised little Rachel. And it wasn't her idea in the first place.

'And you had the gall to feel sorry for me! Don't deny it, I saw the way you looked at me. It's always the little woman who's the last to know, isn't it? Well, actually, no. Gethin Phillips was a good man. I don't know who killed him, or why. But I have *always* known that it wasn't because he couldn't keep his hands off my daughter.'

She rounded fiercely on Hazel. 'Now she's gone off with your idiot friend, and you don't know where they are and neither of them is answering their phone. And maybe it's time to stop worrying about poor little Rachel, and wonder what price the next man who tries to help her is going to pay.'

It was impossible not to take that as a threat. Hazel felt a chill run up her spine and raise hairs on the back of her neck. 'You blame Rachel for what happened to Gethin Phillips? But she was a victim too.'

Pru's eyes were bitter. 'My daughter has always been good at playing the victim, Constable Best.'

Gorman wanted to shake her. He didn't know if she knew what had happened in Highfield Spinney or not. But he believed she could cast fresh light on these events if she wasn't so determined to fight him. 'The more pieces of this jigsaw we fit together, the less the picture looks like the one on the box. I don't think Rachel's told us the whole truth, and I don't think you have either. Why did she go into the spinney that night? And if you really don't know what happened, why are you so angry with her?'

'Because Gethin died for her, and she isn't worth it!'

There was nothing ambivalent about that; nothing maternal either. Whatever the relationship had been between Pru and Rachel before, clearly it had broken down now. Possibly irreparably: Hazel suspected that by the time a mother was driven to say that about her own child, there was no way back. Even Laura Fry might claim a prior engagement rather than tackle that one.

Hazel, for all her native kindness, was not particularly child-centred herself. She was vaguely aware of the ticking of her biological clock, had always assumed that at some point she'd start wanting children; but she was twenty-eight and the moment hadn't come yet, and she was open to the possibility that it never would.

In spite of which, she found herself shocked speechless by Pru Somers' outburst. Most of the mothers she dealt with continued to believe in the innocence of their offspring, even in the face of CCTV evidence and sworn confessions. The depths of Pru's bitterness seemed inexplicable.

And then the shadow of a possibility, the merest hint of an explanation, occurred to her. 'Tell us about Rachel and Gethin.'

Pru's jaw was clenched. 'What about them?'

'How did they get on? It can be a difficult relationship, parenting someone else's children. Did they make a reasonable go of it? Or were there arguments?'

'I'm sure we've talked about this before,' Pru said coldly.

'Let's talk about it again,' rumbled Gorman. He wasn't sure where Hazel was headed, but there was something in her expression that said *she* knew.

Pru shrugged. 'Gethin was good at defusing arguments. He always wanted to make Rachel feel valued.' She said it as if it had been an eccentricity of his.

'He treated her as his daughter?'

She shook her head. 'He treated her as *my* daughter. Fusion families create some tricky problems for everyone, Mr Gorman, but particularly for the new man in a household. He's taking on a father's responsibilities without having a father's rights. Should he discipline the children? If he leaves that to their mother, will she feel he isn't supporting her? Will the children resent him? What about the wider family? It's a minefield.'

Now she was talking about the man she had loved, she was no longer rationing her words. Gorman let her talk. It hardly mattered if what she said was relevant: the main thing was breaking down that protective shell, that iron restraint.

'Gethin had no children of his own but he was a natural. He used to say that just because he and I wanted to be together, that didn't mean Rachel had to like it. She didn't get a veto, but she couldn't be collateral damage either. He was kind, and fair, and immensely patient with her. He wanted her to feel that she wasn't the worm in the apple when we got together, she was the icing on the cake.'

'That *was* kind,' agreed Hazel. 'How did Rachel respond?'

'Slowly. But Gethin didn't mind waiting. At times when I wanted to slap her, he'd say she'd come round in her own good time. And he was right.'

'She never calls him her stepfather.'

'That's because he wasn't.'

'I know,' said Hazel. 'But if you were a family for four years, and they were on good terms, why would she make an issue of it? Because she does. If someone refers to Mr Phillips as her stepfather, she puts them right.'

Pru shrugged. 'She always called him Gethin. We never went in for labels very much.'

DCI Gorman had found that sometimes you learn more from listening to a conversation than by interrupting with questions. Now it was time to steer it back to the area he needed to explore. 'Mr Phillips clearly thought Rachel was worth protecting. Why don't you?'

Pru had found a certain comfort in talking about her dead lover, and she wasn't quick enough to realise it was time to stop. Then too, with all her faults, as a human being and as a parent, she was a woman who took pride in being brutally honest – with herself as well as others. 'Because she's cost me so much!' she cried. 'My marriage may have been less than perfect, but the fact remains that when I had to choose between my husband's wishes and my daughter's needs, I chose Rachel. She owes me for that. And now she's cost me Gethin, and that's a loss she will never be able to make good.'

'She'd probably try, if you'd let her,' suggested Hazel.

'In a parallel universe! Rachel only cares about Rachel. She takes and takes, and never gives anything back. I know,' Pru said hotly, forestalling the obvious objection, 'that's what children do. Except that she's not a child any more, and she's still doing it. Still taking everything that's of value to me, and giving nothing back. Not even . . .' She stopped dead, colour racing into her face.

'Not even love?' hazarded Hazel softly.

The flush travelled all the way up Pru's parchment cheeks. 'All right, yes, that's what I was about to say. That's the unwritten contract, isn't it? You do everything you can for your children, even when it costs you everything you have, because you love them and they love you back. I never had that with my daughter. Most of her life, the best we've been able to manage is an armed neutrality. I made allowances because she has a remarkable talent and I believed she had to focus on it. I encouraged her to be selfish, I suppose, and maybe that was wrong. Maybe it would have been better, for both of us, if I hadn't invested quite so much in her future.

'When I was seventeen I was working nights and weekends in a pub, because I knew I wanted more than that and that was how to get it. Rachel has never had a paying job. She thinks the good things in life just turn up, gift-wrapped. She thinks she's *entitled*. Entitled to unlimited funds of other people's time and money and attention. She honestly believes the world should revolve around her. That she only has to want something and someone will sell a kidney to get it for her.'

Hazel knew they were palpably close to finding the key to what happened in Highfield Spinney. Then things that had been inexplicable until now would finally make sense. 'What does she want?'

'*Happiness*,' Pru replied immediately, pulling a face as if it was a rude word. 'Whatever will make her *happy*. Except it mustn't require any effort on her part. The idea of working for what she wants has never appealed to Rachel. It was even a nightmare getting her to do piano practice: she thought being talented should excuse her from doing the donkey-work. She bemoans the fact that she has no friends, but she won't put herself out for them. She's never had a proper boyfriend, unless you count that hairy youth who mows our lawn. She's always believed that if she sat around looking wistful, there'd be the clop of hooves on the garden path and up would ride Prince Charming on his white charger.'

'Not everyone is cut out to be half of a couple.' Hazel spoke with rather more feeling than she meant to.

'Oh, Rachel wasn't born to be a nun,' retorted Pru. 'It's just, like everything else, she wants it to be *easy*. If she had sisters, she'd be the girl who was always stealing their boyfriends because it was easier than finding her own. Since she hasn't . . .' There she stopped, so abruptly that Hazel and Gorman both stared at her.

And that was it. The thing even Pru hadn't wanted to accuse her daughter of. The unforgivable trespass. The offence that had stoked her bitterness, all the more because it was too demeaning to put into words. You could complain to your friends about your teenage daughter helping herself to your clothes, your make-up, your shoes and even your money. You couldn't utter a word about her helping herself to your partner.

Hazel said carefully, 'Pru – did Rachel fall in love with Gethin?'

'We'd better get moving,' said Ash, glancing at his watch. 'Good grief, it's gone four o'clock. Rachel, do you want your mother there when you talk to Mr Gorman? We could phone her and ask her to meet us at Meadowvale.'

Rachel glanced at her phone – she always knew exactly where it was – and put it away again. 'No signal.'

Ash resumed the search of his pockets. 'Mine may have one.'

'What network are you on?' He told her. She shook her head. 'Me too. There's no coverage here.'

He stopped patting his clothing and stood up. 'Anyway, it's time we were on our way.' He smiled. 'People will start talking about us.'

Rachel stayed where she was. 'I don't care if they do. I like it here.'

Ash looked at the peeling paint on the helter-skelter, the strings of electric bulbs that wouldn't be lit until dusk, the desultory visitors – they wouldn't amount to a crowd until later in the evening – leaving cardboard cups and chip wrappers on the scuffed grass. Even the painted faces of the gallopers looked jaded, and the taped calliope music failed to stir the heart. 'Yes?'

She was studying her knees again. 'I like being here with you.'

He knew what she wanted him to say: that he liked being with her too. A faint prickle down his spine warned him to think carefully about what he said next. He sat down again. 'Rachel, I understand that you're lonely. Seventeen is a lonely age anyway, and you've lost someone who was important to you. It's entirely understandable that you're looking for someone to fill the gap that Gethin Phillips left in your life. But I can't do that. It wouldn't be appropriate. I can't be your father-substitute.'

Now she stood up, so abruptly the purple bear went flying from her lap. Her face was hot with anger. 'Gethin was *not* my father-substitute! He was my best friend. He was the one who listened when I'd had a bad day. Not my mother: Gethin. He was the one who noticed when I got my hair done, when I had new clothes. Who took me out for a meal on my birthday. Who said I could tell him anything. He said he would always listen and never judge.'

'He sounds like a very kind man,' Ash said. 'I wish I'd known him.'

'Kind?' Rachel rolled the word round her mouth, tasting it. 'Yes, I suppose he was kind. I mean, I know that – I always knew – I just . . .' Now the anger died and the sentence dried up.

Ash made a stab in the dark that was actually nothing of the sort. Rachel had done everything but say the words out loud. 'Rachel – did you think it was something else?'

She dropped back onto the straw bale as if her strings had been cut. She couldn't look at him. She reached for the purple teddy and hugged it to her chest. Her voice, when it came, was a breathy whisper. 'You see, I thought it was over between them. Gethin and my mum. I thought they were tired of one another. She's pretty snippy, my mum, and she never showed him any affection; and when she was bitching at him, sometimes he'd catch my eye and wink. And I thought it was all over, they were just staying together out of habit, or maybe because . . .' She swallowed. 'He said he'd always be there for me. I thought, maybe the reason he didn't leave was that he didn't want to leave *me*.'

Listening intently as he was, Ash found himself remembering what Laura Fry had said about cut-and-paste families. About the inhibitions that kept relatives from viewing one another as potential mates, and how they could become confused when the mix got stirred. They'd all thought Gethin Phillips might have been attracted to his partner's daughter. Not one of them had made the leap of intuition to understand that the process was a two-way street: that Rachel Somers had come to see her mother's partner as something other than a father figure.

He said softly, 'Did you ask him?'

Rachel shook her head vigorously, the dark hair dancing. 'I kept waiting for him to say something. I thought it was his job – you know, as the man. I was sure I hadn't imagined it: there were too many times when he said and did things he really didn't have to, just to make me feel good. Still, it's kind of one of the rules, isn't it, that the man makes the first move. I kept waiting.'

Ash felt a deep and sorrowful compassion for her: the love-starved child growing into a young woman without much in the way of guidance or example, aching to be valued for herself instead of her accomplishment, completely misunderstanding when a decent man offered her simple friendship. 'Until that night?' he hazarded.

She nodded, not looking at him. She was talking to the bear. 'I didn't know he was already home. His car was in the garage, and I thought I was the first one to get in. It felt nice having the house to myself, so I went into the drawing room and sprawled on the sofa with a magazine. I was half asleep. The next thing I knew – the next thing that happened . . .' Her voice tailed off.

Ash gave her time to collect her thoughts. But when she didn't pick the story up again, he said, 'You don't have to do this right now. You can wait and tell it to Mr Gorman.'

'No,' she said, flicking him a frightened look. 'I need to tell you. I want to tell you. You'll understand.'

*   *   *

'Gethin noticed it first. He was quite troubled – wasn't sure how to discourage her without hurting her feelings. I thought it was hilarious.' Even now, after all that had happened, Pru seemed in danger of loosing a peal of deeply inappropriate laughter. 'Whatever made her think *he* would be interested in *her*?'

Hazel bit her tongue. She wanted to say, You did. He treated her like a teenage girl instead of a project, and she hadn't enough experience of normal family relationships to recognise his interest as parental rather than sexual. She was used to coldness and manipulation from her mother: when she met with warmth and empathy from her mother's partner, she mistook it for something else. That wasn't her fault, and it wasn't his. It was yours.

She thought all these things, and said none of them. She might have kept her counsel even if DCI Gorman hadn't caught her eye at the critical moment, but it would have been a close-run thing.

Gorman said, 'So what happened?'

Pru bridled. 'What do you mean, what happened? Nothing happened. She trailed round after him with a mooncalf expression when she thought I wasn't looking, and Gethin tried to ignore it. I said to shoo her away like a clingy puppy, she'd soon get the message, but he didn't want to upset her. He brought colleagues' sons to the house a couple of times in the hope that she'd take a fancy to one of them, but she wasn't interested. She wanted Gethin, and she persuaded herself that there was nothing much left between him and me, that he was – or soon would be – available.

'I think that's why this' – she stroked her bump with surprising delicacy – 'came as such a shock to her. I'm not the most demonstrative of people, you may have noticed that, and she thought that because we weren't all over one another where she could see, it was the same where she couldn't.'

Gorman was trying to relate this to events in the spinney. 'Mrs Somers, how do you think Mr Phillips met his death?'

Something inside Pru Somers froze. 'Someone hit him over the head.'

'Do you know who?'

'I wasn't there.'

'Make an intelligent guess.'

She shook her head doggedly. 'That's not my job. It's yours.'

Hazel tried. 'We want to understand what happened. We're not even sure how many people were in the spinney that night. How many do you think there were?'

Pru rounded on her again. 'I know what you want me to say! But I don't have to guess. I wasn't there, I didn't see, I don't know. If you think you know who killed Gethin, I suggest you set about proving it.'

And though both of them tried a little longer, Pru Somers would not be shifted from that position. The detectives left soon afterwards.

'She knows, doesn't she?' said Hazel as they drove away.

Gorman nodded. 'Yes.'

'Has she known all along, do you think?'

The DCI shook his head. 'I think she realised what must have happened when we could find no indication of a third party in the wood. We thought that meant Phillips was the aggressor. She immediately thought it was Rachel.'

Hazel was still struggling with the idea. 'Is this really the best we can come up with? That a frail seventeen-year-old girl beat a man's head in with a fallen branch, because she wanted him to love her and he couldn't?'

Gorman shrugged. 'She wouldn't be the first. She won't be the last.'

'So . . . she made a pass at Phillips, he rebuffed her, she ran outside, he went after her . . .'

'He caught up with her in the spinney, tried to calm her down, but she was angry and humiliated . . .'

'And she killed him.' Suddenly Hazel went cold. 'And now she's with Gabriel.'

'She's safe enough with him,' Gorman said reassuringly.

But her eyes were hollow with anxiety. 'Dave, Rachel's got a crush on Gabriel now. She's been making all sorts of excuses to spend time with him. I told him it was nothing to worry about. But Dave, what if I was wrong and Pru was right? What if Gabriel isn't safe with Rachel?'

TWENTY-THREE

Rachel was half asleep on the sofa, a magazine across her chest, when the drawing room door opened and Gethin Phillips was standing over her. 'I didn't hear you come in,' he said.

'I didn't know you were home,' she countered.

'Have you eaten?' She shook her head. 'Shall I make us something? Your mother won't be home for a bit. She's going to the dentist, then back to the office for a couple of hours.'

Rachel thought, then shook her head. 'I'm too comfortable to move.'

'Coffee, then. I'll bring it in here.'

A couple of minutes later he was back, with two mugs and a plate of biscuits. 'Tide us over till suppertime.' He put the tray on the coffee table; and, so they could both reach it, joined Rachel on the sofa.

She thought it was deliberate. He could have put the tray at the other end of the table and reached it from the armchair.

He took a ginger snap and smiled. 'We should do this more often. Tell me about your day.'

'Nothing to tell,' she answered automatically. And then, seeing the sigh in his eyes that he kept from his lips, she added, 'All my days are pretty much the same. Tell me about yours.'

He brightened again. It never took much. It was one of the things she liked about him. Moodiness was alien to his nature. 'I'm working on a new project.'

'A cathedral?' It was, she supposed, the highest ambition architects aspired to.

'In a way, yes. Since our generation' – they weren't the same generation, but she loved him pretending they were – 'worship the car in much the same way that our ancestors worshipped God, then a multi-storey car park *is* a kind of twenty-first-century cathedral. It'll be built in the middle of the city, people will stream in and out all the time, and every time they find a parking space, they'll bless it. And since nobody wants an ugly building in the middle of their city, the corporation is confiding a lot of trust in me to make it striking and visually satisfying while keeping a thousand cars off the streets.'

She liked listening to him talk about his work. She liked the pride he took in it. She liked the lilt of his Welsh accent, and how he used words like 'confiding' in a way no one else she knew did.

She liked the warmth of his thigh against hers.

She liked having him to herself, just the two of them, in this house where they'd lived for four years but weren't usually alone together. She knew it might be a long time before the stars were positioned this favourably again. Knowing made her reckless.

She said – and her heart was in her throat – 'If you're wondering whether I feel the same way, the answer is yes.'

She didn't dare look at him. If she had, she'd have seen the bemused expression that might have warned her he wasn't sure what she was talking about, what he was agreeing to. 'Yes? Oh – good.'

She read into that what she wanted to. Now her heart gave a great bound. The words came with a rush. 'Will you tell Mum or shall I?'

Gethin went on regarding her with his friendly, faintly puzzled expression and his ready smile. 'Tell her what?'

She honestly thought he was teasing her. She made herself smile in return, though there was a tightness in her chest and an odd kind of prickling behind her eyes. 'About us. We have to tell her. We're not doing this behind her back, and I don't want to wait until she starts suspecting.'

Now Gethin's brow creased in a bewilderment that seemed entirely genuine. 'Tell her what? Rachel? I'm sorry, am I being dim here?'

She rose from the sofa in one fluid movement. Gethin stood up too, putting his mug down on the tray, confused and troubled by her reaction. Rachel felt a surge of heat – which was part anger, part embarrassment and part being seventeen – start behind her knees and work its way up her loins, her spine, her breasts, her throat and finally her cheeks, which blazed like a warning to shipping.

At that moment, when there was still just time to salvage the situation, she knew she'd made a terrible mistake. Or the intellectual part of her knew. The emotional part, which had invested so much in this dream of a future with someone who cared for her and didn't know his Bach from his Bacharach, didn't want to believe it. Insisted that it was a joke, that as soon as he saw he'd upset her, he'd stop teasing and throw his arms around her, loving, full of remorse. So she let the moment pass, and events which could have ended with no more than a bit of red-faced mumbling began to gather the momentum that would carry them inexorably towards tragedy.

She stood tall and straight before him, daring him to fall short of her expectations. 'This isn't funny any more, Gethin. Don't play games with me, I'm not a child and I won't be made fun of. We're not going to make a fool of my mother either. I know there's nothing left between you two, but she has been important to both of us and we owe it to her to be honest. She'll probably be upset, she'll certainly be angry. We can weather that. We have to: we're not starting our life together by sneaking out of the house at dead of night with suitcases tied up with string!'

He finally understood what she was saying. Because he was a good man, and a kind man, he didn't laugh incredulously, or send her to her room, or turn his back without a word and leave her shaking and alone. He tried to make things right. His eyes were full of concern, his voice low and compassionate. 'Rachel, *sidan*, there's been some mistake. Things are fine between Pru and me. I'm sorry if we've given you any reason to think otherwise. I won't say we never disagree about anything, that would be silly, but we try not to argue in front of you.'

'Argue?' she cried desperately. 'You never talk! You have nothing to say to one another.'

'But we do,' said Gethin gently. 'When it matters. We're both busy people – probably too busy, probably we should make more time for one another, and for you – and we're at an age where people have stopped making dramatic gestures, where they're comfortable taking what they have together for granted. So I suppose I can't prove to you that we're happy. All I can do is promise you that we are.'

'But – but . . .' All chance of retaining some dignity was gone now, and Rachel almost didn't care. 'I thought you wanted me!'

'Ah *cariad*,' sighed Gethin Phillips, his complacent middle-aged heart breaking for her, 'of course I want you! I never had a child before. I thought my chances of fatherhood were just about gone. And then I met Pru, and Pru brought you into my life. You've given me so much joy, Rachel. No child of my own blood could have given me more. I am deeply sorry, more sorry than I can say, if I've expressed that so badly that you thought – you believed . . .'

She couldn't bear it. She'd trusted him. She loved him, and thought he loved her. She'd thought he would make her happier than she'd ever been in her life. Now he was telling her it was an illusion? That the future she'd dared to dream was the product of an overactive imagination?

She bent in one swift fluid movement, scooped up the mug from the table in front of her and hurled it at his head. 'I am not a child!' she screamed. Then she turned and fled for the door.

The mug was both empty and cold, and bounced harmlessly off his shoulder. Gethin picked it up, and the handle came off in his hand. He blinked at the pieces, as if unsure what to do about them. Rachel's running footsteps crossed the kitchen tiles and he heard the back door. Awful indecision pinned him to his place. Should he follow her? Was she more in need of space or comfort? His heart made the choice. He couldn't let her suffer alone. Still in his slippers, he followed her through the kitchen, dropping the remains of the mug into the bin as he passed, down the back steps and into the garden.

She heard or sensed him behind her without looking round. Her cheeks were ablaze and she couldn't talk to him any more. She had slowed from a run to an angry rapid stalk, and she didn't stop when she came to the garden gate but threw it open and continued into the spinney.

Half of her hoped Gethin would stop at the gate, the other half that he would follow her into the cool dim greenness of the wood. Though the sun was still up, the light filtered by the leaf canopy was soft, broken into dappled shadows that moved with the whisper of wind through the branches. Here, in the half-light, she could face him, if he dared face her.

He caught up with her at a shambling run, slippers scuffing the leaf-litter, panting out of breath. 'Don't run away from me, Rachel! Surely we can talk about this? We've always been able to talk about anything, you and me.'

That *you and me* grated on her nerves like blackboard chalk, as if he was mocking her mistake by repeating the kind of casual intimacy which had led her to make it. She was furious with herself, but that was nothing to what she felt for him. Right now, for these few crucial moments, she hated him. 'I thought you said there was no *you and me*! I thought you said that was just silly little me letting my imagination run away with me.'

Gethin looked taken aback. 'I never said that,' he insisted. 'Oh Rachel, don't be angry with me. I'm sorry if I've managed to give you the wrong idea. I knew I could never be your father, but I wanted us to be friends. I'm sorry if I got it wrong. Can't you forgive me?'

She might have said Yes. She might have said Maybe, and events would have played out quite differently. There would have been a couple of awkward evenings at home, they might have avoided one another's company for a while, then life would have gone on pretty much as it had before.

Mortified pride swamped the common sense in her seventeen-year-old brain. Rachel spat, 'Not as long as I live!' And once more she turned away and set out resolutely into the spinney.

It may have been the approaching dusk which sealed his fate. Perhaps if this had happened an hour earlier, in full daylight, Gethin would have let her storm off into the wood, hoping that solitude would calm her. But evening was drawing in, the shadows merging between the trees. He was not at ease in nature, had always found the little wood a faintly sinister place. His instincts rebelled against letting a young girl, already distraught, disappear alone into the darkening spinney.

He reached out and took her wrist. 'Come back inside. We'll talk inside.'

'Let go of me.'

He did. 'Please come inside, Rachel. This is silly. It'll be dark in fifteen minutes, and I don't want to be groping around this wood in the dark, tripping over tree roots and wondering where the hell I left the garden gate. I'm a city boy, me – all these trees give me the creeps.'

'You'd better go, then,' she cried, 'while you can still find your way!'

He tried again. 'Don't stay out here on your own. Come inside, and I'll make some cocoa. Your mum'll be home soon.'

If he'd wanted to twist the knife in her heart, he could hardly have done better. Rachel's blood ran cold at the thought of what that meant. Explanations; recriminations; derision. The grown-ups laughing at her. She managed, 'Don't you dare tell her!'

Gethin Phillips regarded her with compassion. 'I have to, Rachel. Not because she's my partner but because she's your mother. She needs to know that we haven't been doing well enough by you, to let you get confused like this. Don't be upset, *cariad bach*. We'll talk about it, the three of us, and clear the air. Tomorrow we'll laugh about it, see if we don't.'

Humiliation swept over her. 'Don't call me that! I know what it means.'

Phillips, whose nerves were also somewhat shredded, gave a surprised laugh. 'You sounded just like your mam then!'

'I'm not little any more!' Rachel yelled; and, much as she had swept the mug off the coffee table five minutes earlier, she dipped and swept up a fallen branch dropped by a nearby beech tree. It made a ready club a metre long and thick enough to fill her hand. She brandished it at him.

Phillips eyed it coolly. 'Now, don't let's get silly, Rachel. We both know you're not going to use that. Put it down, there's a good girl, and come inside.' He turned away, looking for the path back, picking his way over the rough ground in his slippers.

A fury she could neither express nor explain rose through her, filling her belly and her lungs and her throat, born of helpless mortification and the knowledge that she'd made a fool of herself in front of the last person in the world she wanted to; knowing too that whoever laughed about it the next day, it wouldn't be her. Humiliated beyond endurance, Rachel had swung at him before she'd really formed the intention to.

Heavier than she'd expected, the branch acquired a momentum of its own. Gethin never saw it coming. Rachel watched, appalled at her own actions but somehow unable to stop, as the balk of timber turned from woodland ambience into a deadly weapon and found the fragile part of Gethin Phillips' skull, just above his right ear.

Time slowed down. Rachel saw – or believed she saw – how it kept travelling as the man's skull splintered under the impact. Then he was lurching sideways, virtually off his feet, into the trees on his other side. For a moment he seemed to regain his balance; there was time for her to realise that she'd burnt every boat available, and wonder what price she'd have to pay for her lost temper; then he folded silently, bonelessly, to the ground.

For what felt like forever, but might have been a few minutes, she stood bent over him, waiting for him to stir, to sit up. He made no movement. There was blood in his hair. 'Gethin?'

Finally she realised that he wasn't going to respond. She straightened up. Her voice quaked with fear. 'I'll – get help. I'll get help.' And as an afterthought, absurdly: 'Stay here.' She backed away from him, then turned and began to run. But she wasn't running back towards the house. She was running into the depths of the spinney.

TWENTY-FOUR

A sh continued to sit in absolute silence until he was sure that Rachel, hunched on the bale beside him, had finished speaking. When he thought he had mastery of his voice he said, 'You hit him?' She nodded miserably. 'Once?'

She risked a brief, sideways glance at him in which Ash detected just a hint of her mother's trademark indignation. 'What do you take me for? I didn't mean to hit him at all, not really. It just . . . happened.'

'Only the post mortem found two fractures, one on either side of his head.'

Now her gaze was unmistakably fierce and offended. 'Is that what you think of me? That I hit him once to knock him down and again to make sure? I hit him *once*. I didn't mean to hurt him. It was like . . . like throwing the mug at him. I thought it would bounce off his shoulder, or he'd dodge it, but it would get his *attention*! He was treating me like a child, and I'm not a child. I'm old enough to fight for what I want.'

Ash was trying to visualise the scene as it played out in the little wood. 'Is it possible that he fell against something? That, when you hit him, he cannoned off into one of the trees, and that caused the second fracture.'

She was watching him carefully, with eyes that were at the same time wary and yearning. 'Maybe. He did . . . sort of . . . bounce.'

'That makes a difference,' said Ash seriously. 'One blow delivered in anger is a very different thing to a sustained attack, even if the outcome is the same. Mr Gorman will understand that. So will the court.'

That seemed to bring home to Rachel the implications of her actions in a way that nothing before had done. It was almost as if she'd thought confessing would be the difficult part, that now someone would give her a hug and forgive her. As if that was Ash's job, and by mentioning the legal consequences he was refusing to play by the rules. She looked disappointed and upset, and then she looked afraid.

'I don't want to tell anyone else! It was hard enough telling you.'

'Rachel, you have to. A man is dead. There has to be an explanation.'

'It's too late to help Gethin,' she whined. 'But you can still help me.'

'I *will* help you,' he promised. 'As much as I can. I'll talk to Mr Gorman, and I'll talk to your mother. I'll get you legal help. You will get through this. It won't be quick and it won't be easy, but it will pass and then you'll have the rest of your life to look forward to. And I'll still be here to help you then, if you want me to. Find you somewhere to live, help you get your life back on track.'

And then he said the wrong thing. Afterwards he knew it; in the moment, it seemed the best, most reassuring thing he could say. 'The same as I would for one of my own children.'

Rachel shot to her feet, hot rage blazing in her cheeks and in her eyes. If their paper cups had been earthenware, she'd have flung one at him; if there'd been fallen branches at their feet she'd have snatched one up; if someone had left a crowbar lying around, she might have used that. As there was nothing, she went for him with her strong pianist's fingers and carefully shaped nails.

Shocked, because he'd known this girl for two and a half weeks and never suspected the fury that lurked within her, Ash reeled back, and she missed his eye and scored parallel lines down his left cheek. She bent over him, shaking with fury, spit flying in her voice. 'I am not a child! Not yours, not Gethin's. I'm not a child, and I'm sick to my stomach of everyone treating me like one. I never wanted to hurt Gethin: I loved him! And God help me, I loved you too. And he preferred my sour middle-aged mother, and you think of me as one of your stupid children!'

Her passion seemed to pin him to the straw bale in the

shadow of the helter-skelter. He raised a placatory hand. 'Rachel, don't be angry with me . . .'

But it was too late for pleading. She flung his hand aside. 'Don't you dare touch me! I never want to see you again. Don't come after me, and don't try to find me.'

'But we have to see Mr Gorman. You have to tell him . . .'

'I don't have to do anything!' she spat. 'There is nothing I need from you. I can make my own life. Leave me alone!' And with that she turned away from him and stalked back towards the fair. After a moment she began to run.

The spell that had frozen him to the bale was broken, and Ash threw down the debris of their meal and hurried after her. Even if he could have persuaded himself that getting justice for Gethin Phillips was Dave Gorman's job, not his, he didn't think she was in any state to be running off alone into the wilds of Warwickshire. 'Rachel,' he called urgently. 'Please . . .'

There was something inevitable about what happened next. His shout pierced the jangle of the taped calliope and attracted notice. Looking round, people saw a young girl running away and a middle-aged man with blood on his face running after her.

And because some decisions have to be taken instantly, instead of asking questions or trying to figure out what was going on, these concerned onlookers consulted their stock of stereotypes and jumped to the obvious conclusion. They parted to let Rachel through and closed ranks around Ash. Before he could get out a word of explanation, two of the fairground roustabouts had knocked him to the ground and a dark-haired girl with earrings the size of bangles was putting the boot in.

Though he intended returning to Meadowvale himself, Gorman took Hazel home first. They continued to sit in the car outside her front door, Hazel making no move to leave and Gorman making none to evict her.

At length she shook her fair hair in lingering disbelief. 'I still can't get my head round it. Gethin Phillips was beaten to death by a teenage pianist? Hell, Dave, are we sure there isn't another explanation?'

Gorman shrugged. 'It's always possible there's another explanation. But this is the one that fits the evidence. It's also the one Pru Somers believes, which counts for something.'

'No wonder she's been so *angry* . . .'

That was when the DCI's phone rang. All Hazel could infer, from hearing one end of the conversation, was that something had happened at a funfair in a field near Wittering. She went to get out of the car, but now Gorman caught her sleeve. 'You're going to want to come with me.'

She glanced uneasily past his shoulder. 'What about . . .?'

Gorman glowered. 'The damn dog can come too.'

It took a little while to piece together exactly what had happened. Most of the witnesses had been watching the man on the ground trying to defend himself from the steel toecaps of a young woman who looked like Minnehaha but fought like Geronimo. At the back of the aggrieved crowd, however, were a handful of people who couldn't get much of a view and so turned to see what had become of the girl he'd been chasing.

Mrs Emilia Fossett, wife of the sword-swallower, said the girl never looked back. She ran past the hoopla stall and skirted the gallopers, heading for the pirate ship. But she didn't go to the ticket-seller: she pulled herself up over the chest-high fence that kept wandering children and refugees from the beer tent from straying into the danger zone. Mrs Fossett looked away then. She knew what was going to happen, didn't want to actually see it. She thought the girl knew too. The last she saw of her, she'd come to a halt in the path of the great swinging machine and turned to face it, arms spread slightly from her sides, waiting. Mrs Fossett said she was waiting for it as if it would bring her some kind of an answer.

Fifteen-year-old Tony Purvis *did* see exactly what happened. He hadn't wanted to miss it; now he wished he had. The man in charge of the ride saw the girl at the same time he did, and dived to shut it off; but the tons of machinery produced more momentum than could be instantly quelled. The underside of the boat caught the girl on the upswing and knocked her through the safety fence, which collapsed under her.

Lucas Apsley was running the gallopers. He heard the

screams of shocked bystanders and looked up in time to see
the girl's body, still spinning from the impact, coming towards
him. There was time enough for him to stop the carousel but
it didn't occur to him that he should. He continued to stand
on the platform, turning automatically – he'd run the ride for
years – to keep the girl in sight.

He was astonished, in view of how she'd got there, to see
her sit up, nursing one arm against her chest, and then rise
to her knees and stagger to her feet. She stood there, looking
around her helplessly, and Apsley wove his way quickly
between the running horses to reach her before she should fall
down again.

'What happened then?' asked DCI Gorman.

The man gave an uneasy shrug. 'Damned if I know, sir. She
seemed to be pretty much all right, given that she'd just lost
a nutting contest with the pirate ship. She saw me coming,
and took a few steps towards me. Then she went down on her
knees and sort of . . . dived . . . at the foot of the gallopers.'

'You mean she fainted?' prompted Hazel.

'Maybe. Maybe that's what happened. At least that would
make sense. I mean, we have Health & Safety round here so
often we've taken to setting a place for them at the dinner
table. They'll tell you we take good care of our show, both
the equipment and the punters. You wouldn't think it was
possible for a human being to get a hand through the skirts
round the machinery, not by accident. I wouldn't have thought
she could do it if she was trying. And why would she be
trying, you tell me that? Anyone would have known that was
a sure-fire way to get hurt.'

He'd leapt down from the still travelling platform and,
hooking a strong hand under each of her arms, dragged her
clear. He fumbled for his handkerchief, found it none too
clean for the job it had to do, used it anyway to stem the
blood while others squealed and ran for help. She watched
him work, not so much white as with a kind of pale luminosity
to her cheek; and she smiled at him sweetly when he'd done
all he could. He saw her lips move and bent low to hear what
she said.

She was watching the painted horses galloping their endless

circle above her head. 'My mother warned me to stay away from ponies,' she whispered. 'It's what she calls a Dangerous Pursuit.'

Lucas Apsley shook his head, still unable to comprehend. 'Poor lass,' he said sadly to DCI Gorman. 'Still, I suppose it could have been worse. That ship could have killed her stone dead. In the great scheme of things, maybe losing a finger isn't the end of the world.'

Hazel took Ash home, installed him in his armchair and poured him, in deference to his hurts both mental and physical, not coffee but brandy. Soon a little of the colour returned to his face. Admittedly, some of it was bruises. 'What do you suppose will happen to her?' he asked.

Hazel couldn't match the concern in his battered face. 'She killed someone in a fit of temper. She's not going to get away with a caution by promising not to do it again.'

'She didn't mean to kill him. She swears she only hit him once, and even that was more a dramatic gesture than an attempt on his life.'

Hazel shrugged. 'It's not always the thought that counts. Sometimes it's the result. Gabriel, will you drink that brandy? Sniffing at it like it was a bunch of flowers isn't going to do you much good.'

He did as he was told. 'Could she plead diminished responsibility?'

'I'm not a legal expert,' said Hazel tartly, 'but I wouldn't have thought so. If raging hormones were considered an excuse, no one between fifteen and twenty-five would ever be convicted of anything.' Seeing the unhappiness in his eyes, she relented. 'On the plus side, she's entitled to be treated as a juvenile. Due consideration will be given to her state of mind at the time of the offence. If it's felt that counselling or any other kind of help would be appropriate, she'll get it. And she'll be away from her mother, which might do her more good than anything else.'

Ash inhaled the heady warmth of the brandy. 'How can a well-meaning, moderately intelligent, adult human being get things so wrong?'

Hazel elevated one surprised eyebrow. 'Intelligent yes, adult yes, but well-meaning? Pru Somers may have wanted the best for her daughter, but that's not the same thing.'

'I wasn't thinking of Pru. I was thinking of me.' He cast her a furtive look over the top of his glass. 'Rachel came to me for help, and I only managed to make things worse. She opened her heart to me, and I couldn't find the words that would stop her trying to kill herself. If she'd succeeded, her death would have been on my conscience.'

'Well, she didn't,' said Hazel briskly. 'All she succeeded in doing was chopping off her right forefinger. And even that may prove to be a good thing in the long run. She'll never be a concert pianist now. She and her mother have lost their power over one another.'

'You don't blame me, then?' He thought he knew the answer, but he needed to hear her say it. 'So who? Pru? Pru may not be a very likable woman, but what did she do that was so terrible? She'd succeeded in life through using her talents and working hard. Was it so wicked to encourage her daughter to do the same?'

'Not wicked,' conceded Hazel. 'But not very wise, and not very kind either. One of the first duties a parent owes their child is to avoid trying to live through them. They'll have their own hopes and aspirations, they don't need even a loving and supportive mother pushing them to live out her dreams.'

There was a pause while Ash processed that and decided that no, that was one parental sin he hadn't yet been guilty of. His only ambition for his children was that they be happy.

'Gethin, then,' he said at length. 'Was it his fault, for not realising what was happening in time to stop it?'

'Gethin Phillips was a decent man who took on the difficult task of raising someone else's child and did it, so far as I can see, with care and almost unfailing skill. He did his best, and I doubt anyone else could have done much better. He didn't deserve what happened to him.'

'You're saying Rachel is responsible for her own tragedy.' Ash shifted uncomfortably. 'But Hazel, she's seventeen years old. She was brought up with a minimum of love and so no experience in recognising it or tools for dealing with it. The life she had was making her miserable; she saw what she thought was the chance of a better one and grabbed for it.'

'And then,' Hazel reminded him, 'finding herself thwarted, she reacted exactly as her mother would have done – she struck out. Except that she picked up a weapon first. I'm sorry, I have a certain amount of sympathy for Rachel Somers up to that point, but not beyond. If a young woman of seventeen, who's old enough to marry and have children of her own, can't muster enough self-control to avoid inflicting a lethal injury on a man who only ever wanted to help her, then I don't think she can duck the responsibility. I know she was unhappy. Maybe she was embarrassed; maybe she was desperate. There are still some things you don't do, and one of them is beating someone's head in!'

'If Dr Green agrees that the second fracture could have resulted from him falling against a tree, hopefully the jury will accept that Rachel never meant to kill him.'

'But she did,' Hazel said baldly. 'She could have screamed, cried, sworn at him, stamped her foot or scratched rude words in the paintwork of his precious car. She didn't. She went for him with a club. Even after that, instead of calling for help she headed off into the spinney. By the time she found you, she'd worked out a story that would get her off the hook. This isn't about a love-starved girl struggling with her emotions. It's a murder case.

'Think about this for a minute. If Gethin Phillips had woken up with a headache, he'd have told us what actually happened – and sixpence'll get you a fiver that Rachel would have called him a liar. There's every chance we'd have believed her – believed that it was him who attacked her, not the other way round. She could have ruined his life, and he'd done nothing whatever to deserve it.'

'Is that what she's facing? A murder charge?' Sorrow darkened around Ash's deep-set eyes even more than the bruises.

'The CPS may settle for manslaughter,' said Hazel, relenting. 'In view of her age, the impulsive nature of the attack, the fact that she hadn't gone equipped for it, and especially if the FME doesn't rule out the one-blow defence. I'm not sure how much it matters. Either way, she'll be out of circulation for a while.'

Ash was nodding slowly. 'I know you think she doesn't deserve much sympathy. Maybe you're right – probably you are. But I still want to help her if I can. If nothing else, I can get her good legal representation. It may make a difference. Whatever she's done, I don't feel I can abandon her.'

Hazel smiled. The warmth of her friendship bathed his hurts. 'I never for a moment thought you would.'

Sitting beside him on the kitchen sofa, she stretched out her legs and yawned. 'It's too late tonight, but I'll head back to Byrfield in the morning. The wedding's on Wednesday: I'd better check that they're ready, that everything that needs doing has been done.'

Ash looked sideways at her. 'You don't think perhaps they've checked for themselves?'

Hazel's eyes widened. 'Would *you* trust Pete Byrfield to turn up at the right church at the right time to marry the right bride?'

Ash chuckled. 'Well, since you put it that way . . .'

'You will come down, won't you? I need someone to go into the church with – I don't want to feel like . . .' She was going to say *a spare wheel*. But remembering, she grinned and said, 'A gooseberry.'

'Of course I will. I'll buy that new shirt on Monday.'

'Pink,' she suggested. 'It'll look nice in the photographs.'

'So will blue,' he said firmly.

For a little while they just sat side by side, Patience woven in among their feet. Then Ash said, with a sort of studied negligence: 'Talking of things that need doing, it's time I tackled something that's needed doing for a while.'

'Wallpapering your bedroom?'

He wasn't sure if she was teasing him. 'Not exactly. I'm going to take your advice. It was good advice, and I'm sorry I didn't recognise that at the time. I'm going to start divorce proceedings.'

Hazel caught herself staring at him and blinked. 'I have no right to tell you what to do.'

'No. But you have a friend's right to tell me what I should do.'

'What made you change your mind?'

'I think, this business with Rachel and Pru and Gethin Phillips. It didn't happen because of the wickedness of the people involved: it happened because the boundaries got blurred. I think, when it comes to raising children, perhaps it's best to make sure everyone knows where they stand. That there aren't too many loopholes and quick-fixes where confusion can arise.

'Goodwill goes a long way, and doing what seems best at the time is fine, but keeping the books straight is important too. By not facing up to the reality of our situation, I've left the boys and myself in a legal limbo. I need to formalise things before we have any misunderstandings of our own. Good intentions aren't enough. You should try to do the right things as well.'

Hazel was watching him doubtfully. But it wasn't the brandy talking: Ash was finally ready to move on with his life. 'It won't happen overnight, you know,' she warned him. 'I suppose your solicitor will go for desertion. If no one knows where Cathy is, she can't consent, so you could be in for quite a wait.'

'I'm ready for that. It *should* take time. A marriage is too important to be dissolved on a whim.' He paused then, for so long that she thought he'd finished. She was just about to get up and go home when he said, 'Hazel, when it's done . . .'

She had a flash of insight into what was coming. And she didn't know if she should let him finish that sentence or not. She knew how much he mattered to her. She knew she mattered to him too, maybe as much. But they'd been friends – the best and closest of friends – for two years: she wasn't sure if anything else was still an option. She wasn't sure if she wanted it to be.

She actually had her mouth open to voice some of this when outside the window a car pulled into the driveway. Doors opened and closed, tired and fractious young voices complained, then the Ash boys were tramping across the kitchen floor and their father was on his feet, aches and pains forgotten, his half-spoken question apparently forgotten too, arms spread to welcome them. Guy rushed into the embrace and returned it with interest; then he went and hugged Patience. Gilbert, nearly eleven now and too cool for contact, hung back and nodded casually.

'Good holiday?' asked Ash.

'Not bad,' his elder son allowed. 'I liked the surfing. Is there anywhere to do it round here?'

Ash shook his head solemnly. 'There's a reason they call it the Midlands. We're a long way from the sea. I suppose you could have a go at the Severn Bore sometime. Or we'll go back to Cornwall for another holiday. All of us, next time.'

Gilbert nodded. 'Or Bondi Beach,' he suggested hopefully.

'That's in Australia. The surf's good there. Or California.'

'Or possibly Cornwall,' said Ash.

Still dazed by the turn their conversation had taken, Hazel took the opportunity to slip away, leaving them to sort out their laundry and re-establish the family dynamic. As she walked back to her car, their voices followed her through the open windows.

'I can surf too!'

'No you can't, you only sit on the board.'

'Sitting's surfing too.'

'No it's not. It's surfing for cissies.'

'Don't call your brother a cissy.'

'What did you do to your face?'

'I called my brother a cissy.'

'You haven't got a brother!'

'Well, I called my dog a cissy then.'

What Hazel *didn't* hear was Patience say complacently, I know you love me really.

But Ash did, and he bent for a moment and stroked her silken ear – the speckled one – then he took Frankie's suitcase upstairs, and put the kettle on, and set the table for tea.

When the boys too had headed upstairs – he could hear Frankie's oft-repeated injunction about the distinctive roles of floors and wardrobes – Ash went and sat on the leather sofa, and Patience climbed up beside him and laid her long head across his knee.

He said softly, 'You don't talk to me as much these days.'

The lurcher said, You don't need me to. You're doing just fine on your own. By the way . . .

'What?' said Ash.

Can I be bridesmaid?

The postman delivered the final postcard the day after the vacationers returned, as is right and proper and specified by the national postal service contract. It was from Frankie, and it said:

Wish you were here. No, seriously.